ILORAY

A MERMAID STORY

MARY JANE CAPPS

ISBN: 978-0-9992614-2-2

For Mama and Dad

PROLOGUE

*I*t was a story Gryshen had heard a thousand times. Sometimes there were slight varia-tions, depending on which tribe you heard it from, but the bones of it remained the same.

The first children grew from their mother's belly, the Mother of all, deep within the water. She birthed them in the forms of sparkling shells, twelve great oysters, each one holding an iloray babe. They were raised inside a sacred cavern, a place of unparalleled magic and wonder. In this place was everything they needed to grow healthy, fat, and content. Each child, twelve total, was nourished by the abundance of plant life near the cave, nurtured by the powerful love of the Mother, and protected by the strongest gift She could give them, the greatest gift the sea had to give.

The great oysters cradled the babes as they slept and

grew, alongside what is only created when sand gets trapped in the shell—a pearl.

The Sea Mother tucked a grain of sand into each shell as her babes formed, knowing that as her children grew, so would the pearls, knowing that they would nourish her young, and when her young were ready to come out, the gleaming orbs would be there to protect them, like an umbilical cord attached to a placenta.

Except no detachment was necessary.

For many freezes and thaws, the babes wanted nothing more than to be together within this cavern, happy, fed, and next to Mother's heartbeat. But as they grew older, they grew restless. They began to tire of the same games, the same unanswered questions. None of them had ever even left for oxygen, as they all swam to an opening high up in the cavern that reached the surface of the water.

Every morning, the sun shone upon their faces as they drew breath. Every evening, the moon glowed down as they gulped goodnights into the air.

There was land visible in the distance, but Mother had warned them of creatures, of new and strange dangers, of a climate that was unfriendly to ceasids. Most of the children listened, and kept their longings focused in the world that was their own. But two kept going up, gulping air long past the time the others went back, trying to see more of that green island in the distance.

Mother was a good mother, and she encouraged her

children to find their own path—including those drawn to the earth.

And so, brother and sister joined, pairing up until there was no single one left. Except for Mother. She was the only constant in a sea that was only fluid. And these babes were grown and off on their own.

They ventured into open waters, but they found that they grew sick and weak the farther they got from their birth cave. Each pair took a pearl for their vitality, and they agreed to leave six behind in case they needed them.

One pair made their home in the Mediterranean waters. Another traveled toward the Caribbean Sea. Another toward the rocky Celtic coast, another to the balmy Pacific, and the fifth pair took to the iciest waters they could stand in the Arctic.

The sixth went to shore, and practiced basking in the sun for as long as they could. But they soon learned that being out of the water for so long made them tire quickly, even more than when they were far from a pearl. They knew they would need more energy. Back to the cavern they went, asking Mother for another pearl.

Mother asked, "Do the others know? Have they blessed you to take it?"

"Oh yes, yes," the two lied. They thought their siblings might never agree to them taking a second pearl when they had all left home so recently, and when they sensed resentment over their choice to leave their whole ocean family behind.

"Then you have my blessing to take it." And Mother opened her great cavern arms, and they plucked another pearl from its hatchery home.

It worked. They felt better on shore almost immediately. But as time passed, they became frustrated once more, for they couldn't go far beyond the sand of the beach, since they could only use their arms to push their bodies along the ground.

It was known within each of the children that the strongest magic was in Mother's arms, and so they decided to get one more pearl, to see if it could give them the power to move about the planet.

One night they returned to the cavern.

Again, Mother asked, "Do the others know? Have they blessed you to take it?"

And again, they lied. "Oh yes, yes." They were certain that if a second pearl would not be approved, a third would be forbidden.

"Then you have my blessing to take it."

So they brought a third sacred pearl up to shore.

They had the most strength they had ever had, and yet their tails were cumbersome. The brother and sister still had no way to move freely. One evening as the waves drew up high on the beach, they arranged the three large beads carefully in a cluster by some rocks, to keep them from washing away.

The brother accidentally smashed one against the rocks, and from within the white ball, millions of tiny stars burst all over him. They coated his fin in a shimmery glow. The glow burned, and the brother screamed in agony as it began to tear through his tail. His sister watched helplessly as his tail split in two, and the scales began to peel. The pain soon lessened, and in the following days, they understood what had happened as all the scales stripped away to reveal bare pink flesh, and the pink flesh gave way to taut skin.

The ceasid had legs. He stumbled as he learned to walk, and the walk became a run. He reveled in his new body, his new life, as he stretched past all his former limits. He could roam the forest, see the strange creatures of the land. He could climb trees and view the world from a vantage point no one in his family could imagine. He learned to hunt beasts of the land, and brought them back to shore for his sister to taste. He told her of his discoveries, of this earth.

Brother and sister wanted to take the land together, and they knew they'd need one more pearl to do it.

Mother asked the same question, and they told the same lie.

The new man broke the pearl on a rock and sprinkled the stars on his sister's tail. Shimmer led to wretched pain; wretched pain gave way to rebirth.

And so, the first landkeepers came to be.

Life on dirt was dangerous, and difficult. They did not understand the terrain, and injury soon followed.

While searching the horizon for more to explore, the man fell out of the tree and shattered his legs. The new woman, his sister, was desperate. She did not know his legs would heal naturally, so she broke one of their last two pearls over his limbs.

And then they were left with one. It was barely enough to keep them alive. They had not yet discovered fire, and the land was getting cold. Without the magical energy to protect them, death seemed likely.

So back they took to the sea.

They swam awkwardly, and it was difficult to breathe, even though they still had gills in their necks. They had adjusted to the air. Now human, finding the cave proved much more difficult, but they finally did, and Mother was waiting patiently.

"Do the others know? Have they blessed you to take it?" she asked.

"Yes, yes!" they replied.

"You lie." The cavern began to close around them.

"Please—just one more!" they pleaded.

"You have taken four. You have misused the magic. You have taken to my womb to steal from me. No more." And the whirling water began to push them out of the tightening cave mouth.

"No!" screamed the woman. She snatched one pearl and pushed her way out with the man. Upward they swam, but their siblings were all waiting for them.

A battle broke out, with the betrayed family trying to get the pearl from the traitorous two. In the scuffle, the pearl was broken. Out spilled the stars like seeds, swirling around the twelve.

It did some final magic, smoothing the gills out from

the near-humans, thrusting cartilage where there had just been small holes on the sides of their head for hearing, pushing their once broad noses forward to aid their air breathing. But this last change made it impossible for ͏em to stay long in the water. They instinctively held ͏eir breath and swam jerkily away from the rest to gasp ͏ shore, to begin their new life, now banished from ͏ir former home forever.

The star seeds spread over the others, too, and they ͏e what ilorays believed gave them their impressive pan and strength.

Who would want to trade that for landkeeping ͏ay? They gave away their lives, and they turned on blood." These words were almost always part of the of the story—pride and loyalty in sea birth.

ere was another part, too.

͏t was told, Mother had closed the stony gates, had shut away the last pearl for protection. The deepest magic lay in Mother's arms, but no one knew where it was, or how to find it. Some pods had sought it out for the protection of all ceasids so that they may always have one pearl . . . in case. Some had sought it out of greed. Some just wanted answers to deeper questions.

Who *was* Mother, really?

Gryshen's father had always told her that She was everything. She was the salt in the sea, the gleam in hope, the tenderness in a kiss. But was there really an actual Mother, guarding a final pearl deep within the ocean?

CHAPTER 1

"*D*o you need air?" Gryshen asked her father, feeling the familiar rattle in her own chest, her constant reminder. She would feel a burning in her lungs long before any of the others would.

"You both do." Her father's aide signaled from the shadows in the chamber doorway. Even though he was only a child when she was born, Bravis had seemed like an elder since she could remember. No other babe had ever looked so serious. The fact that her dad considered them to be destined for betrothal didn't move her any closer to an iloray so . . . *responsible.*

"I'm fine." Gryshen could hardly contain her annoyance.

Frall considered his daughter. "Well, I am, too, for a little while. Let's go ahead with the plan. Shall we?"

Bravis tightened his already stony features. "Let's not

take too long, then." His brow remained furrowed as his gaze passed between Frall and Gryshen.

Gryshen recalled a recent conversation with Bravis.

"Princess." He addressed her in the formal fashion that was comfortable for him. His awkwardness struck Gryshen as funny, but it had only grown since her father suggested they were made for each other. Maybe it was because Bravis knew it was one more responsibility she had not volunteered for. Or maybe it was because he wanted to distance himself from the idea.

"As you are well aware, your father's condition is deteriorating. The *shun* appears to be taking hold." Bravis cleared his throat, attempting to disguise the break in his signal following the sharp tone. Gryshen thought she saw the beginnings of mist coming over his dark eyes. Bravis had a perfect calm to his face, always. Only his eyes gave him away. He wore his shoulder-length coal hair twisted in a small tail at the top of his spine. It was easy for Gryshen to get stuck staring at him, but necessary for her to look away. She wasn't going to have anyone bound to her because they would do anything for her father. She wanted some part of her destiny to belong to her.

"You are the eldest, you are next in line, and sooner or later, you *will* be our chieftainess. Your greatest responsibility, greater than maintaining order in our tribe, greater than ensuring our food supply, our safety . . . greater than any of these is the oath you shall take to protect our pearl. Without it, nothing else matters. It is your most sacred duty."

Gryshen felt the bone-crushing weight of these words.

It's not my time. It's not my time, and it's not Dad's time. It's like they're all just waiting for him to die.

The thaw season promised warmer skies and a rush of krill for eating, but not much change in the water's freezing temperatures. It carried waves of sunlight that stretched down deep into the ocean. In the dark season, when everything was in line with ice, Gryshen would take to the surface of the water, breathing the frosted air, floating in the stillness, a glimpse of time that seemed to belong to her. And in the thaw season, she took to the surface to take in the life there. There was something about getting out that felt like a momentary escape from a giant net. Gryshen and her tribe took comfort in the knowledge that soon the brightness would return for a half year, and with it, more food for their watery home.

The cavern that housed their pod of about two hundred ceasids was a wild labyrinth that always seemed to have new turns and bends, vast chambers to explore. There was the hub, where the tribe could congregate, where they held feasts, where loves were bound in ceremony, babes were blessed, stories were shared. There were chambers for hunters, for food preparations. Places beneath the water and above the surface where the makers tried to fuse land and sea, landkeeper creations with gifts from the ocean.

There was the Medicine Corridor where many sought spiritual guidance, went on retreat, or participated in sacred ceremonies. It was where healers camped, and farther in, where you could find their shaman's lair. Outside the cavern, not far from two halves of a split ship that seemed as if they had found each other again under the water, lay the bone pit, the place where their dead rested.

And in the deepest, farthest place of the Rone Cavern, so far, one might feel as if they'd reached the other side of the Arctic Ocean, lay the Great Pearl.

The Rone Pearl gleamed a ghostly white, blindingly brilliant. Gryshen was one of the few living to have glimpsed it, and more than once: the first time she was in her mother's arms, one of her earliest memories.

"Look, Gryshie," her mother, Athela, cooed, clutching her chubby-fisted infant and stroking the fin at the end of her little tail. "This is the most sacred creation to our kind. Each pod has a pearl, and each pearl protects the pod—keeping us safe, healthy, a thriving tribe. Look at that . . ." she whispered, fixated on and hypnotized by the glowing orb.

"Never stray too far, Gryshen. Never stray too far from the pearl, especially if you are sick, or there's a lack of food. Its strength only stretches so far past our village."

Gryshen kept these words safe within her heart—not so much for their warning, but for the love they sailed in on.

These words, this knowledge had protected her long after her dead mother was unable to.

Now, Gryshen's second encounter with the pearl was more frightening. They made their way quickly from Frall's chamber to the narrow private corridor that led to open space, before another twist led them down the long path to the pearl. Gryshen gripped the glass lantern tightly in her long, slightly webbed fingers, the blue jellyfish within the lantern casting a ghostly glow on her pale skin and swirling black hair.

"It's good for us all to get closer to the pearl from time to time. It will inspire you as a leader, Gryshen. Its energy will guide and nourish us," Frall signaled, a grate to his tone. He was working with Apocay, their shaman, focusing on his healing. The *shun* was the name for the sickness that had targeted laxes in her family, failing to capture her grandfather. He healed and died a very old iloray with his bride, who gave birth to Frall late in their waves. The *shun* had returned a second time for her father.

Bravis, who had been silent for a few minutes while they swam, nodded to one of the guards at the opening of the farthermost chamber. Gryshen had barely noticed the long cavern hall that had led them here, she was so lost in her terrifying thoughts. The icy walls were flanked by what looked like a pair of golden statues, save for their gentle bobbing as they floated, bedecked with bronze breastplates, helmets with face armor, a spear in one hand, a shield in the other. Their faces were covered in masks of abalone shell, so all you could see was the glow of their eyes illuminated by the jellyfish torches overhead.

They had reached the opening of the chamber, covered in a rusted steel door. Gryshen recognized it as one of the doors that laid in the floor in an old sunken mariner's ship not far from the cavern.

A sharp, barely noticeable nod from Frall, and the two guards turned in a whirl of bubbles, twisting large steel cranks on either side of the doors, creaking them open. All was black in the whirling water, save the soft electric blue glow of one large jellyfish torch above a smaller set of doors, set into the farthermost wall of the room. Steel studs outlined the circular shape, something with markings printed on land, something once used for another purpose by landkeepers. With a flick of his tail, Bravis swam toward it. Gryshen followed, breathless. It was as if she had never seen the pearl before.

In a way, she hadn't. Not like this. Not with the looming, all-consuming pressure.

Jode, her younger brother, had only seen it once when they were little.

Her eyes watchful, once again she fixed her gaze on Bravis's smooth gray hand as he pressed his palm against the circular steel doors, and slid the circle clockwise and counterclockwise, back and forth, until they all heard a loud popping sound. It startled Gryshen, and even Frall twitched, but nothing ever seemed to catch Bravis off his guard.

The doors slowly opened on their own, and as they did, a white halo seemed to radiate from within.

The Great Pearl.

Gryshen gasped. Bravis gave her a small smile. She was so young before . . . it was breathtaking, the most exquisite thing that she had ever laid her eyes upon. It shone with a satin-like quality as it rested upon a crescent-shaped pitch-black piece of shale. It glowed a white so brilliant that it almost seemed like there were other colors in the light-blues, purples, pinks. The pearl gleamed its ethereal gleam, and Gryshen felt a blanket of peace surrounding her. Fear flew away and she was left with an exquisite level of contentment:

"This is what it does," she considered, smiling. "What is it you always say, Dad? Protect the pearl with your life . . ."

" . . . and it will make life worth protecting," Frall finished with a smile.

So much had changed since the first time she saw the pearl, and the rumblings of war were growing louder. The Rone preferred to keep the peace, whenever possible, between themselves and the four other pods of Oceas. Most pods felt this way. Their world was vast, and there was plenty of room for all of them. Occasionally ilorays would marry into other pods, or tribes would barter with each other for beautiful or useful objects. Things like shells from different parts of the sea, good nets, woven kelp wraps for leens, jellyfish lanterns, and certainly human treasures. Ornately carved doors and windows from ships that could decorate a cavern chamber, uniquely shaped glass bottles that made lovely tympanic instruments, sparkling gems from trunks on wrecked boats, and fabrics . . . beautiful textures that could not be duplicated on the ocean floor. Gryshen's mother had given her a silk lavender scarf on her third birthday. She kept it wrapped around the more ornate kelp chest binding she wore on special occasions. The water and salt tore it to bare threads that she wove into the leaves.

Jode brought back a rainbow of ribbons, a small rocking horse, and three green glass bottles for her from his last hunt.

And now, the thought of being the one in charge felt less empowering and more like a massive anchor whose chains had wrapped 'round her tail, pulling her down.

Gryshen saw herself sinking, like a relic in one of the shipwreck yards. She worked guiltily to pull her thoughts back.

"We've got to have our security at its tightest, now more than ever." Bravis spoke earnestly to them both, concern filling his dark eyes. This combination unsettled Gryshen. She nodded repeatedly, feeling her head bob like that of a funny fat little mustached doll she had seen salvaged in the babes' quarter. Gryshen pondered this as her head still bobbed nervously, looking back into his eyes.

Frall considered something. "I'm going to the air

chamber now. Don't take too long behind me, all right, Gryshen?"

Gryshen broke her gaze with Bravis to nod in reply to her father.

Crazy, she reminded herself. *Dad couldn't be more wrong on this one. Bravis is too mature to consider anything besides his obligations, anyway. He's old enough to be your, well, your much older brother.* He felt old enough to be her great-great-grandfather, even though he was only her senior by twelve seasons—six freezes, six thaws.

Gryshen drew herself away from him by a few inches more, as if by floating too closely he might telepathically pick up on her thoughts.

She shivered again. There were whole stretches of the year when she could swim upward, far above home, and burst through the line between sea and earth. The ice would pull back as the glaciers melted, and she could pull up on the rocky shores, among the seals and egrets. She'd stretch out, lay her whole body on a smooth rock, and let the waves lap over her. This inlet was pretty safe, almost barren of people, save for the old man and younger woman who stayed in the tiny gray house beside a larger structure of weathered wood that her father told her was a place where the landkeepers spoke to their Creator. Gryshen wondered how they could hear Her there, when everyone knew their Mother lived deep in the water. Sometimes the older man would pull the rope on a big bell, the pealing drawing a crowd from around the island, like a warmer current bringing in more life.

She would listen for the singing. It came every time, so different from her music. Gryshen would stare at the sky, allowing the water to blanket her, protect her.

Being alone was one of the only things she could do comfortably.

After the singing, the woman would ring the bell, and they would file into her little house, the scent of food carried to the iloray's nose on the salty wind.

Gryshen loved to listen to the lady chiming the bell. It gave her comfort, even if it wasn't meant for her. Anything that welcomed you home had to be a good thing.

Gryshen kept quiet when she heard the tales around Rone. Whenever ilorays from other pods visited, everyone packed into the hub to share the recent news, celebrate important events, and catch up on gossip from all over Oceas. Babes loved to ask guests about land-keeper encounters. Ranging from the mysterious to the funny, to the terrifying, visitors were often all too happy to oblige. So delighted were they to have a rapt audience, the stories occasionally felt recycled.

Gryshen grinned as she recalled one journeying iloray, eyes wild, gestures dramatic, as he told the story of the drunken sea captain who had caught him in a fishing net, hoisted him on deck, and tortured him. "They surrounded me—fifteen, twenty men—shaking their spears and crying out. I tried to reason with them while deflecting their weapons," he said with more than a little bravado. "They stabbed and they poked, and I think . . . I think they were going to sell me to scientists and have me"—he gazed around the room at the wild-eyed young ones—"*cut open*! At the very last moment, I managed to wriggle my way out of the net. As I was heaving myself over the prow of the boat, the mad captain roared and lassoed his harpoon, flinging it at my fin. See here." He gestured sweepingly at his tail while the crowd swam around it and squinted. "Here is my warrior wound. I just *barely* escaped with my *life*." Next, he'd grabbed hold of his fin and was shaking it rather violently for someone who had just undergone such a painful ordeal.

By the light of the torches, the harpoon wound could be generously described as a fissure. It looked identical to Jode's fish hook tear from one of his many entanglements. And the story sounded an awful lot like a very dressed-up version of what had happened to one of the elders of her pod. Only, that lax was missing three-quarters of his fin, and had swum with an odd tilt since anyone could remember. And he preferred not to get into much detail about his misadventure, as the memory was truly painful.

But Gryshen often thought of a grandmother's suggestion that the landkeeper was much like the shark: often unsure, and not wanting to harm unless threatened. It was the consensus that humans were best avoided, and earthly exploration best left to the wise ones of the tribes, for they knew of the safest, most private lands.

Gryshen was again yanked from her reverie when Bravis, rather scoldingly, kept repeating her name. "Gryshen. Gryshen!"

"Yes, Bravis?" she said, trying to sound casual. Trying to sound as if she hadn't been lost in thought when she was supposed to be focusing.

"You don't get it, do you?" He shook his head. "I've been giving you a concise history on crucial battle over territory, threats narrowly averted against our pearl, things a chieftainess must know. Am I boring you? Do you think I just like to hear myself talk?"

Perhaps. Gryshen kept this thought to herself. "Sorry," she signaled quietly.

"I don't need you to be sorry. I need you to care. This is your life. This is about our pod's very survival."

Behind his frustration, she saw the worry. Ah. The exasperation masked his fear. He wore it like a veil. Bravis looked guilty, and softened.

"Grysh"—he never called her this—"I know that losing your dad and gaining a queenship and the responsibility of our pod is a terrible burden to bear. You know that your dad's been like a father to me." His own parents had died in a beast attack when he was small. Bravis never spoke of them. He had to grow up almost as soon as he was born.

Gryshen felt for him. And then the rattling in her lungs shifted to a scraping sensation. She needed air.

"Let's go," Bravis signaled, recognition in his face, "You're long overdue for a breath." As he finished locking up the door to the pearl's keeping, they swam out of the chamber, the guards once again flanking. On they went past the seemingly endless rows of guards. They both remained silent, until Frall passed them, wearing the same tired expression.

"Dad? Are you . . . where are you going?"

"To get some rest, I hope," Bravis signaled, and Gryshen couldn't help but agree.

"Yes, yes." Frall smile couldn't cover the exhaustion that seemed to hang on him no matter how much sleep he got. "Just a little more rest." And despite the *shun's* erosion, his silvery tail flicked merrily, his silver hair blooming down his back as he swam away.

The winged seraphs collected from ship prows smiled sweetly upon them as they entered the mouth of Breathing Chamber Number Three. There were five laid out in the pod's cavern; otherwise, it was easy once outside the cave to swim up for air. They were a triumph of the makers, these oxygen contraptions, marrying form and function. Each chamber was slightly different, using pipes in varying sizes, an array of gears, bellies of ship stoves, and brass tubes from old ship kitchens. Each breathing chamber contained four or five oxygen tubes. These configurations quickly speckled, green with algae and rust, and had to be periodically replaced with other salvaged pieces. The individual spouts connected to arms that reached into a large metal stomach, which was topped with a wide cylinder that stretched up to the surface of the water. A lid with a tightly woven hinge rested on the cylinder like a flat cap several feet above the sea. A steering wheel from a ship sat at the entrance to the room, which allowed the whole piece to be mechanically lowered to avoid being spotted or hit by the occasional passing ocean vessel. Smaller gears sat next to the mouthpieces, allowing ceasids to open the lid at sky level, as well as pump out water that had seeped into the metal belly.

It was a gathering place, a chance to catch up with the tribe during the day. At night they could store an abundance of oxygen in their bodies for sleeping. Come morning, these chambers were often packed, sometimes with lines to breathe. Gryshen preferred to time it so she didn't have to encounter too many others. She was never there for conversation.

Now it was a trickle of ilorays, a couple of mothers and their babes. They spotted Gryshen and Bravis, and the mothers exchanged a knowing look, shooing their young away from the entrance to the air pipes in the back. Gryshen pretended not to notice. Somewhere along the way, other ceasids in their pod had become aware of her more urgent need for oxygen.

They don't have to look at me like a specimen. She couldn't completely shut out the curious glances. She had struggled, waited too long for a sip in an air chamber, only a handful of times in her whole life. It was usually away from the crowd, but secrets were hard to keep in the cavern. Every other iloray she knew could comfortably go with one visit to the breathing chambers upon waking, perhaps another visit mid-day, and once more before sleep. Ceasids breathed in the water through the small gills that rested on the sides of their throats, fresh air from above being a small part of their survival. Gryshen could never be sure if it was her unique problem, or something else that kept her at a distance from so many in Rone.

Bravis offered the onlookers a polite nod, and, getting the hint, they finished their breaths and swam out. Gryshen hadn't wanted them to see her hungrily reach for a brass tube, the sting in her chest more pronounced, the air cooling it as she drank the salt-laced oxygen, propelling out the excess water, drinking clean breaths. Bravis drank the air, too, though Gryshen suspected it was only for her benefit. He always did things like that.

They made their way back to the central hub, where they found Jode surrounded by a gang of friends and gawking, adoring ilorays. Their glances passed over her and Bravis, and returned to the source of entertainment. Gryshen drifted slightly back from the crowd, as usual.

Jode was interrupting his story about his last hunt with his own laughter. Her brother had the same jet-black hair and fair skin as Gryshen's—only where her flesh was grayer, his had a little pink to its tone. A bit more life to it. His eyes were a bright blue with a smile tucked inside them, as if Jode was constantly retelling a private joke in his head. Gryshen loved his sense of humor, loved how light he was . . . except for this moment. In this moment, she resented him. Life would always be easy for the young prince. All the fun of royalty with none of the burden. He didn't even know how bad Dad's condition was. Dad had always coddled him, and she didn't want to be the one to break the news.

"Look what I brought back for my favorite sister!" He was beaming at her while he held a perfectly braided ring of fish bones. "I claimed these from a carcass. Cleaned it and wove them on the way back. Thought it'd be a pretty nice crown, huh?" His ear-to-ear grin answered his own question. The older laxes hoisted their nets on their backs, boasting about their catches of octopus, manta ray, and swordfish; the younger ones held nets full of crab and shrimp. Off they swam into the bleeding chamber to clean their catch. Gryshen shuddered. She preferred to avoid the blood room, especially when they cleaned their hunt. It was so, well, bloody.

Disgusting, she thought to herself, allowing for one more shudder.

Jode chuckled at her, then stopped, taking her in. "You need a break. Let's go for a ride." He grabbed her arm enthusiastically, and Gryshen broke free of her anger. She could never stay mad at Jode. Together they swam from the hub, away from the crowd, to the entrance of the Rone Cavern.

It was a longer route to the stables, but going around the outside of their home meant less eyes and ears. It had been a little too long since she'd taken Misra for a ride. The beluga checked into the stables dutifully when she wasn't cruising in open sea. It didn't hurt that Sodaren, the beastkeeper, always had her favorite white fish from the hunters, even when the supply of krill was low.

"Ah, Frall sent his daughter to teach! Excellent." A mother leen with a brood of babes, some her own, some gathered from all over the pod, tightened one of the many braids twisted around her head. "When we received the signal that your father was going to have to miss our language session, we thought we'd have to just go over what little we knew of landkeeper speak, but now that you're here . . ."

Gryshen froze as the wide-eyed young stared up at her, matching the teacher's earnest expression.

"I'm sorry, I think there's been some confusion. I don't really know very many words."

"Compared to who? Stop being so modest, Gryshie!" Jode grinned wickedly at his sister. He put his arm around her, leaning heavily. "Do you all know that land-keepers have, like, ten different ways to say 'bowel movement'?" Wild giggling ensued. "It's true! And the way they communicate—they can't hum a signal. And it doesn't sound the way we do when we use our mouths out of the water, either. It's choppy. What are some of the words they use, Gryshen? Teach them!" He looked at her with mock excitement.

"You know I don't know, Jode. But you sound like you do," Gryshen hissed.

"Nope. *Kukur* is all I got. That's one of the many, many poop words around this land region."

He pointed upward professorially. Gryshen narrowed her eyes. Speaking to a group made her stomach twist, and her brother knew it. She paused, trying to recall some of the basic landkeeper words her father had taught her.

A low signal hummed across the water, and Jode twisted in the other direction. The deep blue whirled in eddies around them. Gryshen turned to look in the direction he was staring. Flanked by guards draped in black shells across their shoulders, a different sort of king and his company swam steadily toward them astride two of the largest sharks Gryshen had ever seen.

CHAPTER 2

*M*orfal, chieftain of the Rakor pod, had not visited in many seasons. Frall had warned her of this visit.

"He wants our backing in some ocean territory grab, Gryshie. We will not get involved. We certainly won't unite with them. It is open sea space, and that was always understood. There is a possibility something has gone wrong with their pod's sacred pearl, but we never discuss that unless they discuss it with us. We must maintain diplomacy. I want you beside me. You need to see how this is done. Besides, Morfal needs to start seeing you as a leader."

"I'm sorry, we'll have to do this another time," she signaled quickly, and the teacher nodded nervously, the babes moving closer to her, mouths open at the sight of the strange pod.

As the dead-eyed sharks pressed on with their crew,

Gryshen straightened her spine, attempted what she thought to be a regal expression, and begged her stomach to keep down the scallops she had eaten that morning.

"Well, Creepy's just anchored, hasn't he?" Jode muttered.

Gryshen could only nod. She was using all her energy to appear in control. The water around Morfal and his pod seemed to be blacker, if that were possible. No, she was almost sure of it. All around her, shades of azure, teal, sapphire. Around the Rakors, darkness.

As they drew closer, she saw a younger lax with him, about her age. She remembered that Morfal had a son, whom she had never met. His cropped white hair contrasted with his father's long, stringy strands of ash. His eyes beamed an electric green out of his chiseled features. His father's eyes were a muddied blue hue, his face drooping like a jellyfish.

Gryshen suddenly realized the lax noticed her staring.

Embarrassed, she refocused. "Chief Morfal, laxes, leens"—although she hadn't yet seen a single female —"of Rakor: We welcome you to our pod. We have arranged for our best sleeping quarters to be yours inside our home, and we will take you to them so you may get settled."

"Slow down," whispered Jode in a hushed signal. "Give them a chance to say hello."

Gryshen attempted to pace herself. "Welcome." She

reached out to clasp the hands of the chieftain in greeting.

He offered one, barely grazing the tips of her fingers. "Where is your father, child?"

Her annoyance distracted her from her nervousness. Jode had scooped up the net of finest sea glass they offered as host gifts from the entrance of their cavern, and to Gryshen's relief, began handing them out to their guests, gently coaxing smiles out of each of them, including a smirk from Morfal.

"He is in his chamber. I'll alert him of your presence, and he will be down for tonight's feast. We have a fresh catch being prepared in the tradition of your tribe. My father wants all of you to feel comfortable."

Now, she'd have to tell the best cooks of the tribe that the Rakors were here. They hadn't been expected for another wave, but she was not about to appear unprepared.

"Shall we get your beasts quartered? Our beast-keeper, Sodaren, can take--" Gryshen felt an elbow in her side. Jode stared at her, suppressing laughter.

Sodaren was not taking those hulking, dagger-toothed animals anywhere.

Morfal snickered, and the younger lax slid off a shark who was missing one eye. He trilled a short note, and both sharks swam away, back from where they came.

As if on cue, Bravis met them at the mouth of the cavern. He gave Gryshen the nod that let her know her father had been alerted to the visitors.

"This way," she gestured, and swam slowly to the rooms, taking care to give the Rakors time to catch up. One by one, she brought them to their quarters. A withered lax who she learned was their shaman looked like he'd been through more fights than a healer should. The shaman would not take his eyes from her. It made Gryshen shiver in spurts, and she was relieved to leave him at a room, escaping his gaze. The chief and his son were taken to their most elaborate guest chamber. Mother-of-pearl lined the sleeping nest of kelp, and there was a huge conch shell filled with live oysters for snacking. Gryshen allowed herself another look at his son, who offered up a sympathetic smile.

Morfal was sniffing about the chamber, complaining about the oysters.

"Couldn't you provide something a bit more . . . exotic? Some swordfish, perhaps."

"Oh, Chief Morfal, that's what's on the menu tonight!" She made a mental note to tell the cook.

"I'm *sorry*," mouthed the younger lax, who then signaled aloud, "I haven't properly introduced myself. I'm Coss."

"Prince Coss." Gryshen extended her gray-white hand.

"Oh, that. Please, just Coss." His handshake was warm and strong, unlike his father's icy finger-slither.

Gryshen could feel herself sinking a bit. "I'd better be going. You will have escorts arriving to bring you to the feast shortly." And she flicked her tail and hoped the whirl of bubbles that followed would cover the rising blush of purple in her cheeks.

When she went to check in with her father, Bravis had posted himself outside his chamber. He drew a finger to his lips, and let her know that her dad was getting as much rest as possible before the feast.

Gryshen went back to her room to prepare. She had been offered a personal servant years ago, one of the younger hubkeepers, and had refused it. The whole idea of someone's life having to revolve around dressing her and braiding her hair and laughing at her jokes sickened her. Besides, she preferred to be alone.

She braided her own hair. She adorned tiny shells around the sea kelp that wrapped her chest. She inspected her tail for any loose scales. She noticed the circles under her eyes as she plaited a few starfish into her black locks. It had been a long day. Gryshen didn't look like the sparkling, fair-haired, curvy leens that surrounded Jode with her silvery eyes, hair as black as octopus ink, a long, narrow nose, a pointed chin (too pointy, she thought) and fingers that stretched long before the webbing at the base between them.

More bones than curves, that's for certain, she thought as she looked rather forlornly at her flat chest.

Soon enough, it was time for the feast. Bravis signaled just outside her chamber, her father smiling behind him. He did look a bit better. Gryshen took her father's hand and kissed his cheek.

"You look good, Daddy." And she meant it this time.

They swam through the water, down another long passage that opened into a great ballroom. It was almost as bright as the surface of the ocean, even though it lay in a cavern in the depths of the sea. Jellyfish torches hung suspended like electric chandeliers, tied in loops from stalactite to stalactite by thick beads of seaweed. At the far end of the room lay a great stone table carved out of the cave walls. On the cave side was a kind of bench coming out from the rock; on the side facing the entrance to the room, stone stools seemed to grow out of the floor like barnacles.

An especially fat squid lay in the center of the table, its tentacles sprawled out over the table, swirling around heavy silver plates that had been fished out of a wrecked ship long ago. Clams, much lighter fare, were tucked inside conch shell carvings within the stone—a part of the table's creation to keep less heavy food from floating away. The table lay at the north side of the room, and the rest was open space for gatherings.

Gryshen had grown up watching many dances following love binding ceremonies and other celebrations. As a babe, she would hide behind a wall in the cave to witness these displays, since they usually went late into the dark, long after she was supposed to be asleep. She could conjure up the images now, lucid recollections of ceasids swaying to the music—sometimes a musical iloray, sometimes a pair of smaller whales to call out songs in the deep. The whales had a low, haunting melody that suited the movements of ceasids, bodies that twisted and sprang, like two different spirits in one: a flickering tail, long arms stretching in arcs. Sometimes singers or storytellers of the tribe would offer up entertainment.

Gryshen didn't have a bedtime anymore. She knew there would be a ceremony for her when she became crowned leader, but she couldn't look forward to that. Any such celebration just marked the losses that were to come. She gazed to the east end of the room, where a great pit rested.

Here was where crownings occurred. Namings and love bindings took place here, too. Namings were a sacred rite for newborn ceasids. They were not given their true name until this time. So she was named Gryshen at her birth, and a month later, all the Rone tribe, from eldest to youngest, came to this spot to witness her naming. Her mother and father swam out from the circle of ceasids surrounding the pit. One by one, each ceasid holding a torch swam above them, created a fiery blue spotlight above the young family. Gryshen's mother pulled her baby girl close, the water swirling around them, pulling her hair like a blanket for just the two of them. She put her hand to the side of her mouth, and softly whispered Gryshen's truest name into her daughter's ear. It was the name mother ceasids saw written in the eyes of their babes, the wordless stories their infants told them in the hours following their birth. It was never to be said aloud to Gryshen again, for it was hers to discover, as all ilorays did, when she went through her Forms. Her father had tried to tell her what he could about Forms, but what was permissible to disclose was little more than general knowledge until an iloray reached their seventeenth thaw, which she had just touched.

Forms were a series of experiences, ancient paces to prepare you for the next season of life, adulthood. Once you passed through them, you could begin serious training in your vocation. You could bind with another. You could start a family.

The Forms told you what you were made of. She knew that there were parts almost lethal—she had heard about the dangers, not to mention the fact that an iloray she knew had actually died some time back while undergoing his. It was incredibly rare—the whole pod was stunned—but it did happen. The process of Forms involved attempts to control the wild, and the wild was, in its very nature, uncontrollable.

The ceasids believed you were one of six sorts: a hunter/warrior, a leader, a caretaker, a beastkeeper, a healer, or a creator/maker. There was technically a seventh sort, but it was almost never discussed, and an iloray didn't go through their Forms to find it. When the rare iloray displayed highly volatile and dangerous behavior, then they would be marked with a large *X*, a warning to others. There was no one like this left in Rone.

Gryshen knew which one her brother was before he took his Forms. He could be a creator, with his humor and gift for storytelling. But he was a hunter through and through. She knew her dad was a leader—all chieftains were. He bore the mark over his right shoulder blade, like a banner. And Bravis bore his, received after his paces—*healer*—*w*hich always puzzled Gryshen since he was so clearly in a leadership role.

As for what her mark would be, Gryshen knew that destiny had it mapped out a long time ago. She would go through her paces, and she would learn her inevitable function: leader.

Frall guided her gently to the place beside him. He sat at the head of the table, while offering the seat at the other end to Chief Morfal. His son, Coss, and the small band of Rakors in their company kept close. In tradition, her father cut the first tentacle and passed it down to Morfal by way of ilorays, hand to hand.

Morfal took a large bite, piercing the olive flesh with a viciousness that sent a freeze up the neck of warm-blooded Gryshen. Coss looked at his father in disgust. He gingerly reached for his own tentacle, handed it to a stout Rakor to his left, murmuring something Gryshen could not hear. On it went, passed back down the table, until Bravis handed it to her.

"It stops with you," he clarified, an odd tenseness to his signal, as she was reaching out to hand it to her father.

"What?" she asked, puzzled.

A clear, smooth voice glided across the table. "It is my offering to you, young Chieftainess."

"Gryshen," she quickly corrected, her voice like a hammer trying to push down this future.

"Gryshen," conceded Coss. "From a chieftain's son to a chieftain's daughter; may our first meeting be blessed." And his smile melted away the cold on her neck.

Jode's eyebrows raised to the cave ceiling. Gryshen could barely handle a quick nod in reply.

After dinner, Bravis followed her father and Morfal, along with a very skeletal lax Gryshen assumed to be his version of Bravis. Gryshen noted that he even wore the same stiff expression as their aide. But his face was harder, his eyes more calculating.

Her father was weak in his health, but strong in his convictions. She knew he'd stick to what he set up in the beginning; she knew he'd politely refuse to take sides. She just wasn't sure how Morfal would take it.

A bubble popped before her face. Jode.

"It'll be okay, Gryshie. Dad's tough. Always."

"Always?" She softly messaged back. Her eyes threatened to betray her, but she kept her tears at bay. She knew she could not let the Rakor see her as weak, and the remainder of them were coming back from the feast now.

"Gryshen," Coss messaged as though he had known her forever. His tone was the familiar pitch, the kind ceasids used for family, for best friends, for . . . other close ties. Gryshen wanted to wrap her hair around her face. She couldn't stay steady with this lax. Instead, she turned toward him, her loosened braid swirling to the side, baring her expression.

"Yes?"

"I don't know what to tell you, Gryshen. I do not know why my father is the way he is. I know that he is afraid. I know that he is defensive. I know that he is angry. He has always been sort of rough, but it got so much worse after my mother passed." His expression was grave, like a healer reporting the injury of a ceasid to the pod.

"I didn't know you lost your mother, too. I'm so sorry." The memories were faint, but she knew what she'd lost. And she remembered meeting his mother, once. Morfal's bride sat beside him at an Oceas summit between all the tribes. Now she remembered why Coss had that shock of white hair. His mother had the same cropped hair as her son's. She was just as pretty, too.

"Thanks," he responded, and she cringed. She also knew how uncomfortable it could be, having conversations with others about your dead mom: thanking them for their apologies, tolerating their uneasy silence, bracing through insensitive remarks. Ceasids didn't mean to be unkind, usually. So many of them viewed death as the second part of life, the natural transition, that they often forgot that loved ones suffered. They neglected the aching hearts of ilorays who lost a parent, a husband who lost his wife.

"She's stronger than ever!" Some would say, "She'll join us in battles to come!" or "Now he can really watch over the whole tribe, all at once. His eyes see everything now!"

Gryshen lost herself, just once, seasons after her mother's death, when a leen in her pod said that she was happy to now have Gryshen's mother as a spirit guardian.

"Really?" Gryshen's signal frequency was like a wounded seal, "I would just be happy if she could hold me again." The leen looked confused and apologized, but clearly didn't understand how her words were hurtful.

Gryshen, confident that Coss had put up with similar remarks, just left it as sincere sympathy. Coss searched her eyes for several minutes, making her sway between painful discomfort to awkward swooning.

"It happened in the last thaw. She went exploring and ditched the guards that usually followed and protected her. She loved the way the sun shines on the water. I'm sure that's where she was going. To this spot on the beach of an island. Thick jungle. Air so wet you feel like you're still swimming."

Gryshen had only heard of such places. The Rakor came from the farthest part of Oceas, the other side of this great ball they shared with landkeepers.

"The guards caught up to her, but they were too late. She had gotten caught in a mass of stingrays."

A death like this was not uncommon, especially not for hunters. It was, however, more unique for a queen.

"Mine got caught in a whirlpool. It would have been

fine, but her fin was still injured from a deep cut on the reef days before. She said it was better. It's one of the few things I remember about her—she said she was fine to go traveling." Gryshen could hear the confusion that still lingered in her tone. She never understood why her mother insisted she was all right. *Arrogance? Naïveté?* Two qualities that had been passed down to Jode. It was why Gryshen always felt such relief when he returned home from a hunting trip. Too many ilorays died before they even reached old age. Oceas held many dangers, and if you did extensive journeying, you would find that each new expanse of ocean offered a new expanse of terrors.

You could also live long and die naturally at an age past a landkeeper's lifespan. The water held many friends, too. Nutrients in the food. Healing in the plants. If you were careful, if you had a healthy respect for the sea, she could offer tremendous protection.

Without consciously realizing it, Gryshen had been leading him through the seemingly endless twists and turns of their cavern. She had not been to the bone pit in several seasons. It was hallowed ground. It was a place where she kept a part of her heart. Gryshen was like an observer of herself, surprised that she was leading this stranger here. But something inside her knew why. Her heart ached for his heartache, and she could only dull the pain by finding a place for them to commiserate.

And then she was blinded.

Thick black enveloped her, filling her eyes, pouring into her gills. When she realized that blood was billowing into the hall, it only took her a moment to recognize the scent.

Dad.

With a piercing cry, she sent a high-pitched alarm, bouncing off every wall, every corridor of the great cavern. Gryshen followed the rich smell, gagging as it filled her gills. She focused on her father while she kept her arms outstretched, flicking her tail, feeling for an opening to the room where her father had taken Morfal.

Morfal. What did he do?

Did Coss know?

She couldn't think about that now, she had to—*there* —she heard her father, "It's all right, I'm all right, just a little blood." She knew this was intended to reassure her. The only comfort it served was knowing he was still alive. Adrenaline kept coursing through her.

"Morfal!" she signaled down the corridor. "Get away from him!"

A pack of healers sped by her, skilled in their tracking, armed with medicines and wraps, and Gryshen followed. She saw them circling a figure. Morfal was close beside them with a lantern, his expression unreadable, Coss taking up his flank.

"Dad?" Gryshen trembled.

"You just rest. Don't strain yourself," Morfal ordered.

She saw Bravis floating on the other side of her father.

"He's right," Bravis signaled with some difficulty, not concealing his discomfort over agreeing with Morfal. He swept up beside her. "Gryshen, he had a coughing fit. It's been an eventful day. He ripped something inside. But look"—Bravis pointed a long finger—"they're stopping the bleeding."

Slowly, the blood was diminishing. As the water cleared, she could see the room better by lantern light. Her father offered her and Jode, who had caught up, a smile that was weakly reassuring. Bravis offered balms, elixirs, and various tools from the healer's satchels, bags made from swordfish stomachs. The stomachs offered just the right strength and elasticity.

Gryshen had nearly vomited when she tracked her father's blood scent minutes before. Jode always teased her about how when she joined him on a hunt, she kept her distance throwing spears, and always found a way out of cleaning the kill.

Now, she distracted herself from the blood by focusing on her dad. *Wasn't he scared? Why did he seem so calm?* The healers had just pulled a tube full of gooey substance from his throat. He seemed to be breathing more easily. The now broad smile he gave Gryshen did not assuage the sinking in her stomach.

"Daddy?" *Was that her voice?* It sounded as if it belonged to a little girl.

"It's a good thing Chief Morfal was here to alert the guards."

Before Gryshen could ask, her father signaled an answer. "I sent Bravis away. I thought he could use some rest. He's been by me constantly, and it was good for the chief and myself to speak, just the two of us." Gryshen was quite certain that her father being left alone in the care of Morfal was never a good idea. She kept this to herself, though, and hoped the Chief of Rakor had not noticed her earlier accusation.

"You see, Princess"—Morfal's signal crept around Gryshen like an eel—"we are all here in the other's best interests. I look out for your father, and he looks out for me." Never had a statement carried so much forced obligation. It coated the words, stiffening everyone. Coss seemed to twitch uncomfortably. Gryshen was pleased to see his discomfort at his father's attempt to manipulate a crisis.

Her own father, ever a peacemaker, smoothed out the crowd. "Right, Morfal. Thank you for alerting the tribe. I was hardly in a position to communicate. And now"—he nodded in thanks to the healers, dismissing them—"now all I need is a little sleep. I think everyone could use rest." With that, members of the Rakor swam away, escorted to their respective quarters by members of the Rone pod, leaving Coss, Morfal, Bravis, Jode, and herself.

"Please, Chief, let me know if I can be of any . . . help to you." That eel crept again.

Coss glowered in his father's direction. Gryshen would have given anything to know his thoughts.

"That's much appreciated. Bravis, time for bed," replied her father, completely ignoring this exchange. Gryshen couldn't suppress a smile watching her father instruct a full-grown lax as if he were a babe.

"But, Sir . . ." Bravis began to protest, then, observing the chief's weariness, thought better than to argue. He gave a slight bow, and swirled his great gray tail in the water as he left.

"I'm *fine*." He must have known that Jode and Gryshen didn't believe him. But he also must have known that they, like Bravis, didn't want to tire him further with any argument.

So Jode wrapped his arm around his father. "I heard that stuff you have to take is gross, but it'll heal you in no time." He shook the little pouch stuffed with seaberries and a crushed mix of plankton and leaves and grinned at his dad. Frall sighed, releasing a stream of bubbles, and matched his son's optimism.

"Of course. Night, Jode. Gryshie?"

Gryshen leaned in and brushed his cheek with a kiss.

Gryshen and Jode took arms around each other, linking as they headed to the breathing chamber.

CHAPTER 3

*I*t was just she and Jode, since most of the ilorays slept.

"What do you make of the Rakor visit?" Jode asked as he twisted a gear.

"I don't know yet." Gryshen gulped down excess water from the tube, and they began drawing air in large swells. "You've hunted with some of them before. How was that?"

Jode thought for a moment. "I never hunted with that Morfal creep. Or that son of his." The disdain he felt about the latter was clear in his transmission. "They don't really go on hunts, I don't think. Probably think it's beneath them." He snorted, spraying bubbles. He thought for another moment. "Grysh?"

"Yes?" She pulled as much air as her body could store for the night.

"The ones I hunted with were okay. Not so aggressive.

But I gotta say, I don't trust them."

"Either of them?" Gryshen tried to keep emotion out of her signal.

"I know he's pretty, Grysh, but his father—"

Gryshen whipped him with her tail. "Pretty? You think I'm some dumb leen who would be caught up with looks?"

"Ouch!" Jode rubbed his side. "What was that about?"

Gryshen felt sheepish. She hadn't tail-whipped her brother in a very long time. "I'm—I'm sorry. It's just that, well, you know he lost his mother in a stingray attack? Pretty recently. Maybe that's why he didn't join you for hunts."

"I had heard that. I didn't think of it, though. Sorry," he added, still patting his side. "I just don't know how far they want to take this warpath."

"I know, but could you imagine if something happened to our pearl?"

"Do we know if that's true?"

"Not officially. Not that Dad's confirmed, anyway. But why else would they be so anxious to discuss territory now, if something hadn't gone wrong with their own pearl? They now have their entire tribe at serious risk for disharmony, disease, death. We'd probably be that hostile, too."

"You're right."

Gryshen heard the easy concession in his tone, and wondered if Jode wasn't feeling weary himself.

"Let's get some rest."

They cranked the wheel, sealing the water tubes, and swam to their rooms.

Suspended in water, Gryshen's dreams seemed to move with fluidity as she slept. Swirls of blue acted like a closing curtain for each act playing in her subconscious. Jode laughing from the hunt, a shadowy image of her family weaving shells in her mother's hair before burial, embracing her father . . . and then the dream shifted to a crying little Coss, his dead mother, beautiful like him, ghostly blonde, a father growing more and more bitter. She shivered in her sleep; the sea felt icier around this frozen family.

When Gryshen awoke, it was with the confusion that comes from restless slumber. She adjusted the kelp on her chest, and swam quickly down to the water chamber.

The line was longer than usual since they were having to accommodate a guest tribe. Wordlessly, the other ilorays pulled back to the cavern walls, clearly making way for her to go first. This subservience always made Gryshen uncomfortable, and she usually ignored it and took a place in the back of the line to wait with the rest. This morning, however, she felt like her lungs had been rubbed with sand. Perhaps the vivid dreams and wakeful sleep had drained her brain of necessary energy. Regardless, she took the offer gratefully, and rather guiltily, swam to the front. A young ceasid pulled her lips away, saw Gryshen, and backed away nervously.

What is this? Gryshen wondered. Puzzled, she drew

herself up to the tube, and forgot about the anxious child as she wildly gulped down sweet sea air.

Coss was waiting for her as she swam back to her room.

"Can I help you?" she asked, trying to keep emotion out of her signal.

"I don't know. I don't want to bother you."

"What is it?"

"My father is having a meeting with his aides while Chief Frall rests. They were going to summit this morning, but ..."

"But like you said, my father is resting." The very fact that Morfal was still pushing these meetings angered her. *Couldn't he see her father needed to heal?*

"Look, I hope you understand that Chief Frall sent word that he still wanted to meet." Coss responded to a complaint she hadn't verbalized.

"Well, what choice does he have?" It was as if the rush of oxygen to her lungs fueled the fire stoked by Jode the night before. When Gryshen's throat felt especially tight, as it had upon waking, fresh air had almost a heady effect.

She felt a brush on her shoulder.

"I am so sorry. I don't know what else to do." Coss's fingers lingered against her skin for a few moments, holding her in place ever so gently.

"What else?" she asked.

He searched her face.

"Ah, Gryshen. I've just been to see your father."

Bravis seemed to swim up out of nowhere. He gave a nod to Coss, then turned back to her. "He's looking better, Princess."

"Better than bleeding from his organs?" The flames were spreading onto Bravis now, too.

"Right. Better." Only his hair moved in the water, the rest of him stayed still like a hunk of rock. "So will you be joining him and the Rakor chief when they dine later?" His tone suggested that he wasn't really asking.

"Yes. Later. But now I am giving our guest a tour. Father wanted me to help them get the lay of the land."

"Oh, shall I send for your father to accompany you, Prince?" Bravis asked.

"That won't be necessary. He's very busy this morning. I'll report back to him."

"And I'm sure Father will want you in charge of making sure everything is going smoothly with our other guests," Gryshen said.

"Certainly." Bravis raised an eyebrow in one stiff motion and flicked away.

"Shall we, then?" Gryshen led the way in her best effort to conjure confidence. "Have you had air yet this morning, Prince?"

"Oh, please don't go back to that on me. Just Coss. Please. And yes. Early. My pod is very practiced in using up small amounts of oxygen. I can last longer than most laxes of other tribes."

"Is that so? It must be nice to have such fantastic health. I suppose you naturally feel entitled to ours."

"What do you mean?"

They were back down the corridor that led to the bone pit.

"Nothing." *You know better than to pry into another pod's affairs, Gryshen.* She waited until he wasn't looking at her to take a peek at him. The natural light was nonexistent at this point. They relied on the lanterns, now spaced feet apart on the walls and hanging in clusters above their heads, to even see paces ahead.

The lights always stayed lit in the passages to the hub, and openings in the cavern allowed for sunlight and drop-ins from schools of fish or a stray crab. There were the same torches, and often holes in the ceilings of all the sleeping chambers, as well.

There were a few places where no light was kept, where ilorays relied completely on signal. One of these was just before finding the opening out of the cavern leading to the bone pit. The Old Ones said this was to symbolize the darkness when one closes their eyes before being reborn to another part of the sea. They said it was like the darkness of a mother's womb before you come into the light of the world.

Jode's suspicions had stuck to Gryshen as she slept, and had kept her on guard all morning.

And yet there was something about Coss that made her want to apologize, made her want to keep his hand on her, made her want to sink into him.

The lights were getting dimmer, and his eyes glowed as they stared in her direction.

"We're approaching one of the darkest parts of our home." Gryshen crackled into the blackness with these words, unsure if she wanted to break the spell or not.

She let out a call that bounced around the sea, guiding them, narrowing their path in her mind.

"But you know your way well through all this, don't you?" Those eyes were growing dimmer, too, yet somehow it was as if his gaze remained like a spotlight.

"I'm sure you know much more than I. I'm sure you know all about how to navigate in the darkness." She looked straight ahead as she spoke.

"We have many pitch-black portions of our own cavern, if that's what you mean."

"Of course it's what I mean."

"Well then. Yes, I do."

Gryshen had no handle on this conversation anymore. She couldn't be quite sure whether she wanted to, either. Little by little, it was as if the sun was slowly, slowly rising. They swam around corners and bends, moving quickly toward the end of Rone.

The bone pit marked the border; it was the last stop at this part of the cavern before reaching open sea. When the season was brighter, the landscape almost glittered. Now, it still wore a dull polish. The sand was littered with bones of ceasids, but also whales, dolphins, even the exoskeletons of crabs lined the rusted metal entrance.

Over time ilorays had learned methods of preservation: They could slow down decay of many retrieved items by first bringing them above surface to dry, then rubbing them with plant oils. The makers gave new life this way.

Still, nothing could stop Oceas from bringing everything through a cycle of death and rebirth. Eventually, a ship's anchor would become bits of sand on the ground, and sand, as Gryshen understood, could be made into glass by landkeepers. And glass was a coveted item to ilorays—especially if it was thick.

Sea glass adorned their bodies and their chambers. Jars and lanterns and diver's helmets were all used to contain the jellyfish that lit the way. Miles from where Gryshen liked to lay ashore was an aboveground cavern where the makers worked. It had remained far enough from humans to stay a safe place for everything from cataloging new discoveries, to preservation, to construction and repairs.

Of all ceasids, the Rone pod was in the least danger of landkeeper discovery or interference. Living near the coldest part of the world kept things that way.

Now, here, was the safest place of all. The light was blinding as they swam out to open space to meet a wall of ice. The glacier acted like a great tomb, holding the dead close in its crevices. It was a rare place, a place that stayed put in the sea, a place that was close to their Rone Cavern but apart enough to make clear that this was a transition: darkness to light to darkness, death to birth to death.

Some of the graves were easy to see; tucked just

behind a seat of stone you'd find a metal box, or a glass jar, holding the bones of the dead. Sometimes a large glass case or wire cage would hold a full skeleton, or sometimes just a skull or a tail. Perhaps there'd be a piece of jewelry tied to them, or a special shell tucked inside.

Most of the graves were far back, so one had to reach in and feel around, or swim around rocks and a wall of ice that seemed to grow out of the water. Some bones or baubles of the dead remained well preserved, beautifully entombed, but most decayed and eventually faded away to become a part of where they began. Ceasids did not usually grieve this. In fact, the more preserved graves were usually that way for teaching purposes, so that the next generation could have a visual image, a tangible view of a great chieftain or shaman who had long since transitioned.

The important part that remained, only to be recognized by a deeply connected loved one, were the whispers of their soul.

Sea magic stayed preserved in its salty brine, and long after they had been separated from their land-keeper cousins, the ceasids had remained connected to it. They did not really have the option to forget their original power, as they did not have the same distractions that had accosted the landkeepers.

So, the question was never "if" they could talk to the dead, but more like "how much would it help to do so?" or "Do the dead care to share?"

Gryshen's mother's grave had become nearly empty. She did not want an elaborate preservation process, and so all that remained was a brilliant blue bottle. Gryshen remembered it from her childhood. This bottle had kept a post near the entrance to their cave. It sat atop a metal pipe that acted as a welcome, and it was in such a position that it could catch shafts of sunlight filtering down, and send a spray of sparkling blue dancing on the cavern door. When Athela, her mother, came back as Frall's bride, she said the light brought her home. Frall had courted her after having met her at a feast with the Wanaa pod, the tribe who lived a world away in the Pacific. It didn't happen often, interpod bonds, but this time it helped link them further as an ally.

Gryshen wasn't sure what she was doing here, who she was trying to get answers from. Her mother had never spoken to her since her death, not a whisper, a song, a puff of light. All that remained was that bottle.

"This is your mom?" Coss finally spoke again.

"Yes."

"Does she leave you messages?"

"No."

"Not even some energy residue?"

"*No.*"

"My mother's grave just cries."

"What?"

"Yeah. I'd rather she said nothing at all."

Gryshen had no idea what to say to him. Having to

visit a weeping grave? But she wasn't sure that it was worse than silence. She wasn't sure if anything was.

"Let's take a tour of our line."

"I would like that," he signaled with relief.

This time, she led him around the outside of the cavern. Schools of fish swept past them on their way to the line of large mammals kept for pleasure, big hunts, and battle. A starfish came loose from gray rock, and Coss handed it to her. It had four limbs instead of five.

"It's different, like you."

"What? Cause I'm missing something?" Gryshen said tersely.

"No! Because you're unusual." This time, after tapping her shoulder, he moved a billow of her black hair that was dancing in front of her eyes. *No protection now.* "What is it? You've seemed upset with me since this morning. What happened?" As he spoke, he tucked the starfish just above her ear. It was as if the gesture was totally separate from the question.

"What do you want?" she blurted out.

He just stared.

"Like what you just did. You are so comfortable touching me. What are you doing?" She couldn't believe herself.

Again, he just stared, boring through her mind with his eyes. Then her vision was blurred with bubbles and waves as she felt two hands grip her face, his own moving in swiftly, his lips cutting through the cold, sending a signal she had never heard down her throat and into her belly. The message swirled around her heart, binding it up. And she reached back, returning a call she had not known how to make before now.

It was like lightning cracking against the sea. It was like the fire that burned from a maker's torch when they fused pieces together, taking broken bits and sealing them whole, making them sing in their newfound identity.

No one had kissed her, not in this way. No one dared without permission and a formal courtship.

She never wanted it to stop.

But stop it did, when a beluga nudged up against the pair, like a chaperone at a ball.

"Misra!" She felt completely caught. Luckily, whales couldn't talk. At least, they couldn't gossip.

The beasts frequently stopped by for treats and pats. They pulled up to the line when they left the coastline, which was where they usually stayed. There were six narwhals that took turns posting themselves as well, in addition to three orcas and one massive bowhead whale. At any time, one could find eight or more beasts near the post, maybe less if Gup the bowhead was there. He was just that big, with a great suctioning mouth that he drew along the sea floor.

The ceasids had an understanding with these creatures. In exchange for their services, the Rone pod would help protect them from both landkeeper and sea predators, as they kept a watch for themselves. The orca would be tied by seaweed to a kind of chariot, or be ridden astride by ilorays, since the beasts could go farther distances than their part-human friends. Narwhals were also for riding, but the unicorn-like horns on their heads could be used to pierce a seal that a spear missed, or help fight off an aggressive shark.

The bowhead just *looked* impressive, and of all the different pods, he was by far the largest beast that stayed in close contact.

"Misra, I was just going to introduce a visiting prince to our beasts." Gryshen pointed to the line.

Why was she making excuses to a whale? Gryshen attempted to shake off her embarrassment. Misra cocked her head in a way that Gryshen could have sworn suggested suspicion of her claim, but began swimming alongside them toward the posts of animals.

"Okay, right now we have the three belugas—Misra, of course, she's my riding partner; Jeer, he's the one ignoring us; and Kess, she's got the big scar above her eye. A bad run-in with a shark." Kess gave a timid glance their direction.

Coss gave a polite nod to each creature as they stopped to greet them.

"Only two of the six narwhals are here today, Sol and Ry—they're brother and sister. A few others are out today, including a baby."

Sol was brighter and whiter than Misra, who was a pearly gray, and Ry, who was dark silver and appeared to be missing a small chunk of her horn.

"Next, we've got just one of our orcas, Sillar. He's the

smallest of the three we work with." Sillar looked like he was anxious to go after his friends.

"And lastly, Gup." Gryshen swept her arm and head into a kind of bow, as she showed him one of the biggest, ugliest creatures in the Arctic Circle. Gup looked like he was more interested in a nap than anything else, although his half-open mouth appeared to turn into a crooked smile when he received a gentle rub on the forehead from her.

"Very nice to meet all of you." Coss addressed them personally. The effort was not lost on Gryshen.

Suddenly, a swarm of bubbles signaled the arrival of Sodaren, a female at about the midpoint of her life with shoulder-length brown hair and a round torso and tail.

"Princess, I didn't know you were here. I just had an early lunch before I gave our friends theirs."

"Oh, of course. I was just showing our visitor what sort of beasts we kept."

"Yes, yes. Aren't they wonderful? We work with some of the largest anywhere. And so in tune with us." She attempted to wrestle a net of salmon from Jeer's engulfing mouth. "Everybody gets some. This is a snack for everyone!" She got it free, making it a point to hand fish to the others before finally getting back to the pouting beluga.

"I understand the Rakor tribe work with some more *unusual* choices." Sodaren signaled "unusual" as if what she wanted to say was too offensive, so she had to settle for that word.

"We do. But if you know how to work well with sharks—"

"I beg your pardon, Prince, but we work on an ideal level with all *agreeable* creatures—and that certainly includes many kinds of sharks!" Now she was huffing.

"Of course. I am sure you do. It's just that some of the more aggressive ones require a certain kind of—"

"Hostile nature?"

Gryshen was open mouthed at Sodaren's boldness. It was typical of her to be . . . forthright, but with a chieftain's son? She also had the feeling that she was supposed to object to such behavior, but quieting another iloray was far beyond her comfort.

"I was going to say firmness." Coss flashed a vivid smile. It seemed to soften his opponent a bit. But she pressed further.

"Yes, but the monsters? They're different from sea beasts that you can engage with, even reason with." She slapped Jeers away as he dug his nose back into her net in search of more treats.

"Sometimes it's not about reason. Sometimes it's about control."

"Only in life and death circumstances, self-defense, should it be about control!" Gryshen had to protest his remark.

"But isn't it all life and death? Leens, we keep close tabs and tight reins on our more dangerous ones—our monsters. Our beastkeeper knows where all twelve of our larger sharks are at any time." Gryshen knew by "larger sharks," he was referring to a dozen massive great whites. Many tales had been told at the hub's circle about the more sinister sorts that Rakor did dealings with.

"I understand you keep a huge net of stingrays sedated, ready to strike." Gryshen's curiosity took over, now that it seemed he was happy to offer up information.

"What? You don't drug your jellyfish? They're just so docile they let you use them as lanterns?" He was right, of course. Along with their healing abilities, the medicine keepers of all the pods were experts in many everyday uses of sea plant life. A black eel released a venom that poisoned its small prey on direct contact, but when the gland was cut out and a tear was made, it could be released into a vast flock of jellyfish, making them drowsy enough to scoop into nets of metal and sea grass and drop into lanterns. When they came out of it, it was too late.

"But that is for light, not as a threat. Not as some wild expression of power."

"And what is Gup?" As he spoke, the bowhead let out a belch that pushed the water past the three of them.

By the time lunch was signaled, Gryshen felt starved. She was almost willing to get past the fact that she would not be joining the main pod for this meal, but would instead be expected to share food with Morfal in her father's chambers. She and Coss had been debating everything from the use of beasts to tribal customs since they left the line that morning. She had shown him the corridor leading to the healers and the rooms that prepare the next generations of chieftains, and had taken him past the great rotunda of rock near the hub that held most of the tribe's chambers, marked by smaller and larger openings going up the walls like a disjointed reef. They spoke of favorite dishes of the different pods, exchanged tribal lore, and laughed over recollections of the exaggerating heroes who recalled all-too-similar tales. They spoke of quite a lot, but they never spoke about the kiss.

The midday meal was a portion of leopard seal, the larger of which was feeding the rest of the pod in the hub. Ilorays did not eat a lot in one stop typically, because they snacked on plant life and the occasional fish as they swam about, but Gryshen was hungry, and opted to ignore the stares from the rest of their party as she scarfed down three portions of seal flesh and two handfuls of scallops. Bravis kept passing more food to her father like a worried mother, trying to get him to eat, but he waved it away. She felt Bravis's watchful eye as Coss touched her shoulder to ask her a question, but soon realized his weren't the only eyes to contend with, as her father's brow seemed to raise slightly when Coss adjusted the starfish in her hair.

Morfal was oblivious, smacking his lips and eating in the most disgusting way possible.

After Morfal and Coss retired to their quarters to rest, Frall asked Bravis to give him a moment with Gryshen.

CHAPTER 4

"Gryshie, I wanted to speak with you." Frall's words were hesitant.

"Yes, Dad?"

"I understand that you've been very cordial, very welcoming to our guests. And I appreciate the effort."

"Well, I'm trying my best. But it must be nearly impossible for you to have to be civil with Morfal. You're so kind to him. I have no clue how you do it."

"Practice, my girl." He chuckled. "Practice and practice, years of tolerance. There was a time that we didn't get along so great with the Wanaa, either."

"Yes, but that was different. Those were old, small quarrels. The difference is that the Wanaa are caring—unlike Morfal. They wanted to forgive. And they wanted Mom to be happy with you."

He nodded. "I hope she was. I did love her."

"Of course she was. Of course you did." Why was her

father saying it like that? But before she could ask the question, he brought up a different one.

"You keep mentioning Morfal as the issue here. Why just him?"

"Well, he's in charge, isn't he?"

"Yes, and his son is next in line."

"But you saw how tyrannical his father is! He's impossible."

"And you seem to find the young prince quite tolerable."

Gryshen did not like the direction this was heading at all.

"What are you implying?"

Her father held up a hand. "My little kelp, no one is attacking you. You seem on edge. How long has it been since you've visited an air tube?"

It had been awhile.

"Gryshie! I have to trust you to do this. I'd put Jode in charge of you if I thought you would listen to him."

"Jode has his own priorities—like spearing swordfish and having his hair braided by leens," she joked.

"This is not a game. You cannot afford to go too long. You don't have the same tolerance to withstand a lack of oxygen."

"I know, Dad!" She was exasperated. He spoke about her breathing... situation like it was some sort of handicap.

"I won't always be here, Gryshie."

"Just stop it. Please." Her exasperation turned to fear.

"All right. What were we talking about before? Oh yes. Your tolerance for Coss."

Gryshen was back to exasperation. "Dad, you said I should make them comfortable. He wanted a tour."

"And, again, I appreciate that. But I do want you to learn the line between cordiality and unnecessary friendliness. Coss is a very polite lax—he does appear to be nearly an opposite of his father. I am glad he will be the one taking the throne next; it bodes well for our alliances. But for now, he is not in charge. And Gryshie, his father might not take too kindly to your friendship. You can see that there is a bit of a power grab going on here. But now we know more. They have lost something far more important."

"The Rakor pearl is missing, then?" She spoke in her pod's signal.

Her father looked steadily at her, and switched over to Rone signal as well. "You didn't ask the young prince this already?"

"No, Father, I'm not an idiot. I know the one thing we never discuss with other tribes is the condition of their pearl." It was well she should know this, because it was driven into her mind since she could remember.

"Of course you're not. I'm sorry." He looked so tired. "But this information must stay with us."

A nervous trill sang up Gryshen's back.

"Their pearl was stolen. Apparently, an aide that had been close to Morfal for many, many seasons made off ith it in the hopes of starting his own tribe with a leen from the Calaarns."

Morfal really was good at keeping secrets. *But what about the new pod? Why hadn't they been in communication with anyone?*

"The reason you haven't heard about this is because the aide only just got to the Calaarns when another leen, who his mate had apparently confided in, went to Gracke."

Gracke, with a glowing orange beard that came down toward his fin, was the chief of the Calaarn tribe. Gryshen usually could not think of him without smiling. He kept a group of blowfish that he trained to make different sounds when he tickled their belly. He was constantly in the process of starting a band. Jode had turned him down numerous times—not that he could sing or play anything. Gracke didn't care.

"You'd look cool as a pounder. It's easy. Just hit rocks together. Leens love you, and you could really help us get a following."

"Yeah, like you need help with that." Jode would laugh.

"What did Gracke say? Which leens?" Gryshen was sure she would recognize their names at least. There were little more than a hundred ilorays in that pod.

"Cennyn and Sae."

She didn't need to ask who did what. Cennyn was quiet, so quiet you could easily forget she was around.

And Sae? She wouldn't be ignored. If anyone was

feeling revolutionary, if anyone would be an accomplice to a pearl-take, it would be her.

"What happened to Sae?" she asked.

Her father raised a brow at her swift assessment. "She was crossed, and banished."

"Oh no."

"Just for a season of freeze and thaw. Gracke is more generous than I would have been."

"How can you say that? Banishment could kill her." Banishment was one of the most extreme punishments practiced in the sea. A ceasid was left to their own resources, without the protection of pod or pearl. Most made it back when their time was finished, but a few did not.

Crossing wouldn't kill an iloray, but it could destroy their spirit. A chieftain would carve a deep X, crossing out the mark the criminal had received during Forms, so that whatever they had been, they were no longer. Not a healer or a hunter, just *crossed*. They could serve in their pod. They could change their ways, but it was a constant reminder to all. They would never really be trusted again.

Gryshen thought that might be worse than being sent away to die.

"Stealing the Rakor pearl could have wiped out an entire pod, Gryshen! You know that. Without it, they would be susceptible to disease, even famine or war. Without our pearls—"

"We will perish. I know."

He looked annoyed at her interruption.

"Dad, it's just . . . how do we know for certain that they need their pearl to live? Maybe they'll just be a little weak. What if they could survive without it?"

Frall drew in water, eyes wide and white, bubbles swirling.

"Gryshen, do you know a chieftainess's most important task?"

"Protecting the tribe?"

"We are not the warriors! And I am not their father, Gryshen!" He bellowed the signal, and it shook the schools of pale fish darting by. Frall gave a nod, like an apology, in the direction of a crab who seemed like he had lost his direction in the noise. He dropped his shoulders and looked back at Gryshen with a steadied gaze.

"We light the path that leads all ilorays home." He paused. "We are a peaceful pod, a careful pod, a wise pod, and I am trusted to show our pod who we are, like a reflection shows the surface of the sea. I am a guide. I am their reminder."

Gryshen floated, thinking.

Frall continued, "The Rone Pearl is our greatest, clearest memory of who we are, what we are made of, where we come from, and where we'll return." He offered that sad smile again. "Our oldest story tells us what to do, shows us the way, and our pearls are like great lanterns, tethers to Mother. Protect the pearl with our lives . . ."

"And it will make life with protecting," Gryshen signaled softly.

Frall nodded, squeezing her hand.

"Father, I understand."

"I don't know if you do. You seem to take a lot lightly these days, Gryshen." He was drawing himself up to resemble the kind of stately manner he once always carried himself with. Only now she could detect a wince as he did it.

Gryshen repeated herself. "I understand, Dad. I really do. So Sae is banished for two seasons. And the aide?"

"Kosten, I think his name was. They punished him twofold, Gryshie. First a Drying, and then a Ripping."

Gryshen gasped. She had not heard of such a combination of execution.

"This sort of thing is extremely rare, kelp"—he gave her arm a gentle squeeze—"but I fear I have done you no favors by keeping you in the dark about the details, the darker details that swim alongside leaders."

"But you would never—"

"No, I would never. Of course, I've never had to deal with a killer in my tribe, but I can't fathom performing both of the most brutal forms of execution."

"How did that work, exactly?" Gruesome curiosity had taken hold.

Frall took a small gulp. "They brought him out to a barren spot—a rock farther out from the islands, and tied him up—it was a traditional Dry at first, but after two days out of water, when he was almost dead, they didn't wait for the sun and air to finish it. They pulled him back into the water, and just when he thought they were showing mercy, they paraded him in front of their stock of sharks to feed." He wore a look that suggested, for the briefest moment, that he wasn't holding the highest confidence in his ability to work with someone who could do this.

Gryshen stared.

"I know, Gryshie, it's absolutely barbaric. But I would have done something, too. Banished him permanently, I imagine, after retrieving the pearl, and finding a new place for it." Gryshen couldn't argue with this, especially after what she just heard. Banishment almost seemed like a tame treat.

Frall met her eyes and nodded, as if to silently acknowledge the vast universe between his version of "doing something" and Morfal's. "But Morfal has members of his pod bringing it back from the thief's hiding place. So they *should* be safe."

"Should?" Gryshen narrowed her eyes. "You don't believe him, do you, Dad?"

"Well, would you?"

"You think something else happened to it?"

"I think it's very possible that it is damaged, or missing, judging from Morfal's behavior. But you know how I prefer to handle matters of suspicion."

"Watch and wait."

Frall nodded.

Gryshen paused. "What would they do if it were gone permanently?"

"Well, I would have consulted with our elders, but I think the right thing to do would be to share our pearl's energy with them. Ours is the farthest reaching. I would talk with the Calaarns about sharing theirs, as well."

"How would that work?"

"We would move ours to a more central location. It would be a sacrifice, a drain on our resources, but it would be the right thing."

Gryshen smiled in pride at her father. "So who knows the pearl was stolen?"

"Morfal, of course, Coss, another aide, and the executioner," said Frall.

The Rone tribe didn't have an executioner. It simply never came up. Then again, they rarely had violent crime, as her father had just reminded her.

"How did he explain—"

"Morfal said he had been poaching from the food supply, and had conspired to assassinate him."

"And no one questioned this?"

"Did those Rakor look like they'd question him?" Frall asked.

This needed no answer. Of course they didn't question.

"So, what exactly is he after?" asked Gryshen.

"Territory, power. Listen, I don't mean to cut this short, but Apocay will be here soon to check on me after last night."

Gryshen attempted to wash away the recollection that Apocay only appeared so often in a sleep chamber when the living were dying. He had a long, withered face, with a beaklike nose. She couldn't really think of a time when he hadn't appeared ancient. She also couldn't think of a time when Apocay had spoken more than a few words to her: "Pass the seal belly, please," or "Your father is changing course," (dying), or "Yes, the beluga dance is impressive. Who took the last of the scallops?" His bony figure never betrayed his appetite.

"He's so weird," Gryshen said.

"What, you want your medicine keepers to be as charming as your brother?" Her father laughed. "Not me. I want the strange ones, the ones who are so obsessed with healing that they have no time for social graces."

"True. But even Jode manages to be an incredible hunter."

"Jode is very unique. Like you."

"You mean he's unique, and I'm . . . a little broken."

"What are you talking about?" Her father was sharp, and his anger almost made him look healthy, so much so that Gryshen was tempted to say something to stir it again, but when she thought of the rest he needed, she thought better of it.

"Nothing, Dad. Just that it sometimes gets to me, my lung thing."

Her father put his hands on her shoulders and spoke with his usual tenderness. "It only requires an adjustment, Gryshie. Little tweaks. You must make it a priority to stay fueled. No one would know the difference. You can swim just as fast as anybody else."

"Why am I supposed to hide it then?" Her question startled him, and herself a little. She didn't know that it was waiting there.

"You—you don't have to hide it," he signaled a bit defensively. "It's simply that it's nobody's business but your family's. That's all. No one knew I was ill until they had to know."

Gryshen nodded, then thought of another question that had been sitting back behind that one, but she didn't dare ask. She'd upset her father too much. Another time.

And with the realization that she was running out of "another times" with her father, she felt the sting of ink in her eyes and turned her head quickly to hide it.

"Okay, Dad, well . . . I know you're expecting Apocay, and—"

"And you have somewhere to be." He gave a small smile, tilting his head in the direction of the nearest air chamber.

Gryshen obeyed, and the minute the oxygen hit her lungs, she felt wrapped in a comfort that had been missing for hours.

And in the days that followed, Gryshen tried to heed Frall's warnings.

She made it a point to frequent the air chamber much more often than was even necessary, mainly to keep him from worrying. It was a small gesture she could make to seem up to the task of leading. Of course, she was dubious about proving her ability, since not only was she certain she didn't have it, she was even more certain that if she swept confidently into a leadership position, her father might mistake it for permission to die.

Gryshen also strived to remain civil with Morfal, and polite with Coss—the latter proving more difficult than the former. She could fake her way around dealing with the cold chieftain, but his son . . . there was now an unspoken intimacy that threatened to unravel her if she was around him for too long. Mother forbid she wind up alone with him again—she had no idea how she could handle it.

They shared meals with the royal groups, or in the evening with their pod in the hub. Coss remained consistently warm, as if he was completely unfazed by what had transpired between them. Sometimes she would catch that glow in his eyes, but turn away quickly as if he were a mythological monster that could transform her. Only instead of stone, that look threatened to peel everything back and reveal her innermost feelings.

She pretended not to notice or care when the leens of her tribe flirted with him. Unlike Jode, he didn't seem to appreciate Rone's most eligible and beautiful ceasids offering him food from their hands at feasts, showing off treasures they'd recovered from sinkings, or demonstrating their often-questionable singing abilities. It wasn't that it bothered him; he just didn't seem to care. And this pleased Gryshen more than she'd admit.

When she was around him for too long, she practiced excusing herself, rushing away in a similar tone to the way she did when she was moving to the air chamber for a draw of oxygen.

Gryshen often found herself on her shore, on the rocks and bricks of ice that jutted out and sheltered her from view. The larger building was the only thing in sight sometimes, but when she felt bolder, she'd heave herself up higher on flat sheets of rock to soak in the rare sunlight, and when she did this, she could see the tiny stone cottage that lay directly behind it.

On these stark winter days, the lady did not come out as much. Gryshen might glimpse her walking with the old man into the wood structure, a group following not far behind. When the warm season was upon them, she could see the lady hanging her laundry on a line, or picking wildflowers. In both freeze and thaw times, in rougher weather or clear skies, she would hide behind the largest rock and watch the lady staring out to sea. Sometimes the woman would shade her eyes from the sun and peer intently; other times it seemed like she was just absentmindedly watching the water. There was only a small dock on this edge of land, and boats rarely came to it. Gryshen would turn to look in the direction of the woman's gaze and wonder what it was she saw. The humans here seemed nonthreatening, peaceful . . . a small village on an icy land.

But Gryshen was careful, always careful.

She had known that humans feared what they did not understand, that landkeepers had forgotten what the ceasids always knew: That they were brothers, cousins, maybe even twins, so long ago. That in the beginning one chose to stay in the water while the other explored on land.

When it came to landkeepers, there was always a deep sense of mistrust. The old tale suggested that it was because of the memory of long-ago treachery that sat deep within an iloray's bones, that the landkeepers could never really be trusted.

But Gryshen had never actually known one . . . all she knew was what she could glimpse of the old man, the woman drying her clothes, and the groups that huddled into the old worship house.

For her, there wasn't really anywhere that was perfectly safe. Between her passing father, the descending crown, her growing feelings for Coss, and the stretch of shore that sat dangerously close to the humans, sanctuary was tricky to come by.

CHAPTER 5

*R*estraining her emotions whenever a certain iloray was around had become a necessary challenge.

It had been about seven sleeps since the Rakor first descended upon them, and Coss was only becoming more interesting. When she was asked to accompany them to a meeting in the following days, she did her best to avoid his gaze, did her best to keep herself contained during some incredibly dull discussions on territory history, interpod history, and laws of tribal goodwill, that were only livened up by threatening innuendo and barely veiled power grabs from Morfal.

It was after a midday meal that Coss asked for her help.

"I've seen all within your home, but I have yet to really explore around it," he signaled as she trailed a crew of ilorays leaving an air chamber.

"But you joined Jode on his last hunting expedition." Gryshen was not going to be swayed. She was grateful to be freshly filled with oxygen. It helped her feel less woozy around him.

"Yes, but that was hunting. We were focused on the kill. I would just like to spend more time focused on . . . other things."

Gryshen felt her pale ash cheeks fill with a purple hue, the blood drawing from everywhere in her body. She looked away for as long as she could without appearing obvious.

"Well, let me see if Sodaren is available to take you on a ride." She signaled louder than she meant to, attracting the attention of the others swimming ahead.

"Gryshen, please. Let us show proper hospitality! Take our guest for a ride." Her father nodded at her.

Gryshen knew Frall was trusting her, and she would not fail him.

The water was smooth and clear, as if Coss had made it so for their travels.

Gryshen waited for him by the line of beasts. She greeted Sodaren, who couldn't help but raise one eyebrow when Gryshen explained what she was there to do.

"If I may, he is very unusual, isn't he? I never knew one of their kind to be so charming."

"We are ALL of the same kind, Sodaren." Gryshen rattled off her father's words without a pause, even if she didn't agree with what she was saying. Morfal was nothing like her. The Rakor might as well have come from a different planet. But Coss? He wasn't the same as her, but he wasn't like them, either. His very being made her question her prejudices like nothing else.

"Yes, I'm sorry. Of course. But—he is so very charming." Sodaren hung on to her surprise in these words.

And as she signaled these in the language of the Rone, the iloray in discussion had pushed through the water like lifting a curtain. Gryshen felt the burning in her cheeks again, and it dropped down through her chest and belly and fin. She hadn't said anything to be embarrassed about, but Coss didn't know that. He didn't receive their signal, their frequency, so there was always the underlying sense that all sorts of things might be said. This was why it was always considered rude to speak in a singular pod's frequency in front of another tribe.

"Well"—now Sodaren spoke in the main signal —"you know where all the reins and supplies are, of course. But there was rumor of a pair of hungry sharks, unconnected and wild, that were farther out. The hunt mentioned them to me."

"Yes, Jode had told me he spotted them. Not familiar at all. But they were very far out. We're perfectly safe, Sodaren," she said, although she got the feeling that Sodaren's anxiety was somehow more connected to her riding partner than to the dangerous beasts she spoke of. Why did everyone seem to think she was incapable of self-control around this lax?

Misra was napping. Gryshen considered one of the orca, but knew it would be unwise—they were only ridden for major hunts, and were otherwise for emergency battle. She chose a narwhal, Feln, and offered the more mischievous beluga, Jeer, to Coss. Sodaren helped them saddle the beasts, tying the fibers and metal links strung together from freshly retrieved fishing nets and anchor hoists, twisting them around the horn of the narwhal while he waited. She began patting the snout and coaxing treats into the mouth of the beluga until he finally opened up and let her fasten them at the rear of his mouth.

"We'll just be circling the perimeter of the cavern mostly—we won't go out much farther than that." Gryshen said this to both Coss and Sodaren. Sodaren nodded, still wearing a nervous expression, and adjusted their reins for the second time.

Coss sat astride the white whale, his long pale fin like a sleeping ghost resting alongside the beast's great body. Jeer began to bob up and down like an impatient babe that had to relieve himself. But for all his bouncing, he barely swayed the young lax, who just smiled and petted him commandingly. Gryshen attempted to take charge, pushing forward with Feln and gesturing for the pair to follow. They swam along the edge, the rocky home to their left, wild open water to the right. Schools of fish changed in and out with the cycles of waves, and seasons of freeze and thaw, and now palm-sized silver ones fanned in between throngs of smoky purple-and-black fish.

It felt like it had been forever since Gryshen had been out in the open water like this. It was a freedom many in her pod enjoyed when they came of riding age, but it was something that she never seemed to have time for since her father's illness. Being trained to be chieftainess didn't leave much room for anything else. She had a sizable gulp of air just before heading to the stables, but that wasn't what made her feel so relaxed. No, it was resting confidently on the beast's back, sensing her moves, releasing the reins, and barely touching her horn with one hand while she stretched out the other, letting her fingertips get tickled by nipping fish, feeling the silky strands of sea grasses caress her open palm. Gryshen cocked her head back and looked up. Pools of brightness formed in the water above, and as they swam higher, she realized the dark patches existed from swaths of clouds passing overhead. She was startled to see how high they had gotten. She turned around to see Coss following close behind, taking in all that surrounded them. She had been enjoying herself so much she had nearly forgotten about him, about the twisting in her chest and the pounding in her heart whenever he was near.

But this was too close to the surface for these animals, who were trained to keep their riders beneath water unless otherwise commanded, so they tugged the ilorays back down to a comfortable level. Gryshen looked around again, and the water had clouded. She couldn't see the cavern from here, but she knew it had to still be close. They hadn't gone that far. Between the ceasid signaling, and the superior tracking abilities of the beluga and narwhal, being out of vision of the Rone never made any grown iloray uneasy.

She slid off Feln's long back, tying the reins around the rest of his horn. "There. That should make it easier for you to move without them getting stuck on some-thing." Then she let out a high squeal and tilted her head to let the creature know she could forage for food, but to stay close.

Coss followed her lead, tying his own metal and rope around the body of the beluga, and using Jeer's lower-pitched signal to tell him the same. Both mammals slowly turned away from their riders.

Gryshen looked up again, through the darkened sea. The tiny cousins of the silver fish occupied this space, but then parted as if to open a channel between her and the ocean. The deep blue and green shifted to puffs of lavender; the water seemed to be giving her the things she felt she had misplaced this past season. And in that moment, black hair sweeping around and a grin stretching the sides of her face, Gryshen took it all back.

Out in open water, she could finally swim again.

Without the beasts, she could fly through the water toward the surface. She didn't have to worry about their trained protection. No guardians, no negotiations, no expectations. Just the free fluttering of her body, spin-ning and twirling in the water.

It warmed to the touch ever so slightly the closer she came to the sky. She broke into the air, the sun washing all her fears, all her anxieties from her. She was not near her shore. She could not see any shore from this point. Just endless sea.

Then there was Coss.

"You need this, don't you?" he asked.

"Need what?" She shivered involuntarily.

"Open water. Escape."

Gryshen said nothing, only focused on taking steadying gulps of oxygen.

"And this." He held a finger to the wind that seemed to curl around them. "You go to the breathing chambers twice as much as the rest of us. You need more, don't you?"

Gryshen allowed herself a glance upward, waiting for the judgment on his face, but all she could see was curiosity.

"Just . . ." Why was she suddenly out of breath? She was surrounded by oxygen.

"Just what?"

"Another disappointment. I can't breathe right, I can't fit in right, I know I can't lead right . . . " She tried to swallow tears along with the cool salt air. Gryshen closed her eyes, wondering why she said the things she did. She heard a splash; Coss had disappeared.

She stuck her eyes in the water and saw him, or at least his tail. He was burrowed in sea shrubs, foraging for . . . flowers?

He pulled back, his arms now full of vivid orange petals that curled. Before Gryshen could think about what he was doing, he was a blur beneath her and a splash beside her. Without a signal, he tucked the delicate flowers into plaits he wove into her hair, behind her pointed ears, nestled into knots along her jaw.

And he kissed her and kissed her and kissed her.

Something opened within Gryshen. She felt herself unfolding like one of the dozen flowers he had placed on her. The only crown she had ever wanted.

And she was in a way she had never been, free and happy and unafraid.

The crushing pressure released, the grief swam away, and only this remained.

Gryshen let herself smile as he cupped her face in his hands, let herself bury her head in his chest. They wrapped themselves around each other, dropping like a stone into the water.

Something within blossomed, then lit aflame. And in the swirls of flame and water, lips and eyes, teeth and hands, she released completely.

It took longer than it should have for her to hear it— the piercing signal, a warning cry.

Jeer burst into them, which for a moment was comical, until she realized she couldn't see the narwhal.

"What is it?" she signaled, as if he could answer. The white whale just turned swiftly, and they followed obediently. There was no sign of Feln as they made their way back toward home. Even the fish that had been swirling about moments before seemed to have vanished. Gryshen kept looking out behind, trying to make out a shape of a horn, something. In the now darkening water, as they swam deeper toward home, she spotted something. Actually, she smelled it first. The narwhal's blood.

She had smelled it before, as a babe, when one had been accidentally speared on a hunt. She remembered watching them lay it on a table, the hunters helpless as it writhed and seized, a weapon pierced straight through its head. The fragrance was strong, musky, and metallic.

Like now. The blood began to trail toward her like smoke, not billowing out the way it usually did. Then she saw her narwhal coming up after, like the blood was a kind of leash. He appeared all right; there seemed to be a small, jagged gash that barely punctured his skin, like a . . . shark bite.

And the fin that followed, pointed like a hoisted sail, confirmed the sinister realization. She turned to warn Coss, but he was gone. In a moment he had moved behind the narwhal, letting out a series of low calls.

"What are you doing? You have no weapon!" she cried. But he was not listening.

To her horror, he threw himself on the back of the great white animal, gripping that blade of a fin, continuing to trill out those low notes. Gryshen suddenly recognized the shark as the single-eyed beast the Rakor rode in on. The shark turned violently from side to side, and Coss seemed to have lost his grip on the fin. Gryshen's mouth filled with water as she opened it to cry out, but it was as if she lost the ability to make sound. The shark's eyes remained eerily dull as his huge head tilted upward toward the lax.

Then Coss stretched his copper arms upward, turned them in, and plunged his fingertips into those vacant eyes.

He kept digging, pushing into the brain, tugging at the skull. Gryshen couldn't look away.

Here was the warrior. Here's where the legendary barbarism of his pod came out—not with ceasids, no, with dangerous beasts. She wondered if she should be more disturbed, but she couldn't feel it. The relief was too great. Coss was all right. He was better than all right.

She was free. She could feel safe forever, as long as she was with him.

They were close to the cavern now, and others had been alerted.

Jode was one of the first to appear. He couldn't keep from looking impressed when he saw how very dead the great shark was at the hands of this one iloray.

"Nice work. A little messy with the skull and sinew, but—"

"Next time you single-handedly tear apart a huge fanged beast, you can show me how to properly dismantle its head." Coss smirked.

"Right." Jode waved to two others to help them carry the body back.

"Feast!" they called gleefully as they swam.

Coss had remained for a moment, patting the

narwhal, who seemed better. The wound was releasing less blood. Jeer waited by her, as if to be sure.

"And what about you?" Coss dropped that inescapable gaze back on her. "Are you all right?"

Gryshen nodded dumbly. She continued nodding until she wasn't sure how long she had been doing so, and made herself stop.

Coss grinned again, put his arm around her as naturally as if they always did this, and together they swam with the white whale and narwhal back to the stables where Sodaren was waiting, fretting.

"I KNEW I should have stopped you. I had a bad feeling about this." Word had already spread to the beastkeeper of their peril and Coss's daring battle with the shark.

It was so strange to Gryshen, who was just thinking she could hardly remember what feeling bad felt like.

Then she brought her mind back to double-check on Feln.

"She'll be okay, Sodaren? See her wound, right there?"

Sodaren kept pausing between lightly pressing around the bite to shake her head admiringly at the lax.

"Oh yes, it didn't go very deep. It's almost stopped bleeding. Some algae salve should fix her right up," she assured Gryshen. "Are you all right, Princess?"

Gryshen was about to bob her head like a seal again, but it was time to force out a signal.

"That's a relief, thank you, Sodaren. Are you coming to the meal?" She did her best to sound normal.

"Oh yes, yes. They are supposed to have four different large fish, in addition to . . . shark."

"Right. Of course."

The beastkeeper expertly applied ointment to Feln, while Gryshen rubbed the beast's forehead and gave her a small kiss.

Sodaren waited for Coss and Gryshen to swim into the main opening, and then trailed behind them.

The whole pod was at the feast that night, celebrating Coss's daring catch of the shark. By the time it got back to Gryshen, the story suggested that the shark was ten times his actual size, even though anyone taking a moment to look at the creature laying across the table could see that storytellers were taking liberties.

She just sat and listened to the tales all around her, wearing a smile she couldn't take off. Her appetite had finally returned, something she didn't know she had lost. Happiness filled her, a return that her father noted immediately.

"It's good to see you like this, Gryshie," he murmured beside her, as she took a second helping off the fin. "I suppose you were in greater need of a break than I realized."

"It was just what I needed, Daddy." And she couldn't help but dart her eyes to the one opposite her, the one who wore a grin through all the commotion, who nodded encouragingly as Jode told the story for him, adding embellishments and pausing in all the right places. But while his head was turned to face Jode, his eyes kept going back to Gryshen.

Morfal wasted no time using this adventure as opportunity to brag of his son's might and its reflection on their own pod, emphasizing his boy's killer instinct.

"Well, we can all agree that Coss is very brave," her father said after Morfal's boasting.

Gryshen was grateful, grateful that he saw this, that he made it about Coss's courage, rather than whatever ugliness Morfal tried to twist it into in hopes of intimidation.

"And then he bit the eyeball out! One steady chew." Jode was shameless now with a jaw-dropped, squealing audience of little ones. "And the shark, seeing him with his only good eye, knew he was finished." He brandished a shale blade in front of them, as if this was the weapon used.

Jode was officially another admirer of Coss's. That warmth inside of Gryshen remained, as her belly filled. She felt it pouring through her limbs. When the white whales began swirling and sounding out a tune, and Coss immediately took her hand to dance, she didn't even notice the deadly glares the other leens gave her. She wouldn't have cared if she had. She had a place to be now, and it was here, hand in hand with Coss, wherever that led. Forget Morfal, forget her father's droning about decorum, forget Bravis's constant nervous watch, the only eyes that mattered were the ones that pulled in her heart now, the ones that sank her every time.

It wasn't until Sodaren had switched the singers a third time, complaining that it was past their bedtime, and that they needed to keep their throats rested, especially with threats like what they had seen today, that Gryshen allowed herself to be pulled away.

They had danced every single dance together, her and Coss, and the two pods were humming about it. She could hear the chatter on the way out of the feast room, in the cavern corridors, even from a pair of barely older leens beside her at the air chamber. They signaled so quietly, they must have thought she couldn't hear.

"Looks like we'll be getting a new king before long. The princess makes quick enough time."

She knew the pair, sisters Helda and Velda. There wasn't much that their dark eyes missed. Gryshen placed a hand over her heart, as if it would hide this one thing, protect this connection she shared with the prince. This wasn't for prying eyes or chatty sisters. This was for her and Coss alone.

CHAPTER 6

"*P*rincess, a word?" Bravis's tone was difficult to read. Gryshen considered what he might want as she held up a hand to let him know she was nearly finished. She took one last draw of oxygen, but it barely tempered her nerves. The billows of silver hair couldn't hide the two pairs of eyes that kept making furtive glances her way.

No one needs that much oxygen, she thought to herself, as the leens remained in position while she joined Bravis.

"This way, please."

She followed, knowing why he swam farther than would normally be necessary from the air chamber. Once they were safely out of range of the sister's hearing, he still signaled quietly. "Princess, I—"

"Bravis, no one can hear you. You've made sure of it.

Please, you know it makes me uncomfortable to be called by my title."

"I needed to get you far away in order to maintain discretion."

"We're discreet. What is it?"

"I would like to begin by offering something for your consideration, Princess," he began, with an edge of coldness that was unlike him, "If I may—"

"Speak *plainly*, Bravis. No one can hear you."

"If only *you* would, Gryshen!" He seemed to have startled himself. He took a quick pause, steadying himself in the water. "It appears that you are getting carried away into something. It appears to most. And your father—"

"Basically gave us every blessing." Now her arms were folded tightly. *Encouraging her to take Coss for a ride was the same as a blessing, right?*

Didn't Bravis want to be free from obligations? Losing her father seemed inevitable. The heavy crown, inevitable.

At least if she was with Coss, she could feel some kind of power in her life, some measure of control in all that was uncontrollable.

Bravis closed his eyes for a moment. Gryshen felt a twinge of something she was not going to pay attention to.

"Your father, being the wise leader that he is, looks out for the good of his kingdom. He strives to unite and comfort. He recognizes an opportunity here, but—"

"Are you saying my father isn't looking out for me? Are you accusing my dad of being opportunistic with me?" Gryshen thrust her face in his. She'd never been close to him like this, the waters muddying between their eyes.

"Will you stop interrupting me? What are you so defensive about?"

She pulled back a few paces.

"Gryshen, when have I ever questioned your father's heart? Ever?"

She couldn't help but notice a wounded expression in his usually composed gaze.

"I'm sorry. I didn't mean that. It's just that it's none of your business." She straightened her back in her best authoritative impression.

"But it is my business, Gryshen. Your father asked me to be his eyes and ears with the pod when I took this position, and this situation is what the pod is discussing at the moment."

"Let them. Who cares what they think of my love life?" She couldn't believe she had just used those words.

Apparently, Bravis could. "You need to care. You *will* be their leader, and they must respect your judgment. Gryshen, there was talk of a Rakor prince in the tribe's counsel!"

"What, Helda and Velda are your sources now?" she scoffed.

"Go ahead and mock, but those two are almost always an accurate gauge for the feelings of the pod.

They're just a bit more . . . vocal." A tiny hint of a smile threatened to creep up on his face.

It started to threaten Gryshen's, too. "Those harpies," she sighed. "But Bravis—can we keep something between us? As in, you won't tell Father? Not until I'm ready to?"

Bravis said nothing. She went ahead just the same.

"Bravis, he *is* different. I think he loves me. Even Dad seems on board now. Wouldn't this be a good thing for everybody? We could deal with that father of his together. He'd be on our side!"

"Do you love him?" It seemed to be the only word that had caught him.

"Yes." And there it was. Her cheeks filled with dark blood, but she didn't care. She was free of secrets now, too.

Bravis floated, perfectly still.

She narrowed her eyes at him. Why did everyone question her ability to judge character? If he spent a minute with Coss, instead of robotically assisting her father, he would see what he was made of, just how special he was.

"I know what I'm doing. Really. Truly."

Bravis considered her for a minute. "Gryshen, it doesn't have to be me."

Gryshen was silenced.

Bravis's signal carried something with it she couldn't decipher. "But it cannot be him." Bravis handed her his lantern and swam into the dark.

"I wondered where you were, I thought that maybe you, well . . ." The voice that lit everything up inside her signaled from behind. Coss pulled up wearing an anxious expression.

Gryshen looked at him, waiting for him to say more.

"I kept hearing whispers. I know what people think of my father. I know what they think of me."

"Then you must be extremely arrogant, because those leens in there—"

Coss grinned. "No, I mean, your pod is suspicious."

"Not of you. Not after how you protected me." She couldn't help it—she kept swimming closer to his face. Or was it he to her?

"But your father—"

"Doesn't hate you." She smiled. "He's protective, but he trusts my judgment."

"Your judgment? And how do I measure up? How do you find me?"

Just as he was getting the words out, her face was pressed against his. No telling who moved there first, but with her new freedom came a wild courage. She would kiss him and kiss him, and she didn't care.

A sharp whistle emerged, and Gryshen pulled away to see maybe the one iloray who could muddy her spirits. Had Morfal been waiting for a while, or had he just come upon them? Time was so tangled with this lax. But there was his father, and if it wasn't clear from the tone of his interruption, it was certainly clear from the look on his face that he wasn't planning a binding for them anytime soon.

"Son." There was no warmth in his address. If it weren't for the word he used, one wouldn't assume any relation between the two at all. And yet, there they were, Coss bowing slightly in submission, as if his father's gaze was lecture enough. But it wasn't enough, not for a Rakor. The water pulsed in and out in bullet-like movements as Morfal used his own tribe's sacred signal.

Of course, Gryshen couldn't decipher what he was saying, but no real translation was necessary.

Coss lifted his gaze at one particular burst, eyes widening, meek no more. Fluid spears now shot between the pair, their tones sometimes audible, sometimes out of range for Gryshen's untrained ears.

Their faces seemed to come as close as hers and Coss's had just before they shared a kiss. It would have been a little funny if it weren't for the rattle of whistles, grunts, and . . . *blood?*

It took a moment for her to realize that Morfal had just slammed his palm against his son's mouth. The chief let that be his goodbye as he swam away.

Before Gryshen could think, Coss had grabbed her hand, pulling her farther down the quiet corridor.

"Are you okay? He hit you! I can't believe your father—"

"You can't?" Coss asked.

"Well, I guess I can. But, are you—I just—you're bleeding." She reached out to look at his lip.

"It doesn't matter," he said.

"What did he say? What did your father say about us?"

"That doesn't matter either. Not to me, at least." His hands now felt warm as they wrapped around her thin face.

"It doesn't matter to me, either."

"Marry me."

"What?"

"Will you bind with me, Gryshen?"

"Are you serious?"

"Look, I don't care what my father thinks, you don't care what he thinks, and I know your father wants you to step into your role as leader. I love you. I believe that you love me. We'll both have more power in our tribes if we're married. We'll have more respect, be able to make more decisions. We'll unite the tribes in peace! Finally." His hands seemed to almost burn.

"I think I'm ready," she said.

"I know I am," said Coss.

And again, they kissed, tying up their secret. It was a secret she would tell her father when the time was right. *Maybe he'll be relieved.* The thought comforted her. Maybe he would see the power, the strength in her move. *The leader.* Finally, she was stepping into her place. She didn't need more guidance, and she didn't need the instructions from her mother's grave that never came.

She just needed to keep hold of these twisting fingers that curled around hers. It was more than a long trip to the oxygen chamber, this rush. It burned and it burned in this coldest of cold places.

Now she floated like a steady ship, like the ones that flanked the bone pit. The instruments in her mind whirred, knitting together a plan. Coss was right, of course; a union unites. Still, this was hardly on her radar. Gryshen hadn't exactly considered the possibility of being a bride, not this young. Her own mother was a dozen seasons older when she bound with her father. But with Coss, there was no question for her to ask; she knew she had to. She had to lock herself into this. Her only fear was that he might change his mind.

The ugly idea crossed her thoughts in the time that followed, but every moment she spotted him staring into her at the hub, or in a corridor, it swam away.

She wouldn't tell her father. Not yet. Morfal had gone from enraged back to cold indifference, as if he hoped that by ignoring it, this little "problem" might go away. Coss had not told him of their plan, of course. No one knew.

Gryshen could keep a secret, and she loved keeping them with him.

Her father and Morfal had spent another morning discussing technicalities of territories surrounding the channels that stretched between the Rone and the Rakor's tropical home, another morning in which she and Coss tried their best to not look too long at each other in front of the chieftains, when her father asked her to stay behind before they rejoined for lunch.

Morfal, Coss, and finally Bravis filed out of the room.

"I've sent for your brother," Frall signaled as they waited in his chamber.

"What are we doing?" Gryshen asked, now wondering if her father had grown suspicious. Perhaps Morfal had said something.

Jode swam in. "Yeah?"

Frall studied the both of them. "Have you ever heard of *tea*?"

"What?" Jode asked, while Gryshen just stared.

"Tea. Have you heard of it? You know, from this?" He untied one of the nets that hung on his walls and fished out a pot. Gryshen recognized it. It was a teapot. It held lava sand beneath its lid. The stuff was hard to find, but when you got it, you used it. Sparingly.

He smiled at Gryshen. "You remember when this was rubbed into a maker's fin after he was stung so badly?"

That's exactly what she recognized it from. The maker was a lampworker, and it was a risk of the profession, but his attack was especially brutal. It was as if all the jellyfish had conspired against him. The iloray still bore some scars, but when the healers applied the lava sand to his wounds, they probably saved his life with the poison they drew out.

"I've seen that used before, after that coastal hunt a few years back. With the stingray. But why do you have it,

Dad?" Jode asked. "I thought only shamans kept that kind of potion."

Frall grinned. "Well, I am the chief. And if you hadn't noticed, I'm not the shark I once was." Any attempts at humor surrounding his illness were always wasted on his children. "So Apocay set me up with some. A small sting to you could be . . . a little worse for me. But you know this has other properties." Frall held the sunshine-colored ceramic pot in his thinning fingers. He grasped the handle with one hand, and began to pour a little of the potent granules out of the pot.

Flecks of glittering back swirled in a tiny cloud, and their father leaned into it, whispering, "Jode."

It was as if the bits of sand were slowly pulled into a straggled formation.

"Can you see it?" he asked them.

"See what?" asked Jode, but Gryshen saw immediately.

"The spearhead," Frall said.

The sand had formed the shape of a triangle pointing skyward.

"Warrior," Gryshen quietly signaled. She now realized they had all been speaking in their native code.

Was that how their father had called them in? No one was around. What was he concerned about?

"Cool." Jode reached out to touch it, but as he did, the particles of sand scattered into the current.

"But I thought I had to go through my paces first," Jode signaled. "I thought that was the only way you could find out what you're made of." Not that it wasn't obvious to anyone who'd ever met Jode what he was.

"Oh, this is just a good guess, what you get from working with lava sand. It's not always accurate. But usually, the sand seems to get it right, if you know how to use it," Frall said.

"What about Grysh?" Jode asked. Gryshen hadn't bothered, because she knew. At least with Coss by her side, being a leader wouldn't be so painful. *Coss.* She let herself drift into the warm thought of him momentarily.

Frall paused and looked over at his daughter. "Would you like to see, Gryshie?" he asked, already pouring out more from the teapot. He blew gently into the granules, murmuring her name just as he had her brother's.

The tiny bits of sand spread and swirled.

And washed away.

"Wait, what was that?" Gryshen asked, trying to catch a glimpse of some shape, some hint as they separated and drifted.

"Can't tell," her father replied.

"Have you done this before? Try again." Now she was curious.

"I have done it before, for the both of you. After your births."

"And?" Gryshen asked.

Frall looked from daughter to son, and back again.

"And the results were the same."

"So, what am I? I don't understand."

"Maybe you're some weird spirit that hasn't been

discovered yet. The quick-scatter kind. The I'm-not-telling-so-go-away kind," Jode signaled.

"The nothing kind. The nobody kind," Gryshen replied, feeling that familiar weight return to her belly.

"Aw, Grysh, I was just kidding."

"It's just like with Mom."

"What's with Mom?" Jode asked.

"Yes, what is it, Gryshie?" her father asked.

"No connection." She murmured, staring off past the point where the remaining black sparkles had disappeared from view.

"What? What connection?" Jode asked.

"Nothing. It's nothing," she quickly replied.

"Gryshen, there's something important, something all ilorays should remember, but you especially," signaled Frall.

"And what is that?" Gryshen asked distantly.

"There are other ways to find out what you're made of."

Well, obviously. The Forms spelled it out clearly for everyone, every time. She just didn't like the promise of the tie-down she saw looming. Gryshen reminded herself again of the very thing that was making all this bearable, the only thing that was allowing her to breathe through this.

"I'll speak with Apocay and we will set up your Forms soon." Frall nestled the pot back into the net and turned back to face his children.

He reached out his hands. Gryshen instantly

stretched back and placed her palm in his, squeezing tightly.

She saw him wince.

"Sorry."

Frall just smiled at her, and gently cradled her fingers. He left his other hand still open.

"Okay." Jode reached out his hand and rested it lightly on his father's. "Are we gonna sing or chant or something now?"

Frall chuckled. "You know, son, for someone who has no difficulties showering affection on the leens, you certainly seem to have difficulty touching your relatives."

"Look, Dad, I have no trouble holding Grysh's hand. And I love you." His signal sputtered briefly on those last words. "You know that. It's just . . . I'm a full-grown lax." He puffed out his chest in exaggerated pride. He gave a firm shake to his father's other hand. "Better?"

Frall winced again.

"Oh. Sorry, Dad." He looked over at his sister with a helpless expression.

"All right, you two. We haven't really had a chance to discuss what is to come. Not since . . . since everything first happened."

Gryshen recalled the other times their father had taken their hands like this. When their mother died, and when he told them he was dying. She found herself wishing he would find other reasons to embrace them, reasons that didn't involve death.

"I need you to understand something. You are not being placed in your positions out of obligation."

"But, Father, this is the only way it could go. I am your daughter, I am the firstborn, so I must do this." She couldn't keep the bitterness out of her words.

"Gryshen, enough. You are honored to do this! *Honored*." The edge of his signal was sharp and scraping, like the blade Jode had shown Gryshen from a recent hunt, strapped across his chest like a talisman.

"I am honored." She repeated the words, as if by doing so she could release any pain from her father.

"And I'm speaking to both of you. Both of you. Don't you see how pivotal your places are? Gryshen, a great chief does not rule alone. I had your mother."

And I'll have Coss. The thought relaxed her again.

"And after I lost her, I still had Bravis."

Gryshen nodded obediently.

"You are blessed. You will have each other, and you'll have Bravis. And your betrothed, one day."

He swept what felt like a slightly longer glance in her direction. *Did he know something?* She peeked at Jode, who was looking downward.

"But really, most of all, most importantly, it will be the two of you. Jode"—her brother looked up at Frall at the mention of his name—"do you understand how all this pertains to you? You have a sacred place, Jode, a divine role."

It was words like this that had hung over Gryshen's head like the heavy crown to be heaved upon her. And now they were being poured on her brother. This was different. She had never seen him placed in charge of anything outside of beast kills and escorting visiting leens.

"I am counting on you, son." His eyes were fixed only on Jode. "We will both be counting on you for much in the coming seasons."

Jode looked thoughtfully at his father. He was alert. Not woozy from the burden of these words as Gryshen had felt when she had first learned how soon she would wear the mantle of responsibility.

He carried the unseen crown with strength and grace.

Gryshen was suddenly filled with a sense of over-whelming guilt.

"Well, who's ready to eat? I'm starving." Frall attempted to bring cheer back to the discussion.

Gryshen was heartened to see her father's appetite returning, and the business talk of this feast gave her many opportunities to meet the glances stolen by Coss. He found all kinds of reasons and excuses to brush his hand against hers at the table, to touch her shoulder. His boldness never failed to inspire awe, especially with Morfal so near and so shrewdly aware.

But this lax was so careful. His instincts were perfect. He made his moves just as his father was preoccupied with yelling at a subservient iloray for bumping into him, or snatching a fishbone to pick his teeth with. Coss timed himself wisely with her own father, too. He even managed to whisper in her ear after several leens had just finished laying small nets of mussels in his lap, while they tried to shell them for him. He just stared at Gryshen, who prided herself on never having behaved so ridiculously.

"I want them all to know. Soon they will all know how I feel about you."

"How we feel about each other." She grazed his cheek with her lips as she spoke, impressed with her own daring. Gryshen looked across the table to see Bravis, who was apparently engaged in conversation with a more delicate leen from the Rakor tribe. She realized she was staring when she batted away the twinge that twisted inside, annoyed with herself for feeling it. She was sure he had seen her out of the corner of his eye. That unnamable expression seemed to twist the stone mask that was Bravis's reliable face.

After a few furtive glances his direction, it became clear that he wasn't about to confront her here. Of course, he wouldn't. But would he bring it up to her father later? Gryshen saw Frall looking more relaxed than he had in some time, and for a moment she felt a bubble of hope—the kind of hope she used to grab hold of when he didn't look sick yet, before disease had taken its toll on his body. But she couldn't do that. She couldn't afford it, that kind of delusion. Gryshen knew she had to start letting him go.

Coss seemed to notice, too, because he kept offering Frall more puffer fish and blue weed.

"Keeps the mind sharp," Coss told him as he passed the plant bound in a little brass net.

"As if I need the help," said Frall.

The table chuckled, and Jode brightened at his father's humor and appetite. But Bravis wore a small frown, and Gryshen matched it. She wasn't so sure that he was boasting about his cleverness as much as he was underlining his inevitable exit.

Frall saw Gryshen's face, and helped himself to another chunk of blue weed.

CHAPTER 7

"*R*alo, you're such a welcome sight," her father signaled to a latecomer, a traveler from the Wanaa pod who had come to scout binding prospects for other ilorays. Ralo was a caretaker back at Wanaa, but on this visit he was acting as a matchmaker. This was done from time to time among pods, when everyone of binding age was scooped up and a few were left who didn't feel amorous toward their peers, or sometimes simply to keep options open and goodwill flowing between tribes. Jode seemed to possess some kind of love sonar, since after being settled in at the table next to the royal family, Ralo immediately started asking him, in a veiled attempt at seeming casual, about what position he played in games, what his wildest catch was on a hunt, and would he describe his eyes as more sky blue or lagoon?

Gryshen could barely contain a snicker, and even

Bravis betrayed a tiny smirk as Jode took pause to seriously consider these questions. Frall beamed, patting the guest on his back. "Of course, I would encourage any of our untethered ilorays to look outside our own pod and connect with our sister tribes, but I must admit that I have a particular bias with yours."

He didn't have to push encouragement—a couple of single laxes had used the questions about Jode's hunting skills to bolster him up while bragging about their own abilities. One leen who was in an apprenticeship to be a healer begin to exclaim dramatically about a nearly healed scrape on Jode's forearm, pulling out a pocket watch that had been gutted to contain a kind of heavy purple mud. It stained the water around them as she furiously rubbed the balm on Gryshen's brother, warning him of the dangers of infection with properly untreated shark bites.

"It was actually from some ice I saw him bump into." Gryshen tried to wave the purple out of her eyes as she spoke.

"Now, Gryshie, let her work." Frall's eyes glowed. It was clear that the hope of joyful matches for his son and the other ilorays, and the surge of energy brought on by thoughts of romance, were doing a lot for him.

So Gryshen took to just rolling her eyes for Coss to see when her brother began to elaborate. "It was a very jagged piece of ice. I wouldn't be the first to lose an arm from something like that."

And it took everything to keep her mouth from dropping when a tone-deaf Rone leen, tired of being ignored by Coss, began to croon a traditional Wanaa song while writhing around on the back of a very irritated beluga.

Listening politely was next to impossible, but Frall wore a straight face when he signaled to his newest visitor, "Wonderful, wonderful. Who doesn't love a singer?"

"Ralo, how's Hena? I haven't seen her in so long." Gryshen finally got down the mollusk she had nearly choked on after her father's remark.

"Our chieftainess is who she's always been."

Gryshen grinned at this response. It was actually Hena's idea to feed the beasts redshell—a shellfish that was known as a potent aphrodisiac—just before a major hunt, when the two leens were still too young to go along. The effects of the redshell took hold quickly, and made hunting preparations at first awkward, then quickly impossible. Her father had been angry—it was one of the largest planned forages for food in a season—but she could remember how he and Bravis both seemed to be suppressing smiles. Jode had openly guffawed.

"Who she's always been?" Gryshen asked.

"Yes. A joyful and steady ruler. Pods don't often get both in a leader, present company excluded, of course." He nodded in Frall's direction, who returned a polite nod. It was starkly obvious that he avoided looking in Morfal's direction. Morfal didn't seem to mind, or for that matter, notice. He was licking a cod's spine with his extraordinarily long tongue in a series of mesmerizing, albeit disgusting, laps.

Gryshen agreed with his description of her friend. Hena always had an ease to her—a confidence and a comfort about herself that spread like sunlit water to those in her presence. She was a lot like Jode in this way, but beneath her ribbons of black hair, her strong build contained a cunning that Gryshen's brother did not quite possess. Jode was clever, but Hena was crafty.

Gryshen smiled wistfully, thinking of her friend.

"When will she be joining us? I haven't received a message from her in a season." Hena had last sent her a carved message in slate tied around the belly of a pearl-white dolphin named Sarawa with a symbol expressing her love and support after she had learned of Frall's illness. Gryshen was hurt that her friend had not been to visit since this greeting, even though she knew it wasn't entirely fair for her to be upset. After all, Hena was in the same position that she was doomed to take.

"Well, I have good news," Frall signaled to the table, looking closely at Gryshen. "Hena will be here soon. All of the pod leaders will. We've invited them to join our . . . territory discussion."

Morfal glowered, slurping down a mollusk.

The hub was instantly filled with excited streams of signal. Gryshen was startled to find that, instead of being delighted, the thought of seeing her friend now made her nervous.

With Hena, it was her uncle who had occupied the throne. With no mate, and no children, she was the next in line. Her Uncle Qoah was still alive, but she was appointed chief after his mind began to float apart. Sometimes this happened with ceasids. Their bodies could withstand a lot, and lasted far longer than their human counterparts, but on rare occasions an iloray's brain began to deteriorate before their body gave way to transition.

This was not to be viewed as shameful, and the shamans had sometimes even referred to these types as transcendent beings, because they believed that their thinking had advanced to the next existence, and their body just needed to catch up.

This didn't make ilorays more comfortable with it. Uncle Qoah had picked one too many fights with other ilorays in Wanaa. After his third attack, in which he slashed a broken shell across the face of an iloray he thought was mocking his ideas, the elders of the tribe, along with Hena, agreed that he had to be crossed to protect the others.

He could not be trusted.

Gryshen winced as she thought of Hena's uncle, and her last encounter with him several seasons ago. Really, it wasn't so much an encounter, as she avoided him as much as possible, to the point of ignoring him when he began babbling about illusions.

"Lies and illusions. Lies that snare like a fisherman's net." He sang the words to no one in particular.

Hena just nodded to placate him as healers placed starfish on his body. Sometimes he'd get particularly anxious, and they hoped sea stars would draw out excess nervousness and leave him at peace with himself.

But Gryshen couldn't look at him, a once wise leader now marked. She just couldn't stand it. And this seemed to draw him to her.

"Would you care to know what I know, Princess?" He invited her. She busied herself with a loose pearl on her seaweed wrap. "I know you can hear me."

She didn't know what to say, and paused for too long. Now she felt even further tied into pretending. Her cheeks boiled, and at the same time it felt like a streak of ice was working its way down her spine.

"Now, now, Uncle." Hena spoke as if soothing a child in a fit.

"Oh, Hena. Hena, let me help." His tone had shifted to pleading.

"Let's get you to the oxygen chamber. We need to replenish you after all that excess energy has been pulled," one of the pod's healers gently ordered, and led him away.

Gryshen couldn't have been more grateful.

The memory still sent that chunk of cold down her backside. She warmed herself with the thought of telling Hena about her courtship. Well, not so much a courtship, as they moved so swiftly to engagement.

Was it even engagement? Was there to be a wedding? Or just a binding ceremony in the dark? Gryshen pushed away flowery ideas from her childhood to embrace this rush, this surge of power: she could change her life.

Sure enough, she'd have to rule. But with Coss by her side, she could do it. She wouldn't be alone. She would be loved, supported. She'd have a real partner. Most of all, she wouldn't have to stop feeling this way, this wild way that took over her being whenever she glanced in his direction.

She couldn't wait to tell Hena the news.

But she would have to wait until it was done. She couldn't risk being told it was imprudent, or that she'd have to wait. Gryshen had a gnawing fear that if she waited, it might all wash away.

What if Coss fell out of love with her?

She hated feeling this needy about him. She soothed herself as she saw him brush off yet another leen, a particularly beautiful one, in favor of staring at Gryshen so intently, she suspected he might know exactly what she was thinking.

Hena would be one of the first she'd tell if she could get a message to her before word spread through the tribe and all the pods. Hena would understand her need for secrecy. Hena always seemed to understand things like that.

As the after-dinner entertainment (if you could call it that—the leen who had serenaded them before had somehow negotiated two more melodies) wore on, Coss passed by Gryshen once more.

"Let's do it tonight." He interlaced his fingers in hers, then quickly drew them away before anyone could notice.

"Tonight?" Gryshen's face paled. Her heart seemed to bounce in her ribcage.

"Meet me in the passageway near the bone pit after this. Can you get away?"

She gave a quick nod. Of course she would. She would find a way.

When the food was being cleared, the remains of which were offered to the attending beasts, Gryshen gave her father a kiss goodnight.

"You looked good tonight, Dad. You looked . . . " She wanted to say "healthy," but stopped herself.

"Happy?" Frall rescued her.

"Yes. Happy." That was true. He looked happy.

"I'm feeling happy. Goodnight, Gryshie." He kissed her forehead and began to move away. "And Gryshie? I always look good."

Gryshen grinned and nodded, then paused in discomfort to wish Bravis goodnight. Bravis said nothing about what had transpired at dinner, only gave her a longer look before they parted ways.

"Sleep well, Jode." She rolled her eyes as she watched her brother being practically dragged apart by several eager leens. He didn't seem to mind.

Morfal and his ilk had left on the last note of the singer, and Gryshen was actually impressed they had manners enough to stay for that long. But stay they did, through high-pitched whines in what could only be guessed as an attempt to show off vocal range. Then they parted with an almost-perfect unison of cold nods before parading off to sleep.

There were clusters of ilorays in the main hub, and more still drifting about the corridors, and Gryshen attempted to look sleepy as she passed them, wishing each a good night.

His hand burned against her own as the crowd passed, as she waited in the mouth of the hub, waited for anything and everything.

And everything was here.

"The shamans must bind any ceasids of age." He whispered the words in a steady, sure stream.

And she was of age, just as this thaw began. Besides, she was a princess, and this should give her even more power.

Or far less.

"I haven't been through my Forms yet. And Apocay is tricky. I don't know what he would be willing to do."

She wasn't sure what any shaman would say to a binding that was a secret when it concerned the chieftain's daughter and a prince from another tribe. Such a binding would clearly be going against the wishes of her father.

But it was the law. Until the elder ilorays voted otherwise, the law ruled over all, even over a pod's king.

"Our shaman will. He's odd, but—"

"What is it about shamans?" Gryshen smiled.

Coss returned her grin. "Ours will do it. He'll be back in our guest quarters."

Gryshen nodded, tightening her long fingers around his.

Her father would grieve, but only momentarily. *Right?*

Right.

Because above all, her father wanted her happiness. Gryshen knew this like she knew anything. Although she didn't feel like she knew much right now. But she knew she loved Coss. And she had to believe that such a union would ultimately give her dad peace of mind, relief in seeing his daughter gaining strength in the current, growing into a mature space. Marriage pulled her up on the throne. It would elevate her in the eyes of her people; this was a fact. It could very possibly weaken Morfal's tyranny as Coss gained leverage in his newfound position.

It could prevent war.

Not a small benefit, Gryshen thought as her heart flipped over and over, seeming to turn inside and out. The wisdom she could see as the far-reaching results of her choice made her feel more confidence in her decision.

Not that she needed confidence to make the call. While the rest of the pod swayed in and out of the corridors in a chattering state of distraction, the warmth that beamed from Coss could have burned through the sea. It was like a gulp of the airiest oxygen, a draw of necessary breath; it was the way she had to be with him. There was no other choice.

And for one of the few times in her life, she felt the freedom that she had been longing for.

Maybe this was what it felt like to be Jode.

"We won't take a lantern. It will draw too much attention." Coss murmured. She soundlessly agreed.

Together they swam to the guest chambers.

No other signaling was needed. Everything was spoken through the flashes of energy between them.

Gryshen's heart turned over and under and inside out from itself.

She was to be his mate. She was to be with this lax, and they would rule in love.

Then, through the dark, a pounding alarm sounded, breaking the water between them.

Anxious tones shot through the cavern as the ceasids who were making their way to sleep hurried out of the chambers. Gryshen and Coss plunged toward the main hall in a single streak.

The carriers forming a grim line outside her father's room told her the story.

"Daddy!" She shoved against the crowd, fanning her fin wildly to try and break past them.

"Grysh!" Jode screamed, reaching out for her, tailed by the wild-eyed leens he had left the feast with.

"Move aside!" Bravis commanded the swarm of ilorays packed into the space. With two sure arms, he pulled Gryshen and Jode in. She had never noticed how big Bravis could be. His long, narrow form suddenly became large and imposing to the crowd.

In that same sweep of Bravis's movement, he ushered Gryshen and her brother forward, his arms holding fast to both of them like sinewy shields.

Frall was already being ceremoniously tied at the ankles and crown, a silvery net draped over his body like a veil.

As if they have already decided he is dead, without a pause, without a question.

"Who asked you to do this?" Gryshen shrieked to an apprentice healer who was whispering prayers into the braids he was weaving with grasses into the net. "Where is Apocay? Where is he? Get away from him!" she demanded, breaking away from Bravis's protective hold.

Jode floated against the back of the cave wall, numbly.

Gryshen drew right up to her father, reaching out to touch his face, check his heartbeat. "I can't hear his heartbeat. Help him! Somebody help! Where is a healer?" Her signal was like an earthquake in the small royal chamber. It seemed to push everyone back a few paces.

"Gryshen," Bravis signaled. Her name was coated in grief as he spoke.

"Gryshen." Another voice spoke, one far less mournful. Not sad at all, really. A steady hum. It was Apocay, sitting in a long stone indentation in the wall. Ilorays rarely sat, it was usually only something one did when very sick, or extremely exhausted. He was neither. But he was ancient.

The water around Gryshen suddenly felt like it was

boiling. "Well, look who's here! So, that's it, then? You're not going to try to help him?" She sounded her signal in a shriek, her teeth clenched, eyes wild. "What are you good for?"

"Gryshen"—the same hum—"it is done. He has been helped. We will help him on this next transition."

"He's NOT done! You have to help him. He's not ready. He's not ready." She wailed and opened her mouth wide, gurgling. She could see the stunned looks on faces even through the black paint pouring from her face. "Do something!"

"Gryshen, you're turning purple."

She spun around at Bravis's words. "What? Why aren't you doing some—"

"Gryshen," He repeated her name, his grief over-ridden by urgency. "We have to get you to the air tube. Drink. Please. Now." He gestured toward the tube in her father's chamber, but she could only think of escaping this.

Escaping into Coss.

She swam from her father's chamber, leaving Jode frozen against the wall and Bravis calling after her. Gryshen pushed with a newfound force, but it only lasted for a moment. Bravis was right. She was drain-ing, quickly. Her perception contorted, thoughts scat-tering as she tried to remember what to do, where to go.

She zigzagged past lines of ceasids, searching desper-ately, when she saw him.

"Gryshen!" He spotted her outside Oxygen Chamber Number One.

She couldn't get out any signal. Pointing violently at the gills in her throat as she swam was the best she could do. Coss's eyes widened, and he called out for the crowd in the hall to pass.

"Clear the air chamber! Make room!" he barked at two younger laxes.

"It's all clear, Prince. May we help?"

"No. Just give her space. Move toward the hub."

The hub? Why the hub? Gryshen's mind was in a fog. But there she was, at the entrance to the chamber; the pipes seemed to mesh and knot before her in a blur.

Just one quick swim, she told herself. *Come on, Grysh.*

She reached out to grasp the first tube she could, and suddenly her arm wrenched in pain. There was pressure on her throat—she couldn't signal. Gryshen opened her mouth to cry out, but something covered it. She flailed wildly, thrashing desperately in a hold she could not release herself from. Her wild movements softened, the momentum slowed, and the blurry pipes in the water smeared into gold and blue. Just as her eyes shut, she felt a tightening squeeze around her neck.

CHAPTER 8

The sun was so brilliant, it cast a vivid white glow onto Gryshen and her father as they lay against the rocks beside the lady. She offered Gryshen a steaming cup of something she poured from a pot. Gryshen recognized the teapot, but couldn't recall the name for it. She accepted the cup, her father accepted another, and the three let the hot drink fill their bellies as a breeze broke up the brightness. Frall gently patted her head.

"My little kelp."

The lady smiled at them both and continued pouring their tea. They drank and drank. Gryshen had never experienced anything like it. Like any of it.

The lady put the cups and tea back on a tray.

"Oh no. Let's keep doing this," Gryshen said to her. She spoke like a landkeeper.

The lady gave her cup back and poured the final

dregs of the pot into it. Then she leaned over, kissed Gryshen's forehead, and faded into the glow.

Gryshen turned to speak to her father, who was staring deeply into the sea.

She gazed into her teacup, watching the leaves drift and clump together. They formed what looked like a pair of dark eyes, looking back at her.

"Gryshen!" They began shouting at her.

What?

She dropped the teacup, the sea washed over the pair of screaming eyes, and a purplish-blue swept past them.

"Gryshen!"

Bravis was bruising her arms, shaking her with all his might.

She said nothing, only stared, lost, letting the present come into focus. She was in the breathing chamber, her lips pressed against a tube. Bravis furiously jostled the pipe as if it would sweep more air down to her lungs. She had never seen him like this. Gryshen took in the gulps of sweet oxygen and let them melt her hot, scratched throat. What was happening? She heard the signaling of Apocay. His dark tail appeared to blend with the blanket of seaweed that he held around his figure.

The shaman inspected her carefully, reading her face. He held a lantern to look in her eyes as she sucked in air. She couldn't stop breathing. He kept studying her, and with every drink, new awareness came into focus, following a line from the most recent memory to further back.

She had suffocated.

She had been trapped.

She was with Coss.

She had to warn Father.

Gryshen took one more sip, then ripped herself away to tell Bravis.

"Daddy, tell Daddy . . ."

Bravis's expression was indescribable. His grip on her arm had softened as she had regained consciousness, but he had held fast. He started to signal, but paused, looking helplessly at her.

And the next memory drew up to greet her.

"Daddy," she repeated, as if she could call him back and banish the recollection into myth.

The deep blue sea was a shade of violet. Gryshen wondered dully how long it had been this way. She began looking around.

"Purple," she murmured emptily.

"We'll just get you back to your chamber, Princess, and Apocay will take care of you." Bravis was back to his authoritative tone, but she caught a current running beneath it. The water was turning almost plum, and yet he said nothing about it. Gryshen wondered if her mind was bursting. Maybe it had all broken her.

"Where's Gryshie? Grysh! What happened?" Jode's signal boomed in.

"She's all right now. Help us take her back to her chamber. Apocay will give her a thorough exam," Bravis reassured him. "Come."

Jode followed like a young babe in the haze.

"Princess! Princess!" Two guards tore around the corner, pulling up to the group. They stopped, startled by the sight of Gryshen lying in Bravis's arms, her tail hoisted by Jode, and Apocay circling around them.

"Keep it on our frequency. We don't want anyone outside of this group to hear you," Bravis signaled carefully.

"The pearl! It's—"

"Yes. Follow us, and we'll discuss the next action—"

"We think it was some kind of sleeping plant, something knocked us out. We didn't mean—we didn't know —" one of the guards signaled.

"Yes, yes. Enough," said Bravis. "Our first priority is to bring Gryshen back to her chamber."

"Certainly. Whatever we can do," the guard signaled apologetically.

They flanked the crew, and Gryshen lay like a jellyfish that had been overdosed. She had heard this whole exchange, and she had the sense that there was something she was forgetting to care about.

Once in her room, she was laid across a slab of rock. She felt Bravis pass her hand to Jode, and her brother held it tightly while Apocay gave her a full inspection. Bravis and the guards were in the corner, signaling in low tones.

"It's gone, Bravis. So is Lefke. That shark took it. We couldn't find him anywhere, once we came to."

"We'll have to search thoroughly before we assume

that Lefke holds any responsibility. He could be knocked out somewhere," said Bravis.

One of the guards persisted, a shorter one who had remained silent until now. "One of the other laxes was just complaining to me about him the other day, saying he had lost Rone pride. Rumor's been he's talked about opportunity to move up in ranks—though what could be much higher than head guard of the pearl I don't know . . . a counsel like yourself, I suppose."

"It was about the leen. It's always about a leen, isn't it?" offered the first guard.

"What do you mean?" asked Bravis in a steady tone.

"I mean, she broke his heart. Said she didn't want to bind with him after all. And I heard that Morfal was telling him about *opportunities* in the Rakor pod. But it wasn't just about higher duties. He was bragging about all the beautiful, available leens they have. And you know what they say about the Rakor . . ."

"What do they say?" Bravis posed this like an Elder asking the young a question he already knew the answer to.

"Well, you know, they still like to arrange things, don't they? Like in the old times. They don't call it that, but I hear that chief sets up bindings for his inner circle. You don't say no to that one—he's probably threatened those leens."

Bravis gave a tight nod.

"The point is"—added the other guard—"that Lefke was in on it, no question. And I wouldn't be surprised at all if that Morfal had something to do with it . . . put him up to it maybe. He's always wanted pow—"

"How may we help?" The pod's other healers arrived. Obviously, word had spread.

"Leave us, except for Ruvesell. Ruvesell?"

The boxy leen nodded.

"Go to the Well Chamber and get blue-leaf gel."

"I'm sorry, what container is it—"

"Just grab a hunk of the leaves. They'll be in a net by the whale fat."

"Right away."

Not a minute later three more guards poured in. "Princess! Er, Prince? Bravis?" They looked anxiously down the line of command, noting the injury of the first, the preoccupation with care of the second.

"Yes?" Bravis responded, as Gryshen listened, her hearing coming more into focus.

"Some of the Rakor are starting to clear out."

Gryshen saw Apocay look up from massaging her gills to raise a brow. She wondered how old he really was, how many tragedies and crises he had witnessed. She wondered how much he cared about any of it. She had wanted to be that way, and now it was almost as if she could be, the way the words floated in and out of her head.

But something wasn't the same. There was a pressing in her chest. Her lungs? No, it was something else.

"Coss took it." She spoke aloud, staring up at the dark ceiling.

"Princess?" asked a guard. Everyone else remained still.

"You heard me. Didn't you hear me? Coss *took* it. He fooled me, and my dad died, he died, and Coss—I know he stopped my breathing. I know my father's dead. I know he's dead. And the pearl's gone. And Coss took it." She shot out the words in stilted bursts and sobbing gulps. Black smoke filled the blue around her. Black smoke that poured from her eyes and formed a cloud above her.

"Stop Morfal and his son. Tell no one what we've discussed." Bravis looked to the guards.

"Yes, sir," they signaled in unison. Then, spears still in hand, they returned to their posts.

"Gryshen." Bravis signaled her name, and nothing more, but it carried so much.

"I'm sorry. I'm sorry," she kept saying it, gulping and sobbing.

"It wasn't your fault. If he did it—"

"Bravis!" Jode signaled. "If she said he did it, he *did* it!"

"Hold steady, Jode." Bravis rested a hand on his shoulder. "I'm trying to take this one piece at a time. I'm trying to tell you"—his focus was back on Gryshen —"that *none* of this is your fault. There has been much to deal with. You and your brother and your father have had to handle a tremendous amount, and it appears that this was very carefully planned. I will join the guards to comb the caverns, just to make sure they didn't leave any clues behind, or any of their pod, for that matter."

The last guard to leave was the first to reappear. "Rakor are gone."

"What do you mean? All of them?" Bravis asked.

"They left?" Jode signaled.

Gryshen stared into the black pool, listening.

"Yes. We just learned that Chief Morfal and his son were the first to leave. All of Rone is asking questions. I came directly to you."

"And told them nothing?" Bravis signaled.

"Nothing. I'll get back to my post."

"Thank you." Bravis signaled as the guard swam away.

"That lying, evil—"

"Jode," Bravis reprimanded him.

Gryshen continued to murmur her stream of apologies, the words "I'm sorry" rolling into each other. It was like she was stuck in a whirlpool, the recent memories closing in on her and spinning her deeper and deeper down into the hollowest sort of pain.

It was too much. And she was not enough.

"Jode will have to take over," she blurted out. "He will have to be chief. He can lead this pod."

"I don't think I can do that. Can I, Bravis? I mean, would it help her?" He sounded petrified.

"No, you can't. And Gryshen"—he reached out, brushing away the black cloud of tears above her—"you can. And you will. Your father trusted you. He still trusts you, on the next wave. I can feel it."

It was one of the only times she heard Bravis talk about feeling anything. It tugged her out of the worst of the funnel. Her thoughts were still swirling, but now she had a focal point. Jode looked wide eyed at her. Bravis kept his steady gaze.

Ruvesell had returned with the leaves. Gryshen had forgotten Apocay was even there; he had been so still in his study of her. It was as if he had hardly cared about anything else that was being discussed, his focus and intent were so sharp. He took a handful of the flat navy-veined leaves and began ripping the stems off them and squeezing them into her throat.

"Press your lips flat against them."

Gryshen obeyed, and a horrid, metallic taste flooded her mouth.

"Don't swallow," Apocay ordered. "It needs to fill your lungs. I suspect you've had slight tearing."

"Tearing?" Jode and Bravis both asked at once.

"Tiny fissures, nothing deadly. At least, not when dealt with this quickly. Blue-leaf gel will seal them up. Now, had it been a little while longer . . ."

Gryshen assumed he was delicately leaving it to their imaginations, until after a short pause he said, "We'd have to bury her with her father."

He seemed oblivious to the silence he had wrought with his words. "Well, take a little time to rest, and you'll be ready to be at the gathering tonight. Ruvesell, I still have a net full of oysters in the rest spot just outside the Well Room. I'll share a few with you." And they left.

"I will be back immediately following our search to let you know what I have found." Bravis signaled to Gryshen as if she were completely in control of her faculties. He gave Jode a look that suggested he stay put, and off he swam.

"Gryshie." Jode just spoke the one word, cupping his hands on hers, looking as though he wanted to signal streams of words, but was afraid to do it. He paused, softly squeezing her hand. "Gryshie, everything is going to be okay. You are going to be okay, and we are going to be okay." His signal was hushed in the dark water, and it carried the uneasy tone of a babe trying to convince themself that there is no monster in their chamber. But he forced a small grin, and just kept patting her hand.

"Jode, Jode . . ." She had to tell him something. She needed him to do something. But her thoughts were drifting away again. And she went back into complete darkness.

There were three times that she could remember feeling steady and sure. The first was when she was very small, and her father gave her rides upon his back. Her mother was still alive then, a distant memory in the background of the picture, though.

Daddy gave her reins made of weeds and helped her tie them around his chest. She'd lay across his back, barking out orders while he swam in the wild, zigzag patterns she'd direct. He seemed to never tire, and she never tired of telling him what to do. One day, her father showed her the beluga. It was not yet a season old, but some hunters had found it far out on a hunt, motherless. They'd figured a shark had made it an orphan. Sodaren had been looking after the animal at the stable, getting her acclimated to her new home, when her father spotted her.

"She'll be taken out for rides, on the occasional hunt when she grows much bigger and stronger . . . but you may think of her as yours, if you'd like, Gryshie." The little beluga looked anxious tucked into her father's strong arms.

Gryshen reached out a small hand to pet her, and she leaned into her touch. This little thing trusted her without reservation, and the seasons which followed, exploring the open water with her, circling their cavern home and observing her tribe from a private distance, offered an even deeper sureness. Misra could count on her. She could count on Misra. They could both count on the sea.

The third time? Well, the third time she felt sure was when she kissed Coss. When she loved him.

Not steady, though. Never steady.

The wild rocking movement pulled her back.

"There's no sign of any of them." She saw a small, watchful guard swaying back and forth as she talked to Bravis, her eyes shifting toward the chamber opening, then to Gryshen, then back to the opening.

"All of the Rakor? The whole pod?"

"After the leaders left, the others were tailing behind. That's what I heard at the hub."

"Did they ask you about it? Our ilorays? Did they ask what was happening?"

"Oh yes. But I told them it was all under control, and that all would be answered soon. That is right, isn't it?"

"Of course. Of course it's right." There was that uncharacteristic shaking in Bravis's tone again.

"Sir, may I ask what is going on? Just so I understand what I'm doing."

Bravis gave a short shake of his head, then spoke as if she had asked nothing. "Keep posted by the openings, just in case one of them returns. That goes for the rest of you," he commanded to three other guards behind her.

"Thank you," he signaled as an afterthought while they made their way out.

The room now held only a bleary Gryshen, her torn-apart brother, and the most stable iloray they knew, after the one who had just left them behind.

"Where's Dad?" Jode asked, a twist on the familiar word as he spoke it. But if Dad was where all the lost things go, Gryshen was sure he was in the Blessing Chamber, the place where they prepared the dead for their final ride to the bone pit. It was higher up, closer to the gravesite, but just a few stretches down from a maker station. This one was used for elaborate ceremonies, to put together scepters, sacred spears, special lanterns, or to repair or even recreate crowns.

One of the few things Gryshen had that came out of

there was her necklace. She reached to touch it, and for the first time felt the wringing of her lungs, the tearing along her gills, that up until now she had just been numbly observing, like a bystander of her own body.

They made beautiful gifts in that room, treasures for the living and the dead. The more artistic of the makers made their way into this station. She only knew of one who currently held this job, but he was always busy, as ilorays were always birthing, dying, ruling, and living. She thought about him, the poetic maker, the one who used scraps from the human world, garbage and lost treasures, with the life around them: bones, shells, starfish, and sea.

Did he think of the babes being offered a dressed-up heirloom? Did he ever wish the happy couples well as he fashioned a Loving Lantern for their binding? Did he weep for her father, as even now, he must be using all his abilities to mold a keeper for him, a place to put his withering shell?

Did he cry as he pulled the glass orbs he had probably collected from the lamps on sunken ships? Or perhaps he was using something that would require more maintenance, more care on his part. Maybe the rich teakwood from a freshly found barrel. It would have to be changed frequently, of course. Oceas was especially hard on a thing like that. But that would be part of his reverence, wouldn't it? Gryshen pictured the midaged iloray—a smooth-faced, smooth-eyed sort of lax. His name was Stoey, wasn't it? She was sure that was it.

There was a solace in these thoughts, almost. A kind of peace, nearly. She could stretch her mind away from the lost father, drift past the lost love, and think about how very sad Stoey must be. Just think about him taking artifacts above water, talking with the other makers as they repaired lanterns and common spears. She could just see him mourning her father.

That was right. He would mourn and he would grieve. He would construct something beautiful to lock away Frall's beautiful spirit, so Gryshen could always see his love, preserved. So he could go on being the leader of Rone. He could tease her, and advise her, and even scold her.

His soul would stay put, and she would never be left to die again. She would never be alone.

Never.

"Are you ready?"

"What?" She realized that Bravis and Jode had been holding an entire conversation while she had been busy removing herself from this reality.

"They're going to change out the medicines on your gills." Bravis was holding her hand, so warm. She had thought it was her brother, but Jode still floated like a lost child, only speaking necessary words. She wasn't so sure that he was processing much more than she was.

"Okay" was all she could signal. It felt like an electric eel had wrapped itself around her skull as the ointment was gently rubbed off, then replaced.

"Open your mouth, please," Apocay directed.

She obeyed, feeling something like seaweed pods, but larger, and almost unbearably bitter.

"I know it's difficult, but you'll have to swallow."

Gryshen chewed the pods, finding a new distraction in the horrid flavor. She was sorry to swallow, because it meant she would have to come back to reality in the next moment.

Just as reality broke in, the brutal tearing she felt in her gills almost totally disappeared. Now it only felt tender, sore. The same went for her lungs. It really was powerful, the iloray's ability to heal so rapidly.

"And how is it now?"

"Better."

He kept looking at her. "Better?"

"Yes."

He rapped his fingertips against her throat.

She yelped, and Bravis and Jode both turned in shock toward the healer.

"*Why?*" Bravis asked.

"What is the matter with you?" Jode asked.

"I'm concerned," Apocay said.

"You should be if you're going to hurt my sister!" Jode's signal boomed.

Gryshen was certain this accusation had almost nothing to do with the shaman.

"Why?" Bravis repeated, holding out a hand to steady her quaking brother.

"I'm concerned," repeated Apocay, as if Jode's eyes weren't bulging out at him, "because that tapping shouldn't hurt her. It should be completely healed. That's an incredibly powerful ointment, epsoneem berries. They never fail. Extremely difficult to come by, but an unbeatable pain diffuser."

"Well, obviously it fails sometimes." Jode had calmed down, but his boldness was in place, decked out with a degree of rude her father would have nipped immediately.

Things were already starting to decay.

"I'm sure it will heal quickly. It's almost all better," Gryshen signaled. She started to work at untying the straps in place around her.

Bravis and Jode turned back to Apocay for his approval. He didn't give any consent, just stared at her with a farsighted search in his eyes.

Gryshen kept going, as if propelled. She saw her brother's lost little lax look, the fear and pain in Bravis, and each thought, each pause was like the scalding sting of a thousand rays around the place where she had tried so desperately to keep her heart safe. It was time to make a new choice. No more safety. No more anything. Except movement. Desperation could easily masquerade as duty.

So be it.

CHAPTER 9

"*W*ell, what's next?" she signaled. Jode and Bravis looked beyond perplexed.

"Bravis, see how much more that maker has to go. Our pod will need this burial as soon as possible." She heard how she sounded. Gryshen saw Jode flinch at her words, but she couldn't afford to care. "We have no time." She would have been pleading if she had allowed emotion to slip through.

"Then we will need to take you through your Forms, beginning at daylight," the shaman said.

"Apocay, please. Surely a little more time. She needs to heal more. You just said you were . . . concerned." Bravis's signal was weighted.

"She's healed enough. She needs to find her function. That could do more than any medicine. I will be ready to do the chief's Burial Blessing. We can do it in the dark. It's a very sacred time."

"The dark . . . as in tonight?" Bravis couldn't hide his surprise.

The dark seemed just right. It suited the whole picture. Maybe she could block it all out.

If only everything could be in the dark.

There was a silence. Then Apocay broke it. "The pearl?" He looked to Bravis and Gryshen.

Now with a focus in desperation, Gryshen was gifted the ability to piece together decisions. "First the bone pit, then I begin my Forms. How quickly can those be completed?" she asked.

"It depends. We can pile tasks together, so you can move more quickly, I suppose," Apocay said.

"Let's do that. What if we do them all tomorrow?"

Even Jode came back out of his hurt at this. "Grysh!"

"Absolutely not," Bravis signaled.

"It would be . . . highly unwise," Apocay agreed.

"It could *kill* her," Bravis told him tersely.

Let's hope, Gryshen thought to herself.

"Grysh! Gryshie!" Jode kept exclaiming.

"Of course I wouldn't permit that. Some could, but not this one. Perhaps two days," Apocay said.

Apocay and Gryshen ignored the protests of their companions, and formed a plan.

They all insisted that Gryshen rest awhile longer while they took on the details of her father's burial. The shaman went to prepare for the ceremony, while Bravis left to check in on members of the pod and confirm the burial chamber for Frall.

Jode stayed back. No one had given him a job. It was clear he wasn't really up for it. He floated in silence by his sister while she lay and practiced turning her head from side to side, still wincing at the pain she felt whenever she made swift movements. Slower, steady movements made for less pain. Apocay had given her a pouch of the berries, a handful to be taken tonight, some at dawn, then that was it.

"The ceasid can't handle more. It's too potent. I'm afraid you'll have to just hope for the best before your Forms." His off-putting way of signaling in such a disconnect always had irritated Gryshen. She had never much cared for him. But now, as she practiced signaling clearly, trying to find how loud she could pitch before her throat burned up, she felt like she understood him.

She kept her face smooth and her eyes forward to ignore the tortured looks from her brother as she streamed sips of oxygen from the lone tube in the medicine chamber. It was her best shot at making it.

And "making it" was a simple act of attending her dead father's burial, going through two days of rigorous Forms, finding her function, and getting back the pearl herself.

The shaman was right.

Blackest night is perfect for his blackest sleep, Gryshen thought to herself, in the detached way she was becoming more and more accustomed to.

It was possibly the maker's legacy, this piece of art her father's corpse was to be sealed in. It was some kind of massive trunk, the kind of thing that landkeepers might pack their beautiful, frail fabrics in, made up of boards of glossy wood framed with corner crowns of shining golden metal. That was probably its original state, save for the polishing. Even in the thick darkness, it shone like a trophy from the light of lanterns carried by half the tribe. The other half were occupied with carrying and passing Frall's body from iloray to iloray down the line, toward the end, where Bravis, Apocay, Jode, and Gryshen were posted with his new wooden body-home. The light on it displayed a collection of carvings, ancient symbols of the tribe—some so old that their meaning had seemed to evolve through myth, others as clear as the summer sea in their translation.

Gryshen could see the mark for leadership, her father's mark, at the center of the circle of functions. It told his story beautifully—the lax who was all things to his beloved pod.

Her observations were interrupted by a low moan of a signal. Now the torches had been placed against the wall in this narrower hall of the cavern, and the blue and white washed over her brother's face, the face that always wore a grin. Bravis awkwardly patted his shoulder, like the statue from a sunken ruin had come to life to offer comfort.

Gryshen knew her father would want her to be the one holding him up, keeping him afloat, but she also knew that this weight was better carried by stoic Bravis. She had to keep her expression measured, her face smooth. Even this darkness wouldn't shelter her from the gaping crowd.

She could pull out different signals from the pod, like picking notes from a song. The sisters whispered loudly, of course, spitting and hissing like two writhing serpents.

"Look at the casket. The detail! So exquisite!"

"Well, he was a fine, fine leader, of course."

"And now?"

"And now we have the one who swam away." They both cooed and clicked at this.

Were they talking about her? Was she the one who swam away?

Of course she was. She had left in a panic, a shock of breaking heart and breaking lungs. She had sought shelter in her secret, her lax.

Everything inside of Gryshen began to sear and bubble. It threatened to pour out of her and explode all over this casket and crowd, this garish group who only disgusted her with their wails, their fingers clawing at her dead father, like they were trying to drain one more drop of his goodness.

And who were they, and what did they ever know?

She began to quake, the ink filling her eyes, feeling like a chained shark, unable to bite them all in the way they must be bitten, these useless monsters. Her brother just kept on crying.

And now he was before her, her dad. All lanterns

circled them, her family on display. She could barely
look at him, and she didn't dare to touch him, for of all
the wild grasping and groping that had filled her with
such a sickness, she was positive that no one had the
need that pressed upon her, the need and will to seize
her father's body, to wrap her arms around him, and take
him up to that private spot on the shore, a place where
they could drink cups and cups of tea and live and decay
there.

A place where his spirit would be kept safe. In her
cradling arms, in the sunlight, it could be all the spirit
she needed. It would be enough for the both of them.

There was a moment, a consideration, when she felt
a hand touch her shoulder.

"I'm here now. I'm sorry it took me so long, but I'm
here now."

She didn't need to look to recognize the tone. It was
somewhere between a salty wave and a cool lagoon, and
it was as sweet as the pink flowers that dappled the water
of its owner's home.

Hena had arrived.

Long after the crowd had buried her father and made
their way to their respective sleeping chambers,
Gryshen, Hena, Jode, and Bravis were posted in a nook
beside one of the smaller oxygen chambers deep in the
interior, between the sleeping ilorays and the bone pit.

"Jode, don't you need your rest?" Gryshen finally broke the silence between the four of them.

Jode gave her a look that would have been baffled amusement had the joy not been drained from his face, now puffed from an almost endless stream of tears.

"What? Are you serious?" His snort sent a swirl of bubbles her direction. "You think I need rest? What about you? You've set up quite the time for yourself come light, am I right?" He shook his head, his eyes beginning to burn, fear visible in their flame. "Or maybe you have the energy you need. I guess not giving a damn about anybody but yourself keeps you in peak physical—"

Bravis had placed a warning hand firmly on his shoulder. Hena hissed.

"She's lost more than any of us, Jode. And we've lost a lot." Bravis choked on the last words of his signal.

But something around Gryshen's heart reflected the fire in her brother's eyes. It was a burn in the hollowness, like the fires the makers kept in the earth-level caverns.

"Gryshie, I didn't mean it." She saw the regret washing over him. As if his sorrow could be any greater. "I just—I just . . ."

"I know, Jode. I know I haven't been who you've needed me to be."

Her brother tucked the fear away from his face. "Gryshie, you don't need to be anything for anybody."

Now it was Gryshen who snorted. And no one could argue with the gesture.

"Please, I will come back." She signaled in a tired

tone. Gryshen couldn't believe it had only been hours since everything had been destroyed—such a short time for her whole world to wash away. "I will come back," she repeated, more to herself than to the other three.

"Come, Jode." Bravis gently patted her brother on the back. "Gryshen, I will see you at first light. Before your paces begin."

Jode swam a couple sweeps, then stopped to turn. "Grysh, I really didn't mean—"

She held her hand up.

He accepted this, bowed his head, and the pair moved down the hall, leaving the sea's two youngest chiefmaidens to talk.

Hena was still boiling at Jode's accusations.

"He should never have said that. What a terrible thing to tell you! And right after your father's funeral?" Hena seemed to move as gracefully as any dolphin, every gesture like a dance. But she never danced around the ugliness of things.

"He's just broken. We all are. But I will . . ." She nodded, staring off, feeling that hollow flame grow. "I need a plan." She turned to Hena. "Can I rely on you?"

"For anything."

"I'm going to get the pearl back." And the flames shot up from her heart, licking her throat, warming the water with her words.

Hena nodded calmly, then narrowed her eyes softly at her best friend.

"There's a lax involved in this, isn't there?"

Gryshen just stared back at her.

"I can feel the sting in your signal, Gree." She was the only one who called her that.

"He's not important."

"Oh, I disagree." Hena widened her eyes, brows soaring. "'He' is *always* important."

Gryshen remained silent. What could possibly be said? There was no time. And she certainly didn't have an ounce of room in her mind to open this up. Besides, she was busy keeping her heart tucked deep inside her thin chest.

"I know you. I know you're doing your best to keep afloat. I heard about the Rakor's visit while they were still here with you. Some of your hunters encountered some of our scavengers while on their search for wreckage.

"I met that Coss once before, on a visit they paid us many cycles back. You know they've always left us alone. We are strong like them."

Hena was right. Her ilorays were not barbarians like the Rakor, but they all had a thick, solid build. Even graceful Hena had a wide pink tail and flat, sturdy hands the color of clay, limbs that appeared to be able to take anyone down with one good slap.

"That's not to say we can't all beat them. They don't know what they don't know about you, Gree," she said cryptically, after staring into the electric blue glow of the torch she was holding.

Gryshen was relieved to be wrapped up in the mystery of battle preparations. Hena was exactly what she needed—the antidote to the poison inside her.

"What does that mean?" Gryshen asked.

The jellyfish in the lantern had been pulling in its tentacles, tucking them under its body, curling its exoskeleton within. Now, upon Gryshen's question, as if silently directed by Hena, it unfurled in full glowing glory, acting as a spotlight on Hena's wide face.

"They don't know you're *wild*."

Gryshen thought of the way Coss tore into the face of the shark.

Then she thought of the measured methods her pod used to hunt and kill. Her brother prided himself on bringing back clean kills, a good shot with the spear often doing the job.

War was far from clean.

She could feel her long, skinny form as she crossed her arms and touched her pointed elbows.

"My pod." She had come back into focus enough to imagine her tribe fighting with the most ruthless crew of ceasids. Even the Rone's toughest hunters—how could she put them at risk?

"I'll have to go myself," she signaled it into the lantern, as if it would bounce against the glass and explode into a wish so powerful it could build her an immortal army to back up her bony figure.

"You are an idiot. Stop." No, Hena was definitely not

soft. "Gryshen"—she slowly sounded out her name as if she were talking to someone who couldn't speak her language—"what do you think your pod is doing at this moment?"

CHAPTER 10

"S—sleeping?" Gryshen asked.

Hena shook her head very slowly, her thick hair obediently matching the movement, her eyes never losing that stark wideness. "Planning."

"Planning what? They don't know — "

Hena let out a burst of a sound that was somewhere between a scream and a laugh. "Word spread just after it happened, Gryshen. They are grieving your father, of course, but no, they are plotting. They're all just trying to give you a little time to heal and go through your Forms so you can lead them into battle."

"But no one was to say—"

"I think one of those sisters overheard something. Helda? Velda? I can never keep track of those two. I remember them from when we were little leens. They were just a bit older, huh? But they were *always* wretches."

Gryshen wasn't sure if she was horrified or relieved about her pod's knowledge. If they all knew, then she didn't have to tell them that in the hour of her father's death, she had managed to lose their only hope of lasting survival.

"But no one said anything to me."

"The future chieftainess with the dead king father? I wonder why." Hena switched back and forth, not thinking in terms of feelings; then she would catch something in her friend's face and soften again.

"They don't blame you, Gree." She reached a hand out, then stopped midwater.

"I don't believe that."

"Well, they do not. I've been listening."

"Then it's only because they don't know the whole story."

"And so what? When was a leader's private story a tale for her tribe? They know enough." She pursed her deep mauve lips, her dark brown hair billowing as she set her black eyes on Gryshen. "Will you tell me the whole story? Soon?"

"Soon. But first, I need you to help me get through my paces. And then I'm going to need . . . a lot more."

"Suggestions on how to wage a war?" Hena's face became tightly set.

"I have to get our pearl, Hena. It's my fault it's gone. I have to be the one to get it back. There is no other choice."

Hena stared in that way she had sometimes, through her, past her.

"Hena? There is no other choice, right?"

Hena fingered the pale pink pearls tied around her neck, sliding them back and forth. A gift from her Uncle Qoah, when he still had his own mind. Gryshen remembered when Hena got them. Finally, Hena focused back on her.

"No, there's not. But I will be with you. There's no choice about that, either."

They spoke awhile longer, circling the cavern end with quieted signals. Gryshen wished she could speak to Hena on her frequency so there was no risk of other Rone's hearing, but this was one sacred secret between each pod.

The light hadn't reached the water when it was time for Gryshen to wake. Bravis was posted outside her chamber, she wondered for how long, when she woke to a hushed drumming of a signal from him. Her chest felt dramatically stronger; the pain was barely noticeable now. Her gray fin had some stiffness in its winding rows of vertebrae—possibly an effect of circling around late into the night with her friend.

Gryshen rose and swam to her mirror. A pouch was waiting for her, hooked against a broken chunk of the swirled gilt frame. The small net held the rest of her medicine. A petite shell arrow, like a crude knife, was nestled beside it. A purple shell that had once housed a little creature was the last item in the collection. Gryshen reached in to fish the round shell out with her fingers for closer observation. She turned the deep-hued figure over and saw the opening with something packed inside. She made a guess, dipping in a pinky finger and pressing it into the colored stain within.

Painted masks were for sacred ceremonies. Battles, yes. In sweeter, swirled patterns around the eyes for bindings. In smudges around the heart, to make a window for the soul to move forward, in death.

And for Forms. But unlike some of its other uses, like protection in war, or blessing in a binding, the markings for Forms were an invitation for wild, an opening for the unknown to enter. They were applied alone.

Bravis remained outside while Gryshen tamed her hair into two long, tight braids. She began to feel something again as she prepared. The silence before the pod awoke left a space for the time coming.

Gryshen dove into the paint with two fingers, and it clung to their tips. She pressed it so hard to her cheekbones, defining the angles even further, pushing with such force that it might very well bruise.

Bravis tried to maintain a placidity to his expression, but waves of fear—and something else—kept sliding across his face in betrayal. Something like . . . grief. For a flash Gryshen considered the fact that Bravis had lost his best friend, someone who was like another father to him.

It was almost as if she could relate, if it weren't for the fact that, despite his physical age, Bravis usually acted older than Apocay, whose birth no one could remember.

He studied her, as if searching for a sign of something he could use to stop her from going forward.

"Gryshen . . . "

"I have to—I must do this now."

"I'm going with you as far as will be allowed."

"All right."

Bravis joined her in Breathing Chamber Number Three. It was empty this early. Gryshen drank the air in steady sips, letting it coat her insides. Once a she watched Bravis draw breaths from the next tube over, as if they didn't both know he had fueled himself before meeting her. When she had finished, they turned from the chamber and swam in a nearly straight stream. Small white-and-green fish moved out of the way, their schools like fluid boats that bowed to the steady force. Gryshen passed the chambers of the still sleeping, and saw a face looking out from one of the openings. She knew the room well. She had expected her brother to be awake, watching for her. And there he was. She almost sped past him, but forced herself to slow down. Bravis matched her speed.

"Grysh?"

"Jode, I *have* to."

"I know. I know. But here." He reached to his left wrist to the fine meshed net of linked chain that wound along his forearm, bearing at its center a pattern of bones taken from his first hunt. He had gone with their father, and he had taken down the beast by himself, with a fin whip to its back and a spear twice to the belly. He still wore the scar on his hand from it proudly.

"You can just borrow it—for the day." He managed to retrieve a shade of his grin for her, and it was like a gulp of fresh air.

Gryshen nodded, returning his smile with one of her own. She held out her arm as he wound the piece carefully around her own wrist.

She patted his hand gently as it rested on her arm. "Everything is going to get better. Again." She hadn't expected or planned to say this to anyone, least of all the brother who looked up to her, but it came out. "I promise you."

"I believe you." And past the sadness, beyond the grief, anyone who took a moment longer to look would see that he meant it. Optimism is built into some beings like ribcages, and Jode was one of those beings.

"Thank you, Jode." Gryshen took his words, seeing them binding against her arm wrap as if they transformed the bracelet into the most powerful talisman. He gave a swift wave, and as she and Bravis pressed forward, she glanced back to see him bobbing just outside his doorway, watching them glide away.

Colors of the water shifted and changed throughout the cavern. Holes in the ceiling and sides allowed for more or less light, depending, and in a few meters, she could move from a pale gray to clear water, to a shade of sapphire-blue sea. Growth of algae crept across the walls, plucked back by the hands of nibbling ilorays. Bravis moved in sculpin-like precision as they turned left, then right, far past the hub to where Apocay had told her to meet him. They came to the last oxygen chamber on this end of the long cavern, just before pitch blackness opened into the bone pit.

Last night Gryshen had been focused on staying pieced together just enough to hold her shattered heart in place. Now, she considered that this space kept inviting the significant: her father's burial. The first time she had journeyed with Coss. The first time she opened herself to him. It seemed like a remotely far time and place, a distant event between her and a stranger, the romance between them. Now she began to feed the lick of flame that seemed to keep her fused together for the time being.

The shaman was waiting like an ancient ghost hovering just beyond. She couldn't begin to read his expression, even though she searched for something. Anything.

CHAPTER 11

"This is where you leave." Apocay had nearly closed his eyes, as if he was ready for a morning nap. He pointed back from where they came. Though he never looked at Bravis, it was clear this was directed at him.

"Gryshen, here. To guide and protect." Bravis gave a quick tug at his throat, loosening the rope that held a blue glass disk. His hands felt unusually warm as they grazed her neck, his fingers tucking beneath her twin braids to tie it twice.

"Bravis. You've worn this since I can remember—I'll give it right back, just like Jode's."

"You'll keep it. Please. She'd want you to have it now. And I—"

"Who?"

"Your mother." Bravis looked down. "She looked after

me, too. I'll stay as close as I can. Right by the hub, so if you need to stretch your signal for anything—"

"She won't. Need to." Apocay cut him off completely, still looking sleepy and half-interested in a wolf fish that gnashed its teeth in protection from its menacing shadow. "Everyone goes through their Forms. Everyone finds their function, one way or another."

"But that's just the thing," Bravis protested. "No one has been through this kind of injury before taking—"

Again, Apocay interrupted, his tone sleepy. "Surely you don't believe that. Throughout our existence, as far back as we can recall, we have done some version of these Forms. Who knows how many warriors had broken limbs right before having to swim through paces, so that they could come out truly prepared for wars?" He didn't raise his voice at this. His signal almost always maintained its monosyllabic sound.

Bravis wasn't giving up just yet. Gryshen couldn't pinpoint the moment of this shift he seemed to be experiencing, all she knew was that she could never recall his being so fiercely protective. For a lax who had always struck her as obsessed with rules, he certainly was pushing them here, now.

"But in our history, Apocay, there have been losses." His signal turned down to whisper, as if by speaking too loudly his statement could become a curse upon Gryshen.

"I am here. I am going. And you are leaving." She was tired of this discussion occurring around her, sick of being sheltered. The last one who could really protect her was gone. And as it turned out, even he couldn't save her from her own stupidity and destruction.

Maybe by diving forward, she could begin to save herself.

She surged ahead, startling Apocay's eyes wide open. She couldn't help but grin at this.

Bravis called out, "Gryshen! Wait!" Then he spoke to the shaman. "Isn't there a ceremony before she goes in? *Something?*"

"Usually. It appears that this was hers."

Gryshen could feel her smile, like a stranger's, pressed into her face as she pushed into the black-blue. The water swirled around her body like a tunnel as she moved relentlessly forward, as if pausing could make this sudden surge of strength stop. Gryshen only looked ahead as she moved further into this part of the cavern than she had ever been before.

It took several seconds before she identified the hundred little pinches around her back and shoulders. The thick coil that rode in with them, snaking alongside her, ever lengthening, made it clear enough. A shaft of light burst through. Clouds must have broken for the sun to open up in this dark space. Gryshen was disoriented as it was . . . was she near the bone pit? As she beat against the massive squid, the water continued to brighten, and she got a view of its size.

Its head had to be the length of two of her lying down. Its tentacles flailed, the suckers on them pulsing about in the brine. The creature's movements reminded her of the haunting ceremony dances of ilorays.

Maybe if this was happening three days ago she could have fought it for longer, but her already damaged lungs struggled more than they normally would as two, now three long arms wrapped themselves around her whole figure and began to squeeze.

The eyes were the most startling thing, though. The thing that pulled Gryshen's mind from being choked and into something else in this moment. It was between the two of them. She didn't want to kill him, and she didn't think she'd have to. The small arrow tied to her didn't seem up for the job anyway. Were the spears on the ground lost by previous journeyers, or were they left here for her? Some looked far too rusted to be newly placed. They suggested a stretch of time, an evolving of various "monsters" lured and trapped here to fight. Gryshen knew that few had actually died from these quests, especially in recent generations where the paces had become finely honed. This didn't feel like life and death. Not now, as she had just pushed herself from the tentacle. The trick she had remembered learning from Sodaren was to relax, to stop struggling for just a moment. In that same moment, a giant squid would release its grip involuntarily, ever so slightly ... and there she had it.

Gryshen darted toward the small opening on the far side of the creature, not knowing what lay next, but not wanting to waste precious energy here.

Just as she had circled him, a prod to her back served almost like a courteous warning. It was followed by a swift blow to the head.

Gryshen shrieked, knocked toward the sea floor. Her reluctance to harm the giant beast had vanished. Now, she seized the first spear inside her reach. It crumbled in her hands, ruins of iron and wood and leather. His eye matched hers ... eyes? No, eye. The other had been slashed into a dark-purple bulb. Maybe from another journeyer, perhaps from something else. Gryshen met his lone optic as it stared back into hers. There was a synchronicity, a match in the moment, which she broke by reaching down to grasp another spear. It was shorter than the last, silvery, with broken bits of shell on the end. The jagged arrow appeared to be abalone. She didn't think as she flipped it in her arms just the way Jode had shown her long ago, and sliced one, two of the creature's long arms.

It was as if the massive squid spoke to her, communicating like a stable pet, tingling against her outstretched fingers as she pulled back the weapon, blood and ink pouring in spirals around the beast. She looked at him, just for as long as she felt safe to, his one eye steadily meeting her gaze, as if to nod in some strange sort of mutual understanding. She swam in a circle around him, her heart thudding through her chest as she slid through the opening on the other side. She had managed to defeat him. She had managed to do this without killing the creature or killing herself.

But this was only the beginning, *a taste*, she reminded herself, just as the next opening revealed a glittering storm of electric eels, lighting the smooth water and pulsing as they took turns with her.

A hundred tiny shockwaves spread all over Gryshen's fin, her torso, her arms, her throat. Mother, her throat. She began to spasm back and forth, feeling as though even her hair had current running through it. She held fast to her newfound weapon. She rocked jerkily in an off-beat rhythm.

Where's the exit? Gryshen finally had a flash of coherent thought amid the torture. It loomed just ahead, stretching out much wider than the last one, and yet it seemed more out of reach. The giant squid was huge, deadly, encompassing the chamber, yes, but at least she could gather her brains a bit. And meeting his eye enabled a kind of creature connection.

But this? These serpents seemed to be completely mindless, performing their ancient duty. *Electrocute. Electrocute the enemy until death.*

Right now, she was their only perceived threat. One of these snakes getting you on a voyage or a hunt stung more than a nuisance. It was painful—but you could get away and move on. A healthy iloray could expect to heal completely by the next morning. She had heard of swarms attacking, but in open water, there were many more distractions for them.

Not here. So she'd try desperately to grab for a thought before it seemed to swim out of reach.

*Maybe if I—**Jolt.***

*Is there any space between these eels to—**Zap. Zap. Zap.***

A new fire was attacking her lungs now. External. The electric stabs pierced below Gryshen's skin, just past, and she could feel the lightning trace the outside of her vocal chord, pressing against it in terrible spurts.

It was only getting worse. Exhaustion was beginning to take hold, but in the moment she realized this, the terror that propels survival came right up behind it. She couldn't be tired. It could not be allowed.

If I can just move with *the spasms, push them forward. Use them—**Rip!*** A shock cracked through her silvery body, and she took it, riding it like a wave, thrusting ahead a space.

There we go. Now I need to—

The next wave seemed to torch through her more slowly, and she heard her screams blow through her ears. Had she been shouting this whole time? As each surge bolted its way through her, etching beneath her raw epidermis, Gryshen practiced rolling herself into it instead of bracing herself against it. She moved closer to the escape, but each thrust forward was more agonizing than the last.

She began to time her spasms, preparing. *Jolt—elec-*

tric ripple—push. Jolt—electric ripple—push. As if her progress tipped off the eels, the pauses between currents somehow became impossibly shorter. Gryshen closed her eyes, turning her wild shrieks into steady streams of moaning.

"Move!" she signaled aloud, in a low, pained tone. Another hundred switches turned on her.

"Move!" She insisted on working with all the swirling spears in spite of themselves. She ducked her head to try to get in front of the flock around her black hair, trying to beat them back with her braids. She didn't have time to wonder if it helped before the next blast of lightning.

"Move." It helped.

They were behind her now, poking at the rear of her skull, prodding her spine. They were no longer surrounding her; they were unwittingly helping her. Sort of. In their own nightmarish way.

"And MOVE!" She was there. The eels were circling the bottom of her fin, giving her crippling kisses goodbye as she swept into the next pace.

There was nothing visible ahead, but from behind, she still had some persistent eels chasing her, twitching and jabbing at her silken tail. Gryshen winced, shaking it from side to side to try and bat them away, although this just seemed to make the little monsters more determined to fight back.

Gryshen set her teeth, stretched her long arms out, and began to hit them backward. Her limbs felt like weak wings, but the movement helped take some of the pressure off the lower half of her body.

Was she in open space? A wall appeared before her, a sheet of rock covered in algae and sea sponges. Gryshen searched from side to side, spanning around the water.

What had appeared open was now closing in.

These chambers were always sealed off, kept safe for the next ceasid to make paces. The creatures might change at times, the battles get switched up, but she knew that there were some things that were constant. There was no changing the cavern walls. This was an inevitable path for everyone who passed through. The sides seemed to be squeezing closer, but she knew that had to just be her own anxiety as she kept whipping her tail, trying to slap away the last of the eels, while straining to see where the exit was as the sea slowly boxed her in.

Gryshen finally freed herself of the last stinging little wretch, and the wall before her was washed in a faint glow. Daylight. Now she could almost reach on either side of herself as she swam toward the sheet rock and bent her body upward in one fluid motion.

Relief. She was finally free of pain. She didn't know how long it had been for her, how much time had passed since she'd started her paces. She only knew that this was the longest period free from attack since she'd begun. And this awareness, of course, only made her nervous.

It was such a narrow stretch, the slabs of stone that

she had to swim up, up, and between, that Gryshen wondered how some of the larger ilorays managed it. She craned her neck upward, her painted face drawn to the sky. She could see it from here: muddy, gray, and white.

A web spread across the light as she drew closer. In a moment her fingers were clawing at the ropes and weeds. Gryshen thrust her fin back, trying to slide out the other way, but hands were tying the net closed.

Two, no, three ceasids, whom she couldn't name because of the shell masks they wore, hoisted the sides of her trap and slid Gryshen up into the crook of a small cove. The ilorays wrapped ropes around a tall pointed rock while she howled and thrashed.

"Are you Rakor? We will come for you!" she rasped, trying to scratch them through the holes in the net.

"Ugh!" One iloray paused for a moment to touch his forearm. She had successfully ripped a thin flap of his skin. Gryshen took the movement, pressing her face against the thick cords.

"Who are you? Who are you? Are you trying to leave me here to die?"

The ceasids went back to tightening the net.

"Is this part of my paces? Answer me!" she commanded.

"We—" A stocky iloray with a mess of gray-brown curls began to speak when a leaner one with thin black stripes in his long white hair clapped a palm over his mouth.

Nothing more was said to her. She lay flailing, propped up at an angle against a black slab coated in dark green algae.

The three ceasids splashed into the open water and disappeared. Through the cords and twine, Gryshen stared at the vast sky overhead. The clouds hid it so that it was all the same ghostly shade.

Thankfully, the sun was hidden under full cover, so she didn't have to worry about heat. But there was only so long she could stay in clear open air without a drink, a sip.

Gryshen tried to collect her thoughts, tried to hold the fragments together like a broken shell in her hands. She propped herself up on her elbow and craned her neck, pushing her skull against the net as far as it would allow. If she could see something she recognized, she could get her bearings.

Open sea.

She blinked as if to make something appear. Nothing. Just water beating against water. The veil of fog wasn't helping. She still had some time. Was she supposed to get out of this net? Was this a part of her paces, or were those Rakor?

It had to be her ilorays. The one with the brown curls —she wasn't sure about him, but the white-and-black-haired one had to be Meelo.

This had to be its own kind of test.

Hiding from landkeepers? The rock provided her a good amount of cover.

Lasting without water? Maybe. Maybe they would come back eventually and free her from the net—just before the thin, empty air dried her out to death. This was a strong possibility.

Or was she expected to escape from the net?

Gryshen ran her fingers along the wet, coarse knots. It was rough but well-constructed and tightly bound. She ran her eyes over it, pushing it back away from her face. Gryshen moved against the rock, turning her head from side to side. It all looked like an open stretch of sea.

Gulls swooped overhead. She spotted three porpoise fins across the water, breaking the current. The air felt dry and hollow.

She picked at one of the binding knots, wondering if she could force it apart. It wasn't moving. She twisted her body, forcing her way to the other side of the tiny cove and squinted her eyes, straining to see through the fog across the water.

There was the pressure of her throat. Thirst was setting in, and there was no easy access to water without throwing herself over the high rocks and into the ocean. Still trapped in the net, this could lead to her death. She was more sure that she needed to get out of this. Gryshen began sucking the remaining sea water from her hair as she checked individual knots, searching for the weakest. There it was. An unusually large knot—looking as if one of the net weavers had gotten the tiniest bit sloppy. *Fit fingertips in, draw it parallel to line of vision.*

Maybe they weren't so sloppy after all. The knot was

large, but it was very tight. This had to be her best shot, though, so she committed to it. *Careful, careful*... Tugging too hard, too fast could risk tightening it further. Precise picking was the key.

Gryshen was not accustomed to being exposed to open air, without a water break, for so long. When she poked above surface she was just bobbing, so water was available in immediate gulps. Even on her rock, watching the humans, she just slipped right down every few minutes for a drink.

Her skin began to prickle now. She could suddenly feel her eyeballs pressing into their sockets. The roots of her hair began to tug.

Stay calm, she cautioned herself. *Panicking will only distract you.* She drove herself back into that knot, trying to ever so gently pull at each side, looking for someplace where it would give way. It wouldn't. Her already sore lungs weren't offering much support. The burning along the gills in her neck seemed to be returning. Her nostrils felt arid. Gryshen blinked, trying to moisten her eyes, but it wasn't helping. She paused from her puzzle to grab every last lock of hair and suck the sea from it.

It wasn't enough. Her lips were so hot, her face parched . . . and the air now seemed to weigh heavily upon her whole body.

Frantically, she began to look for an opening she could stretch out in the thread web. She couldn't even fit a hand through. Was the fog getting thicker, or was her vision blurring? She swept her eyes along the net again, hoping she had missed something obvious. Her eyelids began to droop, and she thought she heard the calm of the ocean being broken by a **Thud! Sweep. Thud! Sweep.** She half wondered what it was, half tried to get hold of the big knot again, but her fingers fell as her lids closed. The air pulled the last drops of moisture from her.

"Shh . . . shh . . . shh . . ." A sound like waves crashing in the distance washed into her ears. Water lapped upon Gryshen's tail. Something soft and damp pressed against her forehead, her cheeks. She jerked her eyes open as soon as she felt water being poured in a strange trickle down her throat. *Was this a dream?* A teacup was pressed against her lips. It had to be one of those dreams. She must have passed out. Had she died? Had she? She fluttered her eyes, straining to see past the cup and the blur. Foggy sky . . . and a face.

A human face.

She swiftly drew her whole body back, trying to pull herself up on her elbows and failing.

"Shh . . . shh . . . shh . . . " The face placed a finger to its lips. The human was making the sounds of waves. Gryshen blinked again to put all the shapes into focus. She knew the face.

It belonged to the woman of the island, the woman of the tea-drinking dreams. The woman looked anxious. She said something Gryshen did not understand.

The woman handed something to her; more she set it against her fingers, closing them gently around it. Gryshen laid against stone, dumbfounded.

In her hand was a teacup, with no chips and a gleaming white finish. The sunlight came out from the clouds to reflect on the elixir, its dark amber surface reminding her of a valley of seaweed jewels. Gryshen wasn't shaking; she held the cup steady, looking at the woman, then past her. They were tucked deep in a cove, larger and with taller rocks than the one she had been trapped in.

Trapped.

She spied the net torn open with a long blade beside it. She wasn't about to fight this. Not this woman. Who could fight someone who had clearly just saved their life? From her post, Gryshen craned her neck to see their position: to her south, the wall of rock; a bit southeast were a grouping of stones that must have worked as steps for the landkeeper to walk down to this point. The woman sat against a smaller boulder backing up to the cliff. Just ahead, on the west side, a small boat was resting ashore, a pair of oars haphazardly strewn beside it. Past the boat, open sea. Farther still, more sea. She turned around to glance behind her, and in the distance, she recognized her own looking rock, where she had watched this landkeeper, now a face just before her.

The other side of this cliff must be her island, yes, she thought, recognizing the wall now as a place she had swam past.

The woman kept her eyes focused on her. Her hair was in a loose black braid trailing down one shoulder, her eyes a clear gray, her chin falling to a definite point.

She wore a long pale-blue dress tied with a fringe tassel around her waist. She didn't speak again for some time, only sat against the stone looking back at Gryshen.

The woman began to lean forward, but even in her slowed movements, she startled Gryshen, whose hands now shook and spilled the warm contents of the cup. It felt like sun-soaked ocean on her skin, only a little hotter. The woman reached out her two hands in a cradle, and Gryshen considered giving her the teacup. She went fishing for those old words in her mind, but only the silly ones were floating through her head now. She took a sip of the tea and pulled back the veil in her mind to reveal the words she was taught to use in a crisis:

Danger

Help

Hungry

Thirsty

Get away

I will kill you if you hurt me.

The words and their meanings flashed in her mind. She felt no need, nor did she want to tell the woman to "get away," and she knew she was not in danger with her, so there was no reason to threaten her with death. She just needed confirmation.

"He—help?" Gryshen pointed a long finger at the woman.

The woman nodded, then said, "Yes. Help." She stared for another moment, pressing her hand against her chest. "Safe."

Gryshen recognized that word.

"Safe." Gryshen nodded in return, then pressed her hand to her chest in the same place she had seen the woman do it. "Safe," she said again.

"Mother!" A call came from the top of the cliffs. The woman shot up abruptly. She crouched before Gryshen and this time the iloray didn't flinch. The woman took Gryshen's hand that held the teacup, wrapping her own around it. She spoke a few hushed words that Gryshen did not understand, then lifted her skirts to run up the stone stairs, leaving the teapot and the iloray behind. Gryshen blinked several times, trying to make sense of what had just happened. After a few more moments, she felt sure that the woman would not return for some time. And she was supposed to be somewhere, but she couldn't quite catch her mind up.

Forms.

CHAPTER 12

*G*ryshen startled with the realization. She couldn't shake the desire to understand what had just transpired—her own dreams, the woman's behavior, how she had found her in the net . . .

She would have to get answers later. Gryshen set the teacup carefully in a crevice after taking a long draw of its deep amber contents, laid her spear across her shoulder blades, and dove back into the water to find what awaited her.

She swam toward the rock where she had been trapped, hoping there was a sign to lead her forward. Her hope was rewarded by a string of lanterns leading down, down into the water. She drank up the smoothness, the coolness of the ocean like she never had before. She followed the lanterns on their winding path—it was all in outer places, well past their cavern, off course from typical hunting routes. The way pointed toward what looked like a large boulder on the ocean bed with one lantern at the top, and the last of the rope tied to a large anchor that lay beside a small opening.

It was the end of the line, and Gryshen took in a large gulp of water, bracing herself as she swam into the most obvious of all traps.

Light crackled and danced across the ocean floor and the walls of this place. It puckered through skinny crags in the ceiling, a faint wisp of sunlight pouring in through the way she came; the only way out.

And here she saw what appeared to be a giant shell, an oyster shell. Gryshen swam hesitantly toward the open mollusk that looked just like the one from the stories of her youth.

It was the legend, the force of her ilorays.

She felt awe. She felt wonder. She delicately reached out an arm, stretching her fingers gingerly toward the . . . *sculpture.*

Gryshen sank, noticing how the jagged marks of sunlight illuminated what looked like hundreds of gray shells sealed together to form the likeness of the ceasids' birthplace, empty now. As the real one would be.

Only this was just a wish, an imagining. She felt foolish for getting so excited, for believing for a moment that this was her ancestors' first home, when she had been told her whole life that the original womb had been long since hidden, that they had been unable to find it—surely, many storytellers suggested, because of Mother's anger. Mother would keep them from finding it, perhaps until death. Then they may find themselves back in the Great Womb, not unlike this foreign space she was in, and they would see their cradles and they would lay in Mother's arms, like fresh pearls, waiting to be released into a new adventure.

But the only pearl that mattered right now was gone. She had failed at her most important task before she had begun.

And adventure? Her adventure came and went with love, loss, and betrayal.

Now it was only about the mission: The mission to take back the Great Pearl. The mission to slit Coss's throat. Gryshen's finger's clenched, and her eyes filled up with ink, so it took her a bit longer than it should have to see that a large rock had been placed to block the way she came in. When she did realize this, something began to cover even the tiny stretches of light shining through, crack by crack.

Gryshen looked frantically around for the beast that was surely waiting for her in the darkness, preparing for the fight in which only one of them would swim out of this manufactured womb. She reached around her back to tug her rescued spear from its seaweed tie, and as the lights continued to go out, she swam to the massive ashen oyster shrine. This was where she would wait. At least whatever it was couldn't sneak up behind her here. If need be, she could swim up and trap it with her spear . . . possibly.

Not another giant squid. A fight-trained great white

shark? She shivered. *Or more electric eels . . .* she winced. *No, some sort of shark. Or a more aggressive killer whale. Or iloray warriors? Would they do that? After having been strangled, electrocuted, and nearly dried out to death,* Gryshen was sickened by the possibilities. And as the last light went out, she tried to capture a final image of her surroundings, clutching her spear with both fists, pressing her whole backside against the grainy lumps of broken shells, waiting.

And waiting.

The black water seemed as if it had the power to drown, so dark and enveloping, when not long before she was blinded by daylight and stifled by omnipresent air. Now it all faded off, floated away into the black, like the whispers of bugs and tiny sea pods. Hints of other life seemed to appear before her eyes. But she had to be imagining. All light had been blocked out. Even with a ceasid's eyesight, which was more heightened than their landkeeper brothers and sisters, she could only see suggestions, ideas in the pitch. And she waited still.

Nothing approached. No turbulence in the water. Not a sound past the current *shh* of water in her ears, the soft pressure of her heart thudding in her chest. The waiting began to shift into something else in this womb reproduction.

Something like . . . being.

In the whooshing, in her heartbeat, she could collect her thoughts, curate her ideas. Gryshen tried to steady her focus, as what she had imagined to be specks of life drifted up like tiny, glowing, reflective pieces of her whole existence.

Her father's coffin.

Coss's lips against hers.

Tea down her throat.

Her burning throat.

Coss's pinning grip.

She tried to force this last image back into the black, tried to make way for fresh shards of vision, but the memory insisted. It pressed against her brain like a carving. *Their ride on the beasts. Open water. Freedom. Secrets and heart swells. Her daddy decaying.* The pieces of vision drifted slowly at first, then zoomed into view. She imagined each experience carved into her own coffin lid, much like her father's, inlaid with the stained-glass pictures, the etched-into-wood details, telling her story. *Jode—so hurt. Bravis watching over her. The curiously suspicious Apocay.*

Morfal's anger—just a distraction. She saw a new image: *Morfal pushing his son, pushing a spear in his hands, pushing him into war.*

Gryshen knew that there were sacred times in the iloray journey when you could experience visions, clear visions of reality, even the parts you hadn't seen with your own eyes. Visions of the past and future that made the bits fit together, or turned the entire picture around.

She had heard of such encounters, and it suddenly dawned on her that this was not a physical exercise, but a spiritual one.

This must be a part of her Forms that was supposed to make her wiser, stronger, break her down and build her up into the leader she was meant to be. But at that moment, the very idea of being trapped in this transformation sickened her.

She wasn't looking for depth.

She didn't need breaking down; she had already broken several times over, and this bizarre shell role play wasn't going to save her, or strengthen her, or turn her into a chieftainess.

Getting the pearl was the only thing she could do now. It was the only thing that was going to save anything.

In a flurry, Gryshen leapt out of the shell, piercing straight ahead through the oppressive nothing, straight in the direction of where she had last seen the opening.

"Let me out!" she signaled. Her fists found wall, and she began beating against it. "I have to get out! I need to get the pearl!" Gryshen slammed her palms against the stones, and tucked her fingers in, searching for the rock that barricaded the entrance.

"I get it!" she yelled. "I'm supposed to look deeper, see the whole image . . . honor my father!" She found it. The edge of the rock. Gryshen took a deep gulp, and forced against it. It didn't move. A bigger gulp, and a push of all that was in her. Barely the tingle of movement. They could have warriors sitting on it, guards on top of it . . .

They must have tied it down, she thought, ignoring the

bruise she was guaranteeing herself while she persistently jammed her shoulder against it. *Pointless.*

"I under-STAND now!" she screeched. Now the flurries were back in focus, and this place was beginning to crawl on her skin more than any dry net. *Whatever story I have to tell them,* she said to herself.

Jode as a little lax trying to teach her how to throw a spear, laughing when she missed and her miniature arrow found its way into Bravis's then teenaged tail.

Jode frantically shaking when their father first told them he was dying. Her silence. Her frozen, useless silence. Bravis pulling her brother aside to comfort, doing her job. Just like he had to only days ago.

Her brother, broken over the casket again.

Bravis standing over her wounded body. Bravis fighting her and Apocay, trying to stop her. Trying to make her heal.

Once again, in the presence of her broken baby brother, perilous nothing.

But this? This barrage of memories, coming out like the eels that had electrocuted her hours before?

This was everything.

Sweet freedom on her beast, sweeping the ocean.

A gentle stroking of her hair from her mother, whose face was clearer now than ever before in her mind's eye.

Every image doused her in a feeling, but they didn't wash away with the next one. They just kept piling up.

The incessant singing of the iloray chorus. The judgment she saw from Helda and Velda when she was only a babe, when they were all so small. The looks unsettled her. She knew she wasn't fit to lead even then. She knew she wasn't made of the same stuff as her father.

"Are you ready?" She could feel Coss's warm grip, his eyes pressing into hers, the burning in her heart when he asked her to marry him.

Again, fighting with his father.

"I can't do this to her!" The frame swung forward, so much in her space it was as if she were there.

"Son?" Morfal used the word the way she had heard him call for his food. "Son." Now his tone was mocking.

"Yes, father." Coss's teeth were clenched.

"Do you actually have an attachment to this iloray?"

Coss kept his jaw tight, his gaze low, remaining silent.

"I should have known. I should have known you couldn't handle this. Betraying your family for—"

"I'm not betraying anyone. Surely there's another way . . ."

"Another way? What do you propose, child? Asking their waste of a chieftain to 'share' their pearl?"

"Father, he would. I'm certain of it. I've been listening, and he—"

Morfal broke into Coss's words with a roaring sputter of laughter, spitting bubbles in his son's angelic face.

"Child. You child. They will always hold onto the power. They will always be in control, our pod's destiny left up to them, if they keep it! Is that what you want for us? To be wholly in need of their kindness? Completely reliant on their mood, forever?"

"No, but—"

"Yes, to be sure, Frall would offer us a piece of their pearl's energy. But it would not be enough to sustain us long-term. And its power would be watered down. We'd have to move our whole pod close to them to get anything of sustenance. We'd be like leeches, draining off of their energy."

"I don't want that, you know I don't. But is it so much better if we are thieves?"

Gryshen gazed wild-eyed, gape-jawed at this. *Could it be that Coss didn't want to . . . ?*

Could it be that he cared?

This possibility swung open a fresh door of pain in her heart, but a pain traced with excitement.

Idiot! she hissed to herself. She had fought for days, fought harder than any pace she had faced to keep all entrances to her heart closed. And now, in some dark delusion, she was risking destroying all of it for this crazy, vain wish. *Cared enough to leave you for dead.* Cared enough to steal the only thing that kept her pod alive and healthy, even after admitting that he knew they would have shared.

And they would have. Yes, her father would have had to make adjustments, as the pearls had shared energy with their individual pods for so long, since the beginning of their ceasid existence, that they were spiritually marked, almost like the way an iloray was branded to their vocation.

The pearl's power would be weakened when shared between two tribes, even if Rakor all set up camp in her pod's cavern. The Rakor had to know that it would never quite connect with them the way it did with its true pod, that even in stealing it to take back to their home, they were only going to get a pale version of the full energy that had sustained her own tribe all this time.

They must have considered all this, and counted on the idea that a foreign pearl in their possession was still worth more to them than one shared and kept in its home pod. And they were right.

Gryshen pushed back the reality that faced her own tribe, whose only chance of survival without the pearl would be to ultimately abandon their home, break off into factions, and be absorbed by the other ally pods. The choice was available to them; it had been long understood that should one of the friendly pod's pearls be destroyed, that this was one solution. Each group, depending on its size and resources, could absorb ten to thirty ilorays. It was the last option, and one which could involve the breaking up of larger families, not to mention loss of home and ancient heritage, as well as health risks to the very young and elderly in Rone. It was unthinkable. It was never her father's option, and it was never her option.

Whatever Coss had said to his father didn't matter, couldn't matter.

Her own father was becoming part of the sea, crumbling into the water. Her brother was crumbling, too.

Thank the Mother for Bravis. Gryshen knew he would remain in arm's reach of Jode, trying to keep him afloat while calming the pod. *If only Bravis could be chief.*

The thought popped in Gryshen's brain like a spark. Could she pass the crown to him? This question was answered before it could even quite be asked of herself. She could not. He would not take it. And her tribe would not wish it. Oddity though she was, leadership was her birthright. And ceasids lived—and died—by tradition.

No, of course not, he would never allow it, she thought to herself. Bravis would insist upon her rule.

She was her father's daughter, and her father was everything to Bravis, so to him she must naturally carry some of his blessed being. Some of his leadership, a trace of his magic.

Even if she couldn't find it anywhere.

But avoiding the crown was not her destiny right now.

Saving the Rone Pearl, and thereby saving the pod, was. Fighting anything in the way of that, especially delusions of Coss, were necessary to her sacred assignment.

"Sweet Gryshen," a soft voice cooed to her. The picture was fuzzy, but she could recognize a small fin, chubby little fists, black hair too long for the figure. Before the image came more clearly into view, Gryshen knew she was looking at herself and her mother. She reached for the glass charm dangling from her neck, and it felt warm, like Bravis had just put it on her.

"Why did you give this to Bravis?" she signaled aloud, as if the memory might answer. The woman who wouldn't visit her now seemed perfectly present for the

Gryshen babe, this better version of herself, one with greater promise, vivid royal potential.

The little child cooed and giggled in return, then the giggle turned to gasps, and the young iloray began to writhe in her mother's arms.

"What—what is it? Gree? What's wrong? Frall!" The blonde ceasid called out to her husband anxiously. "Frall!" She searched around frantically. Little Gryshen was no longer making a sound. "Help!"

"She needs air. Now!" A young male ceasid who looked to be about ten years of age seized the little one and rushed her to the oxygen pipe that swept into the next picture. He put her little lips to it, and as the oxygen rushed to her brain, a faint rush of pink returned to her gray-white skin. Little Gryshen was revived while little Bravis fed her air. Her mother looked on.

"Bravis, thank Mother! I had no idea."

"No idea?" he asked sharply. She didn't look offended, but he still caught himself. "I'm sorry."

"It's only that I thought that was just a part of her infancy. She looks so normal now."

"Looks normal. Only appears so."

Gryshen was mesmerized.

"Yes. Yes, of course, that's right." Her mother looked down at the baby version of herself, running a finger from her cheekbone to her chin.

It felt like a hand was squeezing Gryshen's heart as she watched the woman who had loved her and birthed her and rocked her to sleep in a view that made physical contact almost seem possible. Without thinking, Gryshen reached out to the crystal picture, and away it went, running down like rain against a rock.

And her mother was gone.

Stupid! Gryshen scolded herself for her gesture, certain that she could have captured more time with the woman she never knew—the woman who couldn't be bothered to reveal herself to her only daughter, if only she hadn't startled the magical little mirror.

"She would be that way, though." Gryshen's words pushed into the black water, a new bitterness upon her. This was a little surprising; she hadn't realized it was there. Apparently, her sense of betrayal ran deeper than only Coss.

And what was the talk of her "only *looking* normal"? She'd had a breathing attack. That was clear. And yes, it was unusual. But they spoke about her . . .

"Like I'm some sort of freak. Maybe I don't know anyone else with this, but does Radepol know anyone else with three fins? I'm sure that he doesn't. I know I don't." She signaled aloud, arguing with the runaway visions. "I have to visit the oxygen chambers more frequently. I only had three or four times where it was a problem." Before the most recent episode, Gryshen's only other lack of air scare was on a journey with Jode. He was excited to celebrate after a particularly short but successful hunt, and the pair of them had taken their beasts for a ride. A storm had been sweeping overhead, creating whirlpools in their usual path back to the cavern. Gryshen had already stretched her time away from the tube well past what her father or Bravis would condone, and Jode didn't think about things like that. Her brother promised a clear route around a reef. It was past familiarity, where they had swum to—only hunters and scavenging makers came this way.

Her recollection swelled up before her, another display in the dark.

"Grysh, what is it? What's wrong?" There was Jode, riding a small whale, reaching out to touch Misra. Her face took a grayer turn than normal. Her eyes were wide, and she was rocking her head back and forth, one hand touching her gills. So this was what she looked like in a deprived spell.

Images washed up and floated away; some lingering, some flickering past. Emotions rang within Gryshen like the bells on the island, and in a state of hypnosis, she waited as the next came steadily into view.

A woman, seated at the edge of rock, clutching clean white linen from the line.

The face stared back at her. Crystal clear, it shone like sunshine, bright white and yellow hot, deeply into her own eyes. It was like being peeled back by an illusion.

"Why? Why are you here?" Gryshen signaled to it. "Why did you save me? Why were you not afraid of me?"

The image wouldn't answer. It looked so intently at her that the picture seemed alive, like the woman was able to transfer a part of herself down here to this tomb of a room.

"Why are you in my dreams?" Gryshen shouted. The

image stayed unmoving. "Why are you in my dreams?" she repeated, more desperate.

The eyes looked back at her with a soft, searching sadness. Gryshen wanted to reach out so badly, but she didn't want to frighten the vision away.

The woman shifted, and began to cry. She looked downward, and so did Gryshen. She held a baby in her arms, with little puckered eyes returning her intense gaze. She clutched the baby to her chest, speaking mixed with quiet singing words Gryshen did not know, in a gesture she craved to feel. The ache stirred in her belly, pressed on her heart.

The woman ran her hands across the baby's wet hair, down her back, to her scaly fin.

Gryshen gasped and black water gushed into her mouth.

A light in the darkness appeared. The water swirled, and rock was pulled away to reveal the chamber opening. As the light spread through the room, Gryshen saw the giant sculpture far below her. As she had reached for her visions, she had moved closer and closer to the edge of the womb tomb. She half expected to see the memories standing there, living pictures now visible and real and alive, but it was just the shrine and crumbled ruins and wall markings beside it.

"Come," a steady voice, a familiar voice, commanded. Gryshen, still shocked and disoriented, obeyed slowly. She swam in inches, arms before her as a kind of shield to the lit hole, the blue doorway.

Only Apocay waited outside, a pouch in one hand, a

lidded pot in the other.

"Name?" he asked, surveying her.

"Gree—Gryshen," she replied, puzzled, looking around herself anxiously. The mouth of the womb tomb was a hill of rock and ice, and she was resting her tired body against it. Apocay sat with his long peeling fin folded out beneath him.

"Your new name."

"What?"

"Tell me your *function*, Chieftainess." He lifted the lid of the pot. Ashes began rising, just like before when her father had shown her.

"I—I don't know."

It was over. It was over, and she was supposed to know something. The recent images swam in her mind, but told her nothing about this. Gryshen was at a complete loss about what to say. Should she tell him about the rescue? She felt she should not. She would not speak of the human at all.

Was it a cheat? A landkeeper freed her. She didn't get out of that net naturally. Was it a cheat? It couldn't be fair.

Apocay blew the ash again and waited.

The shaman expected an answer, and soon after the dust swirled, she was bracing herself for the grave proof of her self-doubt.

Apocay squinted his ancient eyes, and looked back down at the pot as if it must contain a faulty batch. He lifted the lid a second time and shook it around to release any residue. A puff of the grains made its way out, and he closed his eyes and gave a final blow. The granules swirled into tiny eddies, whirlpools void of any symbol or sign.

Nothing.

"Nobody." Gryshen whispered the word like a curse upon her head, and as she spoke, she felt herself marked.

Apocay stared at her with an expression he had not worn for a long, long time.

"So it is."

He loosened the pouch, and pulled out a plump green kobee pod.

Gryshen knew what this was for. She clung to her braid, closing her eyes tightly as Apocay pressed the pod against her right shoulder blade. The burn was reminiscent of the eels she had escaped hours . . . or days before? She couldn't tell. But it felt a little more like when she'd cut herself on shells. It was a branding, this identity tattoo on her skin. She felt straight, long marks slice into her, curving sharply at the edges. Then it was over.

"What . . . what does it say?"

Shaman looked at her with a strange expression. Was it sadness?

"What am I?" she pleaded. She stretched her hand to touch the wound with her fingertips. She couldn't quite reach it.

"Apocay?"

"You're crossed."

CHAPTER 13

*G*ryshen shook, rasping, sobbing, feeling her insides shatter like shale along the beach.

Crossed.

A criminal. That's who was crossed.

A lax who had a vicious way with gentle beasts, who had promised to steal his mother's eyeballs while she slept—and was caught just before he accomplished this, was deemed too dangerous before his paces were to begin.

The other pods were warned, and he was banished to the open sea. Just before this, he was marked.

Crossed. There was no one else in the pod with the mark.

Unknowable, unidentifiable, or unbelievable.

That's what the sign meant, a universal symbol between ceasids and humans, the sign for mystery, marked off.

The sign of *X*.

And now she bore it. Like she was convicted of a crime she'd yet to commit.

Was it because of her plan with Coss? But that wasn't a crime. Wrong, foolish, idiotic, yes—but not illegal.

"Apocay?"

The shaman nodded, as if agreeing with words that Gryshen could not hear. "This is finished. You will sort yours out." He turned, his ancient tail bending like individual vertebrae, his thin white hair trailing.

"Apocay!"

"Lunch is waiting for me," he signaled without looking back.

This was not in her natural range of nightmares. She had never even considered it, because it was not considerable.

But here it was. She tugged at a piece of this realization in her head, like loosening the weave on a human garment. It was ripe to unravel, but if it did, if she let it, she could never put it back again. And if she couldn't put it back, she couldn't get the Great Pearl. And if she couldn't get the pearl, everyone in her tribe would die.

She stopped testing the edge of her breaking brain.

"So be it." Gryshen spoke in a new tone, with the ring of one who has only one purpose, one mission, allowing everything else to fall away.

The water felt cooler than usual, considering the season was on the dawn of shifting into the closest to warmth the Rone ever got. The mark on Gryshen's back burned, but her eyes had cleared, and she drew herself into a smooth motion, moving purposefully back toward the cavern, Apocay a few movements behind. She had gotten her bearings now, and she knew where she was going.

War had begun.

Who she might be—it couldn't matter. The turn in the pit of her stomach about it, the very real possibility that she was a fraud—no, she was a fraud. Gryshen shuddered at this. She wasn't who anyone thought she was, but she couldn't grip what she took from her vision. *No way. Still fraud.* She cheated through her paces with a human saving her. None of this had time or space to matter. It was done.

She was going to make it all right. She was going to do something right, finally.

A humming teemed from the cavern as they approached it from the side and seemed to pour out all the openings. Chatter? Energy? She couldn't be sure. But it was palpable. Gryshen closed her eyes tightly.

Now is your time. Now is your time to make this right. Just go forward. Just go forward. Just go forward.

These three words became a little chant, a charm, a mantra as she pressed on to face her tribe and face the coming season of war.

There was no hiding the mark. Jode had kept watch at the mouth of their home, and his grin could not have stretched wider when he looked up to see his sister alive, with fin intact. It was as if the past few days' pain fell away for the sweetest moment when he gripped her in a back-breaking hug. "Jode," Gryshen croaked as her brother squeezed the air out of her lungs. "No beast was so violent, buddy."

"Shut up." He wouldn't let off.

She laughed, and in spite of the fact that every bit of her still ached, it felt like a great sigh of relief.

"All right, all right." He held her arms, pushing her back in front of him. "Turn around. Let's see it."

In her moment of happiness, she had forgotten about the mob that had gathered behind him, waiting.

These ilorays were like family, even if a few were akin to awful cousins she was bound to protect.

But could she count on them to protect her as well?

Or would they tear her apart?

There was no postponing this. Gryshen took in a deep gulp, and turned, closing her eyes again as she grabbed her braid and pulled it over her shoulder to reveal the cursed mark.

Gasps of horror would have been better. The stunned silence was oppressive, and offered her no answers to her questions. She let herself open her eyes. She saw Apocay where he had remained as he'd swum behind her to the cave. His eyes wore a kind of resignation.

She asked in return with her own. *What do I do? What do I say to them? How do I explain this?*

He stared back at her, and his expression did not tell her much of anything, so again she placed her own words in their reflection.

Just go forward. It was a comfort to imagine he had told her this. It allowed her to pretend that the one who knew so much knew something for her, too.

Gryshen held herself up, and, like pulling off a salt wrap, faced them all.

Her eyes swept the group, and it felt as though she were silent for some time, moving her gaze to the bewildered babes heaped around a cluster of rocks inside the cavern mouth, the light of the torches casting a blue glow on the wideness in their eyes. The same glow illuminated the crowd. She couldn't bear to look at Jode.

Do it.

No one was more shocked. "You're joking. This is some kind of joke, right?" He leaned in, as if to suggest he'd basically been in on the prank.

"No joke." She lay the signal out in a low tone.

The pod, with their glittering blue circles of shock, had faded into the background while she and Jode spoke. Only now, a shift in the crowd startled her back to them.

It was ever so slight. The little lights had been going out, one by one, as the stunned expressions of her ilorays began to change. Their wide eyes slid into glares. A handful kept innocent curiosity. Add that to the still startled young, and Gryshen could convince herself that only half of her pod saw her through a new lens of suspicion.

You've only begun, Rone, she said to herself, and forward she went.

The crowd moved away, and guards swam in dutifully, holding lanterns in a jagged formation as she made her way toward her chamber, Jode and Apocay close on her tail. Two guards flanked them several spaces before the entrance to her room, where she would part the shell-beaded curtain as she had a thousand times, but this time, as something she could no longer identify.

Jode just stared from the shaman to her, from her to the shaman, waiting for some explanation. But none came. Apocay pressed his bony fingers together in what appeared to be a prayer, and then folded them against his hands. A small crushing sound followed. Apparently, he had been keeping crab legs in his net, and was waiting for the right time to begin gnawing them. And apparently this was his idea of a right time.

Gryshen rolled her eyes. Proceeding to ignore his open-mouthed chews, she turned to her brother.

"We need to prepare for battle. Where's Bravis?" She suddenly felt strange. How was he not there to greet her? Bravis was always there. He just wouldn't go away.

"Calming the mob." Apocay picked flesh out of his teeth with the sharp point of a claw, while he craned one of his ridiculous, ragged ears to listen to murmurs of signal down the hall. "He was in the back when you swam up."

His words send a little shriek through Gryshen, but she only let it escape as a clearing of the throat.

"Bring him in," she commanded to no one in particular. As if by power of her words, the waving shells were pulled aside by a long arm.

"I am here." Suddenly she felt a sense of calm unlike anything she had been living with. It was as if those words were a steadying shoulder to lean against.

"Good." It sounded like a whooshing note, the beginning or end of a song, and Gryshen was taken aback by her own signal. *Go forward*, she pressed herself again. "Now, Jode, I need you to redirect that mob's suspicion into battle-ready discipline . . . where's Hena? Where is everybody?"

"Hena is on her way back. She was out connecting with a messenger from her tribe so they would be ready for her signal."

"Signal?" Gryshen asked.

"Are we going to war or what?" Hena swam in, sounding just like Jode, who couldn't resist a grin.

"We got this, leen," he said.

"You're cute, little one."

"Do you think so?"

His words made her raise her thick brows. Gryshen could have sworn she detected a hint of blush between them, but it was difficult to tell by dark torchlight, with blood and forbidden secrets on the brain.

Gryshen broke through. "Jode, did you hear what I said? I need you to—"

"Grysh, please. What is happening? What is . . . happening to you?" He swam closer to her, moving hesitantly toward the mark, as if it could be contagious.

Hena, briefly distracted by Apocay curling his long tongue to eke out the remaining claw meat from his disgusting food artifact, bulleted over to take a look. "That's right, Gree! Your function. As if I need to look. We'll match, of course. I—" Her words cut off like a blade through the water, and she sucked the dark sea into her teeth while she floated stiff as a pillar.

"So . . . that's what he gave me." The shaman raised an eyebrow at Gryshen's weak attempt to somehow pass the blame to him for her cursed *X*. She looked away from him, and turned to Bravis, still floating quietly at the edge of the room. His face was difficult to make out in the dim light, not that he was particularly expressive any other time. But now, there was something like fresh snow on the island, keeping it soft and silent.

Meanwhile, Hena circled Gryshen, arms folded, once, twice, a third time.

"Well," she stopped in front of her friend to speak. "Are we really that surprised?"

"What?" asked Jode.

"What?" asked Gryshen.

Apocay snorted. They had all forgotten he was still here. He had finally discarded his treat, and was watching the rest of them with a vague sense of interest.

"No, really, are we?" Hena asked of them.

"Yes," said Jode.

"Think about it. Not to be harsh, Gree—"

"No, you wouldn't dare."

Hena ignored this. "Not to be harsh, but it's not as if you've been dying for the position of chieftainess."

"Probably because my father had to die to give it to me."

Hena gave her a warning look. She should listen. After all, Hena was right. Everyone with eyes could see she didn't want this, and anyone with ears might have heard her complain of her fate long before she knew how soon she would have to take the throne. And now, Hena wasn't swimming away. It looked as if she was still ready to treat her like a peer, even possibly still a friend. Gryshen waited.

"Furthermore, it's not as if you've shown a real leaning toward any function, in a traditional sense."

Jode protested. "She's great with the beasts. Always has been. Her pet responds to her like another animal. She could have been a beastkeeper, like Sodaren."

"Oh, Jode." Hena's tone was more than a little condescending. "When has a chieftain's child ever worked with the stables?"

Jode mumbled out his signal.

"What was that?" Hena asked.

Jode coughed, whirling water. "When has a chieftain's child been cursed with X?"

There was nothing anyone could say to this. Gryshen being crossed was, well, unknown territory. It had only been convicts and the supremely insane.

Jode moved around to her front, beside Hena, face to face with his sister. The wounded, funny lax already looked a little older, careworn. Gryshen wanted to wash all the pain from his face as he studied hers.

"Grysh?" he called out, looking as if waiting for something that resembled home to answer.

"It's from all the times I snagged the last of the sweet mussels from you. I knew being a criminal would come back to haunt me." She managed a little smile.

It was like she'd cast sunlight upon him. Jode reached out, taking both of her hands. It was unusually tender for him, especially in public. Gryshen drew a sip of water, waiting for him to speak.

"Nah. You're just crazy."

She couldn't help but throw her arms around her brother, bubbles of laughter escaping her lips. Despite her best efforts, a few tears mixed with them, swirling a little ink between them.

"Thank you" was all she could signal.

Hena gave a nod of approval. Bravis had drawn closer during this exchange, and now he was beside the rest of them. Even Apocay had pulled in a bit.

"All right, then, Chieftainess, what are our orders?" Hena asked.

So they're just going to let this go? Maybe just for now. Maybe they were as hurt, scared, and tired—no, no way they were as tired—but they were ready to do something besides feel stuck in grief and fear.

"You said you needed me to redirect the crowd, right?" Jode handed her something to grab onto.

Gryshen collected herself. "Yes. Yes. "Jode, nobody rallies like you. And that's what we need."

"Okay, Grysh, but they're going to need to hear from you, too."

Before she could protest, Bravis spoke. "He's right, Gryshen. They need to trust you. You're asking them to risk their lives."

"But, I don't want them to. I thought *they* wanted to. I tried to do this myself." Gryshen knew the words were useless as she signaled them.

"Not this again," Hena scolded.

"They will go into battle. They want their pearl. But they're afraid," Bravis explained. "They can't just do this for survival. They need someone to unite them."

"Jode or you or Hena—"

"I've got my own pod to send into battle!" Hena reminded her.

"Of course. I'm sorry. But surely . . . "

"Jode is more like a brother to all of them."

"Or a lover," Jode added, with a look at Hena. She snorted again.

Bravis continued, "And I am not a leader in that way. I am—"

"Lord of the Responsible, borderline ancient, party killer . . . Jode ticked off titles on his fingers.

"I was going to say *quieter*."

"Oh. Sure. That, too."

"What I was saying is that you—"

"Are Frall's daughter." Gryshen looked down.

"And their chieftainess. They need to rally behind *you*, believe in *you*."

"Not a ghost. I know." Gryshen thought of her father's gift to bring enemies together with his easygoing presence. He could make anyone believe him.

It was simple to do when you told the truth.

This thought led her to what she was almost certain she was told by her own visions. She just couldn't even consider it. There was a moment of hope here; her most beloved ilorays were behind her still, and she was going to keep it this way.

"Okay, fine, fine. I'll come in when they've warmed." Gryshen shivered. Whenever that might be.

"All right, so like before a hunt?" Jode looked to Bravis and Hena for advice.

"A bit. Be yourself. You are their friend," said Bravis.

"Be funny—but not obnoxious," Hena said.

"Be the one they can trust," Gryshen said. After a brief pause, she added, "If they can remember how much they like you and trust you, maybe they'll be able to tolerate me."

"Gryshen." Bravis looked at her, Hena's jaw set firmly in agreement with what he was going to say next.

"Okay, they trust you, and we'll make them trust me."

They all seemed satisfied with this answer.

Jode checked himself in the chunk of glass against Gryshen's chamber wall, baring his teeth and cleaning bits of barnacles from his fin.

"For Mother's sake, I hope you have more to rely on

than how you look." Hena floated just behind him, arms folded.

"For them or for you? Never mind, I think I can win over both." Even Bravis chuckled at this. Gryshen felt a little heartened for her brother when she caught the suggestion of a smile on her friend's plum lips. Jode caught it, too, and it probably didn't hurt his confidence when he swam out, followed by Bravis. The guards signaled throughout the cavern that everyone was to meet in the hub for an announcement from the prince.

"Don't you need something? Before you speak?" Apocay finally signaled.

"What?" She was just wishing he would go away. He was too connected to things she couldn't consider now, the things that had to stay hidden. She had an uneasy feeling that he might be able to draw back some secret veil if he chose, and reveal all.

Apocay tapped his throat. *Of course.*

"Oh, right." Gryshen had forgotten again. It was so easy to. But now, even just as he reminded her, she could feel the little cuts in her lungs. She needed air.

Hena swam alongside her on their way to the chamber nearest to the hub. Everyone had moved out to hear Jode. They had probably only moved so quickly two other times, and those had all been over the last few days.

Hena coached her all the way down.

"Gree, you've just got to look them all straight in their faces. It doesn't have to be straight in their eyes if you don't think you can handle that. Pause at each cluster in the crowd, and every single iloray will think you spoke directly to them. Trust me."

Gryshen was glad for her help. She needed all of it, unlike her brother, who she could hear as she gulped oxygen from the tube like it was courage.

"They betrayed us! They slept in our chambers, and they ate at our elbows, and they abused our kindness— your kindness, my kindness." The crowd murmured and yelled in agreement. "My *father's* kindness." They roared. "My sister's kindness!"

The roar turned way down, something between a coo and a growl. "My sister, who doesn't—my friends, my tribe—she doesn't even know what other purpose she has." He was going for it.

Everything in Gryshen's body tensed.

"What is he doing?" Hena hissed.

"She doesn't know what other purpose she has, because the only purpose that's ever meant anything to her is Rone! Her *family*, her *lifeblood*. She rushed to her Forms after our enemy tried to kill her, she rushed— against our warnings, I should tell you—she rushed in so she could be ready to lead us, so she could lead her Rone family into battle to *take back our life!*"

The crowd broke open with cheers. Gryshen almost collapsed with relief.

Hena nodded her head. "Oh."

"He's saving me, that's what he's doing."

"Now, Gryshen." Bravis gestured that the time was right for her to speak.

Just go forward, just go forward.

She stared at her brother's face and took in his triumph, in spite of everything he had been through.

Bless you. Bless you forever, Jode.

Once more, she couldn't help but fling her arms around her brother. It was the truest thing she could do.

And the once-angry mob loved it.

"My brother is better at speaking to crowds," she said, doing her best to be as close as possible to the picture he painted of the leen who existed only to love her pod, and consequently was inadequate at everything else. This was a much better option than a functionless, fraudulent, heartsick Turnic.

Gryshen continued, "But with your help, and with our bravest warriors, we *will* be victorious. I'm taking back our pearl."

Tears spilled over. They were real, and this time she didn't fight them. They helped. They began to spread contagiously through the crowd. She looked above their eyes, because looking any closer was too much.

"Will you help me?"

The spill of warriors, arms raised, had to be contained by guards. Babes cheered. Pride was palpable. It was time to finish, quickly. "We plan tonight. We will set out tomorrow. As soon as details develop, you will be alerted. Thank you." The tears came again. She was beyond thankful for them, for Jode, for the chance. And she wasn't going to let them down.

The guards led her past a still-roused crowd, Jode on the other side of her, his arm squeezing her shoulders.

"I knew you could do it, Grysh."

"Yeah, with the stage you set, brother."

"That wasn't acting." Jode looked confused, and a little hurt as they made their way to the empty hall, the pod simmering in discussion back in the hub.

"I just mean—"

"It *is* showmanship, Jode. Don't deny that. And you are very, very good at it." Hena's admiration was all over her face.

"It's who he is," Bravis corrected.

"It's just his beliefs aglow, like his personality's been lit by a hundred lanterns," Gryshen signaled softly in agreement, realizing something that made her uneasy. Of course, her brother wasn't making that up. He was an entertainer, but he was no liar.

"So that was you speaking completely unedited?" Hena looked even more impressed.

"What? Sure. I mean, I didn't talk about my own fears, or what these last days have been like, because our pod doesn't need that. They need to believe in something."

"Like you believe in me . . . " Tears threatened to betray Gryshen.

"Gryshen, what is it?" Bravis had been watching her,

apparently, and he had moved up closer than made her comfortable, studying her face.

"Nothing." She rethought that flimsy answer. "Everything."

Bravis looked like he desperately wanted to say something, but his mouth had been pressed shut by an unseen force. There was that softness in his face again, but it was matched by unmistakable concern. Gryshen felt herself simultaneously wanting to reach out to him, and swim as far away as possible. She couldn't shake the feeling that he might know more of her story than she did, and here he was, not warning the others, not swimming away . . . *he couldn't know much.*

After they drank their air, the band returned to their respective rooms, with a plan to meet as daylight hit the cave. Bravis was the lightest sleeper of them, so he would be in charge of waking the rest if they weren't already up. As exhausted as Gryshen was from the trials of the recent days, she wasn't confident she could fall asleep easily. Her head was too full. Hena and Jode assured her that with Hena's planning skills and Jode's hunting background, combined with Proggunel's guard training, they would be able to devise a solid battle map. The time now was for rest, since they might not get much once they hit the open water. Gryshen took this as a command, and as she lay floating in her dark quarters, she fought back memories of visions from just hours prior. Her pod needed her. Jode, Bravis, Hena, and the others risking their own lives—they all needed her to be the iloray her brother believed she was.

So, going forward, that's who she would have to be.

By dawn, Gryshen was startled to discover that she had actually fallen asleep immediately, with only a haze of pictures and pieces of stories floating off to suggest that she dreamed. Her lungs felt noticeably better, and the welts that had appeared on her body from the evil persistence of those electric eels had faded. The rough, raw patches on her fingers and hands from attempting to escape the net seemed to be toughening, and the rashes and streaks of bruising from the giant squid were almost undetectable.

Gryshen considered what a wreck of a sight she must have been when she first arrived back from her paces. She was too absorbed in newfound knowledge and heartache to even notice. Only now, with the healing process well underway, was she able to recognize how damaged she had been. Gryshen remembered her medicine, dipped her fingers to scrape the last of it out, and winced as she rubbed it gently on her gills. They were greatly improved, despite the additional beatings they had taken. She would ask the healers for another pinch before they set off.

"Are you awake?" Bravis's voice signaled in a hush through the sea glass and braided twine.

Gryshen gave herself a quick look in the mirror. Sleep had been kinder to her face, and for the first time in days, her eyes didn't look as though they'd been punched. She was skinnier, unhealthily so; she'd barely eaten. The iloray pulled at her braid, letting her black mane flow like a protective shield. She stretched, and finally remembered that Bravis was at her door.

"Yes, I am."

"How did you sleep?"

Even without seeing his face, Gryshen could tell he wanted to ask so many more questions than just this innocuous one. It was perhaps the best way he could ask how she was doing without actually asking how she was doing, which would, of course, be a ridiculous question to ask anyone who had just been choked and robbed by their betrothed, buried their father, and come out of their spirit quest with a personality disorder.

"Okay. You?"

"Fine." He paused. "All right. I slept enough."

Gryshen started a little at the longer-than-one-word answer she had just received. She swam up to the doorway and parted the curtain to find Bravis waiting, a guard not far behind on chamber watch. The guard looked to her, and after she gave a nod, he swam away to catch some sleep before rejoining them later at the hub to hear orders.

Bravis had that look again, but Gryshen didn't hide behind her sweep of black hair. She stared back, exploring his expression.

CHAPTER 14

"*B*ravis, thank you."

"For what?"

"For being here."

"What do you mean? Why wouldn't I be here?"

"Supporting us, I mean—"

"Yes, I know. Why wouldn't I be?"

"Of course. You were always there for my father, and I know how you keep a promise—I mean, I'm sure you talked about looking out for us."

Bravis backed up, his mouth tightening. "Oh. Of course."

Gryshen couldn't take another space of quiet between them. "Is everyone else up?"

"You were the first I checked on. Shall we see?" They swam down the corridor, a bleary-eyed Jode flopping out of his room, a wide-awake Hena waiting just outside hers.

"Should we wake Apocay?" Bravis looked at Gryshen.

She really could go an eternity without seeing the shaman again. "For what?"

"Spiritual counsel—if you think it necessary."

"Your shaman is probably useless until he's had a full breakfast, after his twenty hours sleep," Hena said with a smirk.

"It's true." Gryshen chuckled.

"The crab legs? While we were in crisis? What was going on there?"

Jode began laughing, and Gryshen's heart played a little song. The rest of the way to the hub, he did a disgusting impersonation of Apocay sucking the meat out of the claws. Even Bravis laughed.

It was before breakfast for the rest of Rone, and guards waited outside while two head guards helped them plan, as well as Goshen and Timbaray, two of the best hunters next to Jode. Hunters and guards came from the same function, just trained a little differently based on what the pod needed and their own abilities. They could both act as warriors.

Jode was unique in his skills for how young he was. Most hunters didn't become strong or lead a hunt until they had been through their Forms, but Jode had proven himself long ago. When the time came for him to go on his own journey, it would just be a confirmation of what everyone already knew: he was full of courage, and was the best hunter their pod had seen in many seasons. Goshen and Timbaray, being a little older, had already been through their paces. The two high-ranking guards had been through theirs many seasons back—it was a requirement before you could accept that position.

As they gathered around the table, two leens came from the Food Base, holding clumps of weed and sea berries and carting a net of mussels. After delivering the food, the crowd passed it round, and the hubkeepers swam away. Gryshen looked at Proggunel, the head guard, and then she turned to the hunters. She had not only never planned a battle, she had never seen it done, only knew what her father had told her—and he had never had to plan a war either. The last one her tribe had been in was a brief skirmish with a faction of Rakor that were trying to break away from their main pod and take territory from Rone. This was during her grandfather's reign, her father's babehood, and it was short lived.

Proggunel cleared his throat, coughing and gurgling the water, his eyes staring at nothing in particular, as if awaiting orders.

Jode was talking excitedly with Goshen and Timbaray. "It'll be like going after great whites. Element of surprise. And then . . . *pow!*" Goshen gestured a spear being thrown as Jode described his vision of the fight. Timbaray wiped his hands in a gesture of easy cleanup.

"Chieftainess, if I may," Proggunel spoke.

It was beyond bizarre to have this face-lined warrior seeking her permission to speak on the act of battle, but Gryshen played along.

"Yes. Please." She shot Jode a look, but he was too

busy reenacting the time he fought off two squids to see it, so Hena hissed and punched his arm.

"Ouch! Why . . . ? Oh, right." He stopped to see what was happening.

"We've studied the insides of caves—it's part of a guard's training—"

"Hunter's, too," Jode cut in. "We know all the good hiding places from here to the Mediterranean."

Proggunel raised his eyebrows at such a claim, and Jode corrected himself. "Okay, we know a lot, all right."

"I'm sure you do, but hunting and battle strategy are not the same thing," Proggunel said.

"I have been in more near-death situations than I can count."

"And I have spent *two* of your lifetimes studying successful-and-unsuccessful war strategies."

"Yeah, *studying*." Jode snorted.

Hena could have knocked anyone else over with the snarl she let out, but Jode stubbornly crossed his arms, challenging the guard.

"*Enough*," Gryshen signaled in a lower tone, but they both turned to her. "You think our father would have accepted this?" she scolded her brother.

He bowed his head. The tense pair of laxes behind him backed away slightly.

"He trusted our head guard with his life. And Elder"—Proggunel gave a quick nod, listening to her, watching her brother—"my brother is not a guard but he is quick, and clever, and his ideas are invaluable to this pod, to this battle plan."

"Yes, Chieftainess."

Hena practically beamed at her, and the pride in Bravis's face was unmistakable.

Gryshen straightened her spine, squared her shoulders, and faced the ilorays who counted on her to take them through this like she had a clue as to what she was doing. "Let's begin. Elder, I'd like to hear your ideas, and then we can go around the table."

Proggunel loosened a cove shell from the broad strap of woven eel skins from his chest, and dipped his finger in it. It was holding the same ink they used to mark themselves, garments, and cavern walls, sticking in thick putty to his fingertips. He began drawing curvy lines and scratching symbols across the stone canvass of a feasting table. The rest of the crew pulled the net of mussels farther back to make room. They all leaned in.

"So here"—Proggunel pointed a short, wide finger at a familiar etching—"is, of course, Rone and our surrounding waters." He drew his fingers back, tapping at points around, rubbing small dots on the surface as he did so. "And here are the surrounding islands. They are directly across a wide stretch of open sea. It shifts into a tropical climate, with warmer waters and the Great Reef here . . . "

"But, Proggunel, won't they be waiting? Won't they be expecting us to come just such a route? Their fighters at the ready?" Jode had already forgotten, or was now ignoring, the taking-turns plan.

"He has a point. Maybe we just go back and forth in a civilized way. Everyone knows how to be respectful here." Gryshen gave a knowing look to Jode. "Elder, what about that?"

"It's true. They will be. No matter which way we go, they'll be expecting us."

"But we have a benefit. We have the Wanaa coming. They won't be expecting that at all," Jode said, sharing a grin with Hena. Goshen raised up a hand to clap hers, but she didn't notice. Instead, his friend mocked him while they floated behind the distracted pair.

"We do. And we have something else. We visit other pods more frequently. We have a more extensive knowledge of traveling Oceas than they," said Proggunel.

"Both of our pods do. Wanaa are some of the best at camouflage, too," Hena said.

Gryshen knew this. Hena's tribe was well-reputed for their ability to wrap their hair in reeds, and the colorful inks they had access to allowed them to paint themselves up like coral or seagrasses—long enough to hide a bit for a big hunt. They had used the techniques in water games with other pods, but it certainly wouldn't hurt in life-or-death battle. Gryshen was again sickened at the thought of the Wanaa getting involved in this.

It affects us all, she reminded herself. *Respect for each other's safety and survival and mutual trust is what binds us, is what makes us who we are.*

A signal came through the hall, pounding through the water like fists against sheets of maker metal.

"Did I miss breakfast?" Gracke, his vast bush of a forked fiery beard, bellowed as two guards tried to move ahead of him. "Your guards asked me to wait, but I'm already late. I told them—"

"Please, leave us, thank you," Gryshen told the guards, a smile taking over the faces of their group.

"I spotted Theus and Tollo on my way in. They were distracted. Something about Great Mother intending for some of her children to leave the sea. A debate about destiny." He rolled his eyes, and Jode and Hena chuckled.

The Nereids, ilorays from the Mediterranean waters, were usually more preoccupied with philosophy than reality, and preparing for battle proved no different. Jode and the other laxes moved aside to make room for Gracke's hulking figure and stubby dark blue tail that seemed to whip around on its own. Gryshen returned his grin with a small smile of her own.

"That's an excellent point, Hena," Gryshen continued. "So how do we begin?" She shook a little as she asked this, partly because she was officially opening a war, and partly because she felt as if she was supposed to know this sort of thing. But she didn't, so she looked to Proggunel, to Jode, to Hena, and finally to Gracke.

"Well, Chieftainess, I first wanted to wish your father a safe journey, a peaceful journey," he signaled in a gurgled tone. "I wish I could have made it in time to send him off."

"Thank you, Gracke." She had always referred to him as Elder, but it suddenly occurred to Gryshen that if she wanted to convey authority she might want to start using names.

Gracke bowed his head for a moment, his beard taking over the rest of his face. "I heard about the theft through hunters on my way here. I think the Nereids know, too. We all suspected, before the council meeting. Knew Morfal was up to nothing good."

Gryshen tried not to wince as Gracke squeezed her and Jode's shoulders with a grip that was sure to leave a mark. She heard her brother let out a sigh of relief when the large iloray released them.

"A couple of my pod came with me—decent fighters in their own right." Gracke drew himself up, extending his chest as he signaled, and it was clear that "decent" meant "excellent."

Gryshen again felt the strange sensation of relief and guilt, like floating with a rock tied around her. "I —thank you."

"But was the gift the choice to decide? Is that really freedom?" Tollo's feminine, melodic signal rang softly outside the room.

"Wait, we're here," answered her twin brother, as if they both had just remembered where they were and what they were doing.

A few snickers spurted through the group, and then silenced as the pair swam in. With almost white tails, chiseled forms, and cropped curls, the twins looked like something scavenged from a ship and polished to a glow.

Theus paused and bowed in an exaggeratedly slow motion, with Tollo moving only milliseconds quicker. The water scarcely swayed as they inched through it, like flipping through landkeeper pictures frame by frame, when they were still perfect, before the salt and sea warped them.

Jode nodded approvingly at the army that was assembling.

Hena looked annoyed over the time it took for Tollo and Theus to swim up beside Gracke, but Gryshen remembered what her father had told her about the Nereids, particularly Theus and Tollo.

"They're brilliant. So brilliant, they appear almost stupid."

"We are grateful to have you here," Gryshen said with a slight bow of her head.

"We came as quickly as we could," Theus said.

Gracke covered his mouth with a broad paw. Hena snorted audibly, and both Jode and Gryshen flicked her with the tips of their fins. She winced and drew up quickly.

"Yes, well, we're glad to have all of you here," Gryshen continued. "This is going to be extremely dangerous. The Rakor are . . . ruthless." She stifled the flashbacks of Coss covering her gills, suffocating her, moments after her father's death, the day they were to marry.

"They have no concern for another's heart—another's *life*," she corrected herself, and even though she had to close her eyes to push down the visions of Coss expressing feelings for her to his father, she couldn't ignore Bravis's worried gaze. It seemed to move past all of it, straight to the place she was fighting to keep safe and covered, the place that couldn't take any more injury. "I don't want anyone to assume that this will be a smooth task," Gryshen held up a hand to silence Jode and his overly confident companions from arguing. "Of course we have the brightest, the best, but we are missing something."

"What? Our weapons are just as good. Our warriors are just as skilled." Jode offered a complimentary gesture toward Proggunel, who seemed to respond with one of the most uncomfortable smiles Gryshen had ever seen.

Proggunel signaled low. "Of course, I will be happy to serve in any capacity." He looked to Gryshen, and she realized that he had to be almost as old as Apocay.

"We will need your services here. At home, protecting our pod," she said, looking to Bravis for a reassuring nod.

Proggunel bowed his head, so she couldn't see his expression. "Yes. It will be my honor."

"And we have a variety of abilities," Hena added,

switching back to the subject at hand. "They have just one pod fighting, just a small skill set. What could we possibly be missing that they have?"

Gryshen pressed her eyelids together, as she felt the sting that summoned the inky black well from the back of her brain.

As if knowing, Bravis finally spoke.

"*Evil*," he signaled. "They do not care about anything. Evil. This gives them the ability to always do worse. They will always be willing to commit darker deeds than us because they are soulless."

"Strange. You actually believe they were created without souls? The Mother made them dark?" Theus asked curiously, stiffly.

"Sometimes that dark allows light to shine brighter," Tollo said.

"Would Mother have made them that way, though?"

"If Mother was made that way, she may."

Gracke, having been hunched down on a stone, listening, lifted his head to boom out a signal. "We don't have time for this! The Rakor have been made of bad stuff since I can remember. Since our mothers and fathers can remember. Bravis is right. They are evil. Who cares where it came from?" His beard wove and danced in the water, like an impossible fire.

"We just need to make them go away," Jode growled, and Bravis gave a tight nod. Gryshen could have sworn she tasted blood in her mouth, and she wasn't sure if it was from biting into her tongue to distract from tears, or if it was the fact that somewhere between the cracked places in her heart, she longed to snuff out the life that had essentially ended hers.

Perhaps there was something to fear about *X*, after all.

In between altruistic questions from the twins, and platters full of mussel nets being shoveled into Gracke's gaping mouth, plans were made. Plans that were as good as battle plans can be for a group of leaders who had never seen real war.

"It's time we meet with the makers. Some of my warriors—your warriors"—Proggunel corrected himself as he turned to Gryshen—"have been preparing since yesterday. A couple of our more gifted ilorays already have a small collection."

"Of what?" Gryshen didn't even feel self-conscious in not knowing. There was too much going on to be embarrassed for ignorance.

"Armor," Jode and Hena replied in unison. Jode's crew grinned and began whispering excitedly.

"Oh, right. Ceremonial things? Or . . . ?"

"Oh, we'll have supplements for protection along with spears," Proggunel assured the group. "And yes, as I'm sure Apocay could tell you, those ceremonial masks serve a greater purpose than just looking impressive." He shot a stern look at Jode and company, quieting their chatter. They all folded their hands and bowed their heads like scolded babes.

"Supplements?" Gryshen asked for more.

"Well, my pod fighters are bringing shark tooth grips. They've been good for protection in a hunt; I'm sure they'll be useful," Hena said.

Gryshen had heard of these: skeleton, metal, shell, and a set of jagged teeth facing outward made frightening gloves.

"Good." Proggunel nodded in approval. "And the others?" He looked to Gracke and the twins.

"My laxes are wearing rock fittings. We've used them in game fights." Gracke's pod liked to work out struggles with the occasional fin whacking, and some of the huskier laxes would fit rocks to their fins and knock into each other until they both were so beaten up they were best friends again. "Choice picks of sharp blacks and grays, smoothed on the bottom to fit the wearer comfortably enough." He paused for the benefit of his rapt audience. "But *Boom*!" He pounded his great fist against the rock table, sending bubbles to blind the crowd.

"*Boom*?" Jode asked eagerly.

"Crack a head open!" Gracke said with a wink in her brother's direction as he tore mussel meat out.

Gryshen felt a touch on her shoulder. She looked to see Bravis's eyes upon her. Her face must be turning a strange color.

"Must we use those words?" she asked, her hand on her stomach. All she could see were heads, but none of them were Coss's. Then something occurred to her. "What about the young?"

"What about them?" Proggunel continued marking the surface of his rough map.

"Their young? Or yours?" Hena asked.

"Theirs. Ours. Everyone's!" The bloodthirst for Coss had been replaced by something new.

"We have some of our best fighters staying back to protect all of Rone," Bravis reminded her.

"I, myself, will remain here in case of attack," Proggunel agreed.

"But don't they have innocents?" Gryshen asked, amazed that in everything she had not considered this.

"And we have no quarrel with them. There would be no reason to hurt anyone who hasn't put themselves in battle," Proggunel said, still not looking up from his battle plan.

"But if we end up inside their cavern—that's the point, right? That's where the pearl will be, won't it?" She looked around, pausing to look at the twins, hoping that they would say something more prophetic and less insane.

"The pearl will be where it has never been," Theus said, while Tollo pointed her finger in a kind of dance, following a small beam of light that cut through the ceiling.

"That's handy," said Gracke.

"Gryshen, we won't hurt babes," Jode assured her.

"We'll capture them to keep them out of harm's way, if we must," said Bravis softly, and this seemed like the most reasonable idea so far, so Gryshen let it escape through the top of her head, releasing a bit of the pressure that had been building.

"Okay, so where were we?"

"Extra tools," said Proggunel. "And I'm afraid to ask, but . . . " His eyes darted toward the twins.

Tollo smiled, and stuck her still-moving finger out farther toward the line of sunlight.

"Oh, sun powers. Terrific," Gracke grumbled, and Hena snickered.

Then Tollo swam away and up, following the beam to its widest place, sliding in and out of its glow. Her pale fin was blinding in it, her skin spotlighted. In and out. Then, Gryshen blinked once, twice, to confirm what she was seeing. The glow of sunlight, the deep waters, all seemed to blend and shift back and forth.

"Tollo?" Jode asked, mouth open.

It was Tollo. Changing colors, tones, ever so slightly, becoming more and more a part of the background.

"So, it's true," the head guard signaled in awe. "You do have the ability to camouflage. I've never seen it."

"No, camouflage is meant to stay hidden," Theus signaled without a trace of sarcasm.

"We don't all have it," sang Tollo.

"Five of our thirty. Two of them are prepared to come," said Theus.

"Excellent." Jode drew the word out, and the table of ilorays looked at the twins with newfound admiration.

"When can we expect them?" asked Gryshen.

"They'll be here before you can expect them." Theus

folded his arms, his gaze almost as far away as his sister's, staring at the entrance to the hub. The water shook and swept, the gray of the walls bending, the rocks shifting into clear view. A pair of middle-aged ceasids seemed to come out of the stone walls, the bits of light. Their pale eyes and distant stares were more than slightly unnerving.

"Thank the Mother they're on our side," Hena signaled to Gryshen quietly.

Gryshen gave a stilted nod in agreement. The hidden ilorays drifted in the background, awaiting further instruction, apparently.

"All right, yes, fine, that is actually useful." Gracke held up his shield-sized palms in a kind of stunned surrender.

Tollo now appeared to be playing a game of chase with the spokes of light.

"Useful?" Jode's mouth was still open. He began to reach out to touch Theus, entranced by the pale skin with the shape-shifter powers. "How do you have that? How come we—"

Before Gryshen could scold her brother, Theus turned his smooth face toward her brother and bit his finger.

"Agh! What the—why . . . ?"

Gracke wailed with laughter. "How did I not know the crazies were the best pod around?" His laughter seemed to wash over the crowd. Jode was not amused, shaking his now-purple finger in shock.

"Really, Jode, didn't your parents teach you to ask before you touch?" Hena was almost in tears laughing.

Bravis clapped a hand over his mouth, his eyes revealing himself.

The grin made its way to Gryshen.

Theus's face was back to its chiseled position, as if nothing had happened.

"But, Theus, how do you do that?" Gryshen asked.

"Evolution."

"Now, that isn't necessarily—there's no evidence of your pod's advancement," Proggunel protested.

"Oh, not this same old story. For Mother's sake, twins, we all came out at the same time." Gracke shook his head, his beard seeming to bristle along with his expression. Apparently, his newfound admiration was easily dismissed by his long-standing annoyance.

"Silly, you believe in time?" Tollo giggled, pausing her game of peek-a-boo with a jellyfish lantern.

"Does everything have to be philosophical with you?" Proggunel asked.

"We see time differently. We believe that our pods may have matured differently," Theus said.

"Oh, yeah, with the biting. Sure." Jode pouted, sucking on his wound.

"There, is of course, the idea of parallel evolving, " Proggunel said, looking at the puzzled expressions around him. "We all know that Gracke's pod is known for brute strength."

"And skill! Don't forgot that!" Gracke added, his fat finger waggling in the water.

"Yes, yes, of course, Gracke. But there are other pods known for different attributes, gifts that would prove useful in a battle."

"Like cunning." Hena grinned, speaking for her own pod.

Jode mirrored her smile. They were bordering on a little much for Gryshen now.

Gryshen wracked her mind frantically. Why hadn't she paid more attention to her father's lessons through the years? She was sure this was basic knowledge of tribal leadership, and she was certain to fail the test— and risk looking, once again, like the fraud she was.

Her pod's shaman was admired across Oceas, but spirituality couldn't play a part in bloodshed, could it? Gryshen considered the way her brother whispered silent thanks to the Mother and the beasts just after stopping their pulse.

"Yes, Hena's pod are known for being clever, and an ability to cut right to the heart of a matter. They can size up a friend," Proggunel said.

"Or an enemy," Hena added.

"We have the best storytellers, too. And our music —*well*!" Gracke blurted out. Gryshen wondered if "brute strength" had rubbed him the wrong way.

The head guard continued, "And, of course, the Rakor—"

"Ruthless," Gryshen spit out. This answer she had

down. She knew what they were, even if she did not know her own self.

"And they are good fighters, besides." Gryshen could hear how it pained Jode to state this fact.

Gryshen thought of her pod again. *Was it their maker abilities?* After all, their breathing pipes were the proto-types for the other pods. Most of what was used around the sea had been cobbled together from something that originally came out of Rone.

The knot that had been ever-present began to tighten within Gryshen's chest.

"They are." Proggunel agreed with Jode, "And then there are our ilorays." He gestured toward Gryshen to speak.

"Frall was an example to us all," Bravis signaled in a low tone, looking straight at her.

"Our wisdom," Gryshen whispered this. "Steady temper." She thought about the intricately carved symbols scratched and burned across her father's casket, recalling two she recognized. One symbol was shaped like a nautilus shell, the other like the horizon: wisdom and temperance.

"Clear head, clear vision," her father used to caution her when she'd get angry as a child. "You can't focus when you let your emotions overwhelm you."

The rest of the ilorays at the table seemed to accept this, and Gryshen shot Bravis a look of gratitude.

How did he know she needed that? It was as if he was giving her a clue. It was completely out of character for

Bravis to cut in. He reserved his minimal signaling for the end of only the longest of silences.

Perhaps he just knew she was shaken from days of horror, and could use some extra help right now. Perhaps it was more.

CHAPTER 15

*B*y lunch, a few more warriors had joined them.

Sodaren had checked in briefly to receive orders for preparing the beasts for battle. Trying to picture Sodaren and other tribe members attempting to somehow strap the braided seaweed reins onto the enormous Gup brought a small smile to Gryshen's face.

"So you are to remain up front with me?" She tried not to sound too desperate when she went over the route plan with her brother.

"Yeah, yeah. Of course!" An undeniable spark had returned to Jode, somewhere between time spent using his hunting skills and being in a space so close to Hena.

Gryshen, and the weight that dragged her, felt slightly lifted.

The makers delivered on word of their abilities. When they were signaled, they waited at their workshop in the cove to show off the pieces. The war band made their way up, Hena and Gracke discussing plans for their pods on the way.

"It makes the most sense for mine to meet us at a point outside the Rakor boundaries, yours as well, I assume."

"My Pael would love you."

"Your wife?"

"Yep, she has a battle mind like you. Most of the leens in our pod do. It's just that it usually comes out on their husbands." Gracke's laughter at his own remark flooded their path with bubbles. The energy coming off their crew gave Gryshen fuel, and hope.

This grew as they surveyed the creations: spears of rock and shell, tightly bound, some long for bulleting threw the water with a strong throw, some shorter for hand-to-hand combat. The enormous starfish that lived in their waters had been affixed to what Gryshen recognized as wheels with a metal grip. They still pulsed, alive but trapped, their natural hard exterior providing the perfect shield for battle.

Jode gripped a spear and ran his fingers over the shield admiringly. Gracke picked up the shields, getting a sense of their size.

"We'll bring a satchel full of spirit slugs, too," Jode signaled to the group. Spirit slugs looked like they had wings, and they released an oil that kept predators away. It wasn't a guarantee, but it was good to release a few when swimming through shark territory.

"And looky what I have packed, Chieftainess." Gracke patted what appeared to be a net full of leaves with his massive rosy hand. "Here, we'll just be a moment," he cooed a signal to a white fish he grabbed in an instant. It beat nervously in his grasp. "This won't be permanent, promise."

Gracke reached into the satchel with two fat fingers, and held something gingerly in his fist. He pulled the flapping fish closer, until it appeared to kiss what was clutched in his other palm. "Oh! It'll be over soon, dear."

The fish's eyes misted, and it began bumping into Gracke's broad chest repeatedly. He chuckled.

"What did you do?" Gryshen was mystified.

"Seems cruel, but it'll be over soon." In another few moments, the fish's eyes returned to normal, and he appeared to give Gracke an accusatory look as he swam away. Gracke gingerly pulled what looked like a tiny gray crab from his fist. "It's a parasite. Causes temporary blindness. Got a net full of them, collected when they were eggs. Blocked the holes with leaves so they don't get out until we want them too. Could come in handy, eh?"

"Yeah. Copepods? When did you harvest those?" Jode rushed over to get a better look.

"On the way here. We use them in hunts back at Calaarn." Gracke was obviously pleased by Jode's admiration.

"Yes, good thinking, Gracke." Gryshen nodded, now distracted by Bravis intently eyeing the top of her head.

Bravis swam over to the bone-white pile on the banks, and gave her a nod.

"Which is for the chieftainess?" he asked a maker.

"Here." The maker lifted a bright seal skull and handed it to Bravis, who held it out for Gryshen.

"Your helmet."

The white was broken up by dark streaks all around. Upon closer inspection, they were carvings.

Swirling crisscrosses. A parade of them.

"Unknowable." Gryshen felt the hollow in her again.

The maker nodded once, then began handing out helmets to the rest of their group.

"Gryshen, listen to me," Bravis signaled quietly.

The helmet burned like dry lungs and heat in her hand. She just wanted to send it sinking to the bottom of the ocean, so it all could be forgotten.

"Gryshen," Bravis repeated softly.

She lifted her wounded gray eyes to meet his soft black ones.

"Do you know what this is?" he asked.

"A curse. Shame. They are at a loss over their forced leader." She spat the words out into the water like bits of tin.

He shook his head, holding the helmet up in the daylight sweeping through the opening of the cove.

"Respect."

Gryshen raised her brows.

"Yes, respect. Look at these carvings, the intricate

swirls—there's far more detail on yours than any of ours."

"Well, there technically has to be, doesn't there? I'm chieftainess, whatever they think of that."

"You underestimate your ilorays." He thrust the helmet into her hands, pursed his lips, then swam to help distribute the rest of the armor.

The skull from a beluga was ridiculous on Gracke, but it was the only thing that would fit his enormous head from their collection. The makers wrapped up the shields in a net, and tied the spears up like a bundle of sticks. Each of the band took their respective helmets and swam to meet the day.

The swim there was going to remain cool; there was no warm passage.

Apocay gave them markings, and was to remain with the rest of the pod, along with other elders. Gryshen had made an attempt to get Bravis to stay back, even to the point of command, but Bravis refused, and Jode bucked for him.

"Your father wouldn't hear of it," he insisted.

"My father is dead."

Bravis didn't let the words move him. "You are alive. And you will stay alive. And I will help."

Jode put a long brown arm around him, to apparently attempt an embrace. Bravis's returning hug was so stiff and unnatural for him, Gryshen had to stifle a snort. Hena let it out, and Gryshen was certain Jode would not attempt affection with Bravis for the rest of his life.

The pod cheered them on, even Helda and Velda plaiting rare silver shells into Gryshen's and Hena's hair, a known token of strength. Apocay marked each of them with sacred symbols whose meaning was a riddle to all, and Gryshen wondered if even he knew precisely what they meant. Hers was the most mysterious, the thing she dreaded, in bold, deep green and black across her skin. The *X* spread over her entire face, an immediate warning sign to anyone who approached.

Unknowable. Just like all of it. She gave her brother's hand a squeeze goodbye until they met up at the Great Reef closer to Rakor territory. They made their way through the water with a handful of hunters, pod leaders, and the healers that could be spared. They swam alongside their beasts, sometimes astride them, as the creatures were marked in their own armor—oftentimes bones from their deceased kind. They made a stretch until all went dark, and then found a resting place, where Gryshen took the armor from her beluga immediately and gave her head a gentle rub.

The ones who hadn't joined, who were waiting just behind in case their plan failed and they needed to signal back, were Hena and Jode, along with a couple of beasts, and the blue whale. He wasn't exactly fast, but no one else had one, and he certainly had stature. Hopefully, the enemy wouldn't notice that all he needed was a belly rub and a snack and he'd nap happily.

Gryshen just wanted to see that flash of light return to her brother's eyes again before they parted ways.

"Try to focus on the task at hand, will you?"

Jode, completely taken aback at this, said, "What are you talking about? I live for this task, Gryshie."

"But you weren't counting on being distracted, right?" And she cocked her head in the direction of her friend with the burning eyes, full lips, and silky hair.

Jode was usually shameless, but the purple bleeding through his cheeks revealed something.

"Knock it off." That smile returned to his mouth like an old friend. They held hands and touched cheeks.

Into the wide open nothing and everything, she sailed, Bravis just behind her, beasts, two healers, and Gracke acting like a kind of body shield at the rear.

The stretching sea was the place Gryshen loved most, and at times in this steady war beat, her crossed mark like a criminal tattoo across her face, the seal bone helmet in one hand when she tired of wearing it . . . she almost felt ease. Her long tail curled and lapped against the icy blue. Pale fish that had usually moved farther south by this point seemed to be unaware of their late migration as they bent through the water with their vast, one-minded school. She swooped down to run her fingers against the kelp and sea grasses, their tendrils a slippery comfort to her fingers. Bravis quietly mirrored her every move. He even gave the plants a little grip in passing. Misra swam to her left, occasionally nuzzling in for a pat.

If they weren't going to kill or be killed, with their pod's survival dependent upon their returning home with the Rone Pearl, this would have been a near perfect ride.

"Have we ever traveled together?" she thought the question, and it escaped as a signal directed at Bravis.

He looked puzzled for a moment. "Gryshen, we have grown up together. I guided you around most days of your childhood."

"Yes, yes, of course. But I mean . . . have we ever just gone for a swim . . . directionless? Just for the sake of getting out of the confines of the walls of the cavern . . . just to . . . "

Bravis thought. "No. Just to see what might be there?" He gave her the line she was searching for. She didn't expect to find it in his signal.

"No. Always a purpose. Always intentional." The look on his face was blocked by tiny eels sliding through. It brought Gryshen back, shivering from the memory of their less sweet cousins.

"You'll have to fix that after our little tousle, eh?" Gracke had been eavesdropping from the back.

Gryshen had assumed by his booming tone that his sense of hearing may not be so good, but apparently it was just fine. "Everyone needs adventure. Play. Even leaders. Especially leaders."

"Oh, but I've had plenty of adventure," Gryshen murmured.

Gracke caught that, too, his signal back startling her and making Bravis smile. "That's not the right kind. I'm talking about the kind you seek out, or even just fall into because you're so damn free. Do you know that land-keepers actually toil and save goods to barter with in exchange for travel—travel planned to the last detail, free of adventure, free of surprise, a few lights every twelve moons? They think that's fun." He snorted. "Crazy."

"How do you know that?" Bravis asked.

"I see it! They come through on their boats, with their looking devices, and you know what they do?" He threw his head back in a chortle. "They stare at the water. They lay on the beach and stare at the ocean. They jump overboard in ridiculous getups to spend moments doing what we live doing. Fools should never have left."

No one could or would argue such a statement, as the blue enveloped them, ushering in green and gray, the rushing of the water like the heartbeat of the Great Mother.

By the time darkness had overcome the sky, they only had to circle the edge of the reef a few times before finding a deep overhang they could tuck under out of sight. No one thought the Rakor would be all the way out here, but they didn't want to count on that. All armor was removed from the beasts so that, as they swam and slept in open water nearby, the sight of them wouldn't arouse such suspicion. Gryshen also directed the beluga to separate from the others—they may be companions around the home stable, but in the wild, they were not, and they had to keep up that appearance for any passing creatures.

Sleep would not come for some time, even as the black filled up the space.

Misra came over and prodded Gryshen while she floated, eyes wide open, not daring to look to the others. She patted her gently, and slid the base of her torso upon her back in the old familiar way, sidesaddle. She wrapped her long fingers around her dorsal fin, and without a squeak or signal, she took off into the deep.

CHAPTER 16

They rode up over the reef, gliding upward, until the black turned coal, and revealed a watery veil between them and a sky packed with stars. Gryshen closed her eyes tight and pressed her thumb against the back of the white whale's fin, her signal to continue up. Up they went, the water rushing past them, until there was nowhere to go but piercing through the water and rocketing into the midnight air. The pair arced higher than she had ever dared. Bravis would be horrified.

They were completely exposed.

But to what? Gryshen opened her eyes to see the blanket of sparks above them. Water dripped from Misra's head back down to her fingers, from her hair down her shoulders, turning into tiny icicles on the way down. Rugged white glaciers banked the landscape, cutting into the black and perfect silence. The cold burned her nose, and tears flooded her eyes.

She slid off the beluga, and with a signal told her to play but stay close. The beast gave her shoulder an affectionate nudge, then spurted water threw her spout, and dove in and out of the ocean, weaving to a happy tune.

Gryshen stretched her vision across the water. No sign of landkeepers. For a moment she felt a tug, missing her little island and the strange woman there, and then in the next moment she took in this new view, this endless possibility. Everything had gone so wrong. She only wanted to feel something that was right.

It was here, in this bright and black, clear and uncertain world, this space in the middle of and nowhere near time, this place where she was not Frall's mourning daughter, she was not the burdened chief, she was not the tricked and jilted lover.

She was a wild beast. She was the free and blessed spirit the landkeepers had so foolishly left behind. A laugh escaped her in a cloud of air puffs as she thought of what Gracke had shared, about them needing to travel away from their lives. She understood that. She was like that—always trying to escape, even though she was surrounded by water that never seemed to stop.

At some point, you have to escape into what you are. A wild and free thing. She thought of her father, and wept. The tears came from the sea and fell back into it, breaking down and rebuilding her heart and her body, the salt that surrounded her. She thought of her heart, her careful heart that she didn't know she had been hiding her whole life until she opened it to a beautiful lax, a lax who placed himself like a fortress between her and all that she feared—she was no longer odd or at odds with herself—she was wanted. She was worthy. Until he tore it out of her and took it all back, leaving the hollow shell of the odd leen, worse than before; a half leen, a faded shadow.

The hand that reached out should have frightened her, coming at her and grabbing hold in the loud silence, the clear cold air and stretching waves, but all she did, all she could do was grab hold with both fingers. Bravis's own longer, larger hand felt warmer against the air, but not by much. Gryshen clutched it between her own, the black tears pouring from her eyes and seeping into the cracks between his fingers, rolling over his knuckles, splashing into the valleys of her palms. Bravis came into the cold, and said no words of admonishment at her being here, out, like this; he said no words at all. He bowed his head into the water while she looked straight up to the stars, their individual glows connecting in the wet of her eyes. Sobs broke through her throat, and she didn't care—she just held his hand tighter.

He waited with her, keeping vigil. Clouds passed over the sky, blocking the light, and more poured out of her in this darkness.

"May I?" He replaced the hand that she was gripping with his other, gingerly reaching his free arm around her, the tips of his fingers barely touching her shoulders, as if they were made of fine glass.

Gryshen rolled herself into his arms, face pressed against his shoulder, her eyes resting just above its line, wide open. In the path beyond was a stout and steep glacier, like a formidable giant, watching. There was no moon tonight, and the clouds passed again, freeing the sparks from their cloak. The tears ran and ran, until the flood became a stream, and the stream narrowed into a trickle, and the trickle waned into drops . . . until the last drop faded. The night air was frigid against her now dry eyes, and she could feel a slight shiver ripple through Bravis. He still said nothing, just held her carefully.

Gryshen took a deep breath of the clean, icy air, as if it was helping to mend her insides. Each breath felt like a small stitch across her torn heart.

She realized she was still clutching Bravis's hand, and so she reluctantly let go.

Now to back away. She did so, averting her gaze from his, staring anywhere but toward him.

"Thank you. We should get to sleep. It will be light soon." She croaked out the words, her throat glazed by the quiet arctic breeze that attempted to ruffle her now rigid hair. The white whale, right on cue, slowly swam up to her, tired from her own adventure. Gryshen wouldn't meet Bravis's eyes, and so she gave one last look at the sky, then turned and rode back down to the overhang, where she faced the ice wall. She pretended to sleep until sleep eventually came.

"Not too bad." Gryshen awoke to the sound of Gracke chomping on a cod. "A bit thin, but it's got flavor."

She waited to feel the pounding in her head, the heaviness of her lids, that she usually felt after a night with so little sleep. But only energy ran through her veins. Her eyes snapped open, and a smile played at her lips while watching Gracke share a bite with his orca, the one he'd ridden into Rone on. She noted how the grin didn't feel weighted down; it came easily as it stretched a bit.

"Good morning." Bravis greeted them both, and Gryshen immediately pretended to be preoccupied with a purple sea sponge clinging to rock.

"Ah, morning, Bravis. You look like you didn't sleep a wink. Fish?" Gracke tugged at a full net to reveal his morning catch.

"Oh. Yes. Sleep well, Gracke?" He avoided the original question, and Gryshen was certain she could feel him looking her way. She dared herself to lift her eyes for a moment. He was. Back to the sea sponge.

In spite of her strange feeling around Bravis, she felt more hope than she had in . . . *maybe it hasn't been that long. It only feels like forever.* She bit hard on her lip, watching the curls of plum roll out and in from the plant, effortlessly. *If I'm going to be a wild thing, I can't be embarrassed. What do I need to be embarrassed for? I let myself be free. Nothing has changed between us.* The idea was laughable. *Nothing.*

Gryshen looked defiantly back at her travel companions, and grabbed one of the bigger fish from the net, tearing into it and spitting out the bones in a way that would have disgusted Morfal.

❦

The light shifted and the space grew open as the sea carried them along their journey.

Flat, paddle-shaped fish in shades of pink and deep blue swam opposite, one occasionally straying from its school and darting in front of their faces. Gryshen's eyelids kept blinking, threatening to shut. No one had slept well on their swim across the globe. There wasn't time for proper rest. She gripped her narrow spear tightly with one face in her mind. *Could she get him before the pearl? How many might get in her way? How protected might he be?* Gryshen wondered what kind of vicious guards would be the wall between her and her target.

"Let's break," Bravis suggested. They gathered near a reef, and a healer pulled a pouch from his net. He plucked small, flat worms from it.

"Oh. Sturs, right?" Gryshen carefully accepted one between her thumb and forefinger. "I've never had them."

"No, Chieftainess, we usually reserve them to give hunters energy. They have been harder to come by in the past few seasons. We took our reserves for this."

Gryshen nodded in thanks, and watched Gracke pop

one into his wide mouth. She followed, and soon adrenaline pumped like electricity through her veins.

"That'll help." Gracke nodded. "Theus? Tollo?" He gestured toward the twins, offering.

"Yes. I'll take one, if you'd like." Theus folded his fingers around one.

"All right, then." Gracke stared at him a moment. "And Tollo?"

"Oh no, no. Those will make me fall asleep." Tollo backed away, giggling.

"Course they will." Gracke shook his head and hoisted his pack on his shoulders. The net caught on a branch of coral.

"Aargh!" The pouch full of blinding parasites had come loose, releasing them in a burst. Gracke tried uselessly to scoop them up and contain them.

Gryshen's vision began to take on a haze, the colors closing in.

"How long will this last?" Bravis signaled, unable to keep testiness out of his tone.

"Not *quite* sure. Dangit!" Gracke waved his arms comically in an attempt to scatter the bugs away.

"You don't know?" Gryshen asked with a panicked edge to her signal.

"It's just . . . it depends. The babies release more venom than their parents." He was still flailing to no avail.

Just before darkness took hold, Gryshen saw the blurred outline of Tollo patting Gracke gently.

"Good. Now we can finally see!" she trilled.

After a few moments, the fog began to lift.

"Did you hear that?" Gracke asked, turning his large frame. They all followed and listened. A faint signal penetrated the water, figures in the distance coming their direction.

Gryshen squeezed around her spear as tightly as she could, her heart pounding

"Gryshie! It's us."

Jode. She let her shoulders fall and loosened her grip. Jode, Hena, Tollo, warriors from other pods, and the last of the stable beasts.

"Grysh!" Her brother darted toward her, his grin taking over his face. "Everything looked clear."

"We trailed behind just enough. Didn't see any Rakor following," Hena added.

The smallest orca wouldn't let himself stay more than inches behind his annoyed siblings as usual.

Sol and Ry seemed to make their own sibling connection with Theus and Tollo, who had not brought their own beasts. Their tribe was another that didn't keep a regular stable, but unlike Rakor, they were more respectful of their beasts, preferring to hop on an animal when the creature seemed agreeable.

Most of the Rone animals stayed back with the pod, just in case—but they brought Jeer, despite Gryshen's protests.

"Of course he's obnoxious, but he's clever. It could

prove useful," Bravis insisted when they were prepping the pack.

With her brother's arrival, Gryshen felt another surge of strength.

"All right, I guess we can fight now."

Jode beamed at his sister's first attempt at cracking a joke in days.

"Yeah, thanks for waiting. Not that you had any choice." Jode stuck out both arms, flexing his muscles and turning in a somersault.

"Ha." Gryshen almost laughed. Hena rolled her eyes, but Gryshen couldn't miss the fact that she kept her eyes on her brother as he played bullish warrior. She shot a knowing glance at her friend.

Hena turned a hint of rosy purple.

Bravis pulled up alongside Gryshen, and suddenly Hena's expression mirrored Gryshen's own accusing look.

She turned to see Bravis floating, waiting, but she couldn't look him in the eye for long. It was too much.

Gryshen turned back to Hena with confusion, and received her friend's second eye roll of the morning.

They collected their weapons, swimming up in pairs and groups of three to the water's surface to replenish their oxygen before entering deeper into unknown territory.

Gryshen and Jode went up while Misra splashed nearby.

The sun bathed the whole sky in white, reflecting the

brightness from the sea below. It was blank, vast, and foreign.

The air here tasted different, somehow. Grainy on her tongue.

"I think Hena was checking me out." Jode chuckled.

"You think, brother?" Gryshen asked. Modesty was not a part of Jode's character. With every leen who wasn't a close relative fawning over him, humility required a bit more effort from her brother.

"But she's not like the other ones," Jode said as if to finish Gryshen's thought.

"No, she certainly is not." Hena was perhaps the one leen she would like to see arm in arm with her sibling.

Jode's smile was replaced by a grave expression. "What is it, Gryshie?"

She had been lost in the prospect looming before them.

"It's this. What's waiting for us." Gryshen squinted at the brightness, willing it to blind her thought. "Jode, some of our ilorays will die."

"I know. But they'll all die if they don't fight back."

They slowly slid down beneath the water.

Jode stared at his sister. "I'm going to kill him for you, Gryshie."

What felt like rope twisted around Gryshen's heart, pulling tight.

"Jode, please. This isn't about avenging me. Don't put yourself in more danger."

Her brother said nothing, looking past her for a moment.

"What is it?" Gryshen turned to look. The water rippled deep greens and golds, marked by coral gardens.

"You never see her, do you?" Jode asked, distantly, still staring.

"Mom?" Gryshen asked, using her lips, the word suddenly strange on her tongue and catching a little in her throat.

Jode nodded slowly. "I can't understand. You need her now, too. More than ever."

Perhaps she knows about the other one watching over me . . .

"Have you seen Dad?" Her signal broke out.

Jode hesitated.

"You have." Her tone was bitter. She couldn't hide the hurt.

"Only in flashes. A ripple, and then he's gone. You know how that goes. He's busy swimming to the other side."

Gryshen did know how this went. Apocay had warned ilorays that a ceasid could risk getting stuck, a ghost in the water, if they didn't allow themselves to move on and flow with the current to the next place, the next season. It was one of the reasons that "too much" mourning was frowned upon.

"You don't want to hold her back, do you?" Gryshen recalled an old leen saying to her granddaughter when she made the whole hub black with her unending well of tears.

Her sister had passed from an internal shutdown the night before.

Gryshen remembered how that had struck her, too cold even in their arctic depths.

"She's just trying to help her move on," her father had explained to her later.

"But she died so recently. And so suddenly." Though the leen who died was a few seasons older and Gryshen was never good at playmates, she suddenly felt a strange kinship with her. A missing organ. Gryshen had felt like part of herself had always been misplaced. To actually have something that never came through with her insides made sense to her.

Whatever was missing, she could be certain it wasn't her heart.

How could something that was shattered continue to break, over and over again?

"Yes, I know," Gryshen signaled to Jode, now more numbly. It stung too much. But there was a deeper truth, and her brother revealed it to her.

"Come on, Gryshie. You know why you haven't seen him."

Gryshen panicked. Did Jode know what she wasn't even sure of—that she was not made of the same stuff?

That she was unworthy?

It hurt too much to consider the idea that her father wouldn't visit because she wasn't enough like himself.

And frankly, it didn't seem like the lax she had known, to treat her this way. To ignore her in death, in her most desperate times.

Jode clasped his hands around her shoulders and gave her a little shake to pull her out of the whirlpool her thoughts were plunging into. "You know why, right?"

She waited for him to deliver the blow.

"He's not invited."

"What?"

"Grysh, you wouldn't come with me to the bone pit unless I pushed it. And you only did it for me."

Who did I have to visit? Gryshen asked herself. *A woman who didn't birth me—and probably resented pretending to be my mother?*

She clapped her hand against her mouth at this thought that she had just permitted herself to think.

Jode gave his sister an odd look, and repeated, "He's not invited. You don't want to see him."

"That's not true!" Gryshen protested.

"No, it's not about your love for Dad. It's just . . ."

"I'm sorry." Bravis swam up near the top, where they had been floating and arguing just below the surface. "It's time for the others to refuel before the journey."

"Right. Of course." Now Gryshen was eager to get out of where this conversation with her brother was leading.

"Bravis," Jode signaled. She winced. He was going to involve Bravis. "Brav"—he was the only one who felt comfortable giving the lax a nickname—"help me explain this to my sister. I'm just making her angry."

"New and different," Bravis replied drily.

"Yeah, well, here I am again. You know I see the dead. More than some do."

"More than most," Bravis corrected.

Jode twitched at this for some reason. "Yeah, sure. I can't help it."

"What's the issue?" Bravis asked, not particularly concerned with making anyone feel more comfortable.

"I was trying to explain to Gryshen why she hasn't seen Dad and we have."

"*We?*" asked Gryshen, turning toward Bravis. His dark eyes softened at her look. A bluefish swam between them, giving her an opportunity to break the gaze.

When she glanced back, Bravis was still looking, explaining, "Only shadows in dreams. The way most ilorays see their loved and dead." His signal caught slightly, and Gryshen realized that she'd never heard Bravis use the word love—not even with fresh mussels or hunting or taking a ride in open water.

Just this. And recognizing his own pain, she forced herself to meet his eyes, and not leave them.

For as long as she could take.

"I think what your brother is trying to say is that you don't want a visit from your father just now, because a visit from him on his Soul Journey would make it all true."

"His death would be real," she whispered into the water, a wisp of bubbles riding on the sounds.

Now she broke their gaze. There was only so much a leen could take.

"That's it." Jode looked relieved. "And I think that's okay."

Bravis gave them both a small smile. "I'm going to bring up the others for air. Shall we?"

They swam back down to the overhang to gather armor and weapons and prepare the beasts, who had woken and were snacking and playing.

Attempting to put any kind of plating on Gup was ridiculous, so they left him alone. Gracke produced the paint, and Hena swam from iloray to iloray, marking them in the sacred symbols that had transcended translation.

Gryshen pulled up to Misra's back. The seaweed reins felt foreign in her hands. Ceasid and beast both wore armor, and their small army spread out in a fan across the sea. Onward they moved in a fluid, alternating sway, spreading out to cover as much space as they could. Their weapons at their sides, they had nowhere else to go but forward into a battle no one really knew how to fight.

Everyone had their method of distraction. Gryshen led her whale up, down, side to side, stretching in the water, listening to her small army. Jode flirted with Hena. A few warriors exchanged dramatic hunting stories. The healers checked and rechecked their supplies. Tollo and Bravis discussed iloray lore. Gracke persisted in asking

Tollo questions about herself and the Nereids, and took turns gaping and snorting at her answers.

Schools of fish in a multitude of sizes and colors scurried by. Stingrays kept their distance. Even the sea sponges curled away. It was as if all the ocean was giving them some room.

And then, again, the room stretched wider and wider, into another open space, even blindingly brighter than the one before. No fish, only specks of plankton and creatures that made up sea dust. The sand somewhere below. And ahead and around, Gryshen could only see Jode to her left, Bravis to her right, Hena just behind.

"It's close now." The signal was Theus's. Tollo moaned somewhere off to the side. Gryshen knew he was right. There was something almost like poison on her tongue, in this place where nothing seemed to grow.

They couldn't be far.

The chieftainess relaxed the awkward reins, and pressed her palms flat and firm against the sides of Misra's head, resting her tail against her beluga's back. Two of the orcas flanked her, as if obeying a command. Gryshen wondered with a note of annoyance who had sent them up front to guard her.

This was soon put away, because the water showed no clear destination ahead, and the uneasy feeling this gave her only grew.

"Be ready," she murmured a signal, turning up the volume just enough to reach her immediate group. They echoed it to their neighbors.

Gryshen strained her eyes to see, but nothing appeared. Only water and light and particles. Beasts and the group that gathered. It could have been only them in all of Oceas.

Then it appeared, a long gray-red rock, like a fortress wall.

CHAPTER 17

*G*ryshen hissed, but everyone else saw it, too. Despite all her instincts commanding otherwise, she leaned forward, pulled her helmet down over her eyes, turned side to side to see the others doing the same, and gripped her spear with an anxious force.

She gave Misra a slight whip with her tail to move faster.

There was no way she was going to let anyone die before her.

As they approached what must be the Rakor hub, Gryshen began searching around frantically for a band of warriors, but she couldn't see one. She couldn't see a cave entrance, either.

Since the private Rone signal couldn't be understood by half their party, and they didn't want to risk the universal signal being picked up by their enemy, the

263

group had developed five basic tones that would mean something specific in this fight.

The tone Gryshen chose to use now, a high, soft note, meant, "Look sharply."

She scanned the crags and pillars of rock with her eyes. Every few feet, roughly carved black holes opened like mouths ready to pull an iloray in—or spit one out.

Try as she might, she couldn't see a hand, a poised spear, a quivering fin. Not a shadow.

All was still.

She looked in puzzlement at her companions. They were equally curious, equally guarded, all moving slowly toward the wall of entrances and exits.

Sunlight sparkled on the water meeting sky, sending beams like spotlights down upon each of them. Gryshen became very aware of how exposed they were. She swayed uneasily from side to side, hand still gripping her weapon firmly.

Finally, she dared another signal, this one a series of low tones.

"Wrong way?" It had been meant to be used as an alert, but she shifted it at the tail end to sound like a question. Her black hair billowed as she turned her sharp profile back to view their entire crowd. Bravis looked thoughtful, Gracke narrowed his eyes . . . but then shock, followed by terror, washed over their steady features, and in a moment Gryshen knew why.

A boiling column shot up just beneath her, pressing and burning against the thin silver edges of her fin like someone had sliced across it with a hot dagger.

A shriek escaped her lips.

The whole group was shouting.

Moaning.

Then growling.

Torch paths.

They weren't around Rone, but Gryshen had spotted them before on her few childhood journeys—usually behind her father's warning cry and protective arm. But then there were one or two.

There had to be at least twenty here.

And between the scorching channels, a new threat revealed itself.

The Rakor Cavern looked vacant because it was—at least of warriors.

They shot up, alternating the explosions of scalding water, beneath the ilorays. Some with spears, some viciously grabbing their fins with oddly sharp talons. They had been waiting beneath, in the sand, knowing how this amateur army would be blinded by this place.

They counted on it.

A hissing hag of a ceasid had a death grip on Gryshen's fin and groped her shockingly sharp talons along the slender end. She pierced through the tender flesh between her ghost-white scales.

Gryshen screamed.

Someone bellowed.

In a flash, another set of arms were fighting. She

soon realized they were on her side, beating down the creature, pulling her unbelievable nails out of Gryshen's bleeding body.

Gryshen ripped her fin back, and without a thought, grabbed the leen's hair and thrust her long fingers up the nostrils of her attacker, pushing her upward and sending her tossing back.

Blood began leaking in clouds from her broad nose, the hag's eyes rolling up into her thick, sleepy lids.

Around her, she could see their group battling other attackers. Gryshen watched her own enemy slide down, her fin bending strangely.

Gryshen's scalp stung fiercely, and she looked back up to see a brutish lax grabbing her locks and wrapping his fingers around her helmet. She opened her mouth wide, crying out and spitting bubbles in his face. She swung her long, thin fin, curling it back and whipping at his like an octopus's tentacle.

Where she expected scales, she was instead met with a hundred tiny spears. Gasping, she gazed down to see that he was wearing full armor on his tail, constructed of fishbones and arrows.

He grinned menacingly at her and reached to rip off her helmet. Then, just as he was laying his fat fingers upon the white edges of beluga skull, he froze.

The hulky lax squeezed his eyelids together, letting out an indiscernible yowling sound. He was suddenly framed in thick black pools. He fell forward, almost tumbling into Gryshen were it not for her drawing back quickly.

Her brother's determined face popped up behind him, long spear in hand. The tip of the arrow protruded through the surface of his chest. Jode had used enough force to drive it all the way through the fighter's heart.

"Jode!" Gryshen cried out, sick. "Thank you." But she couldn't feel much relief. It was overcome by the fact that she had just watched her baby brother kill someone for the first time.

Defending her.

She remembered the wild leen, and looked down to see if she was still knocked out. The female's back was arched, arms hanging limply, bobbing in the water. Blood still billowed from her face, but now her eyes were open, glassy.

"I killed her." Pronouncing this made the water colder.

"Yeah. Did you *see* her? You did what you had to do," Jode said, pushing away the clouds of blood with his fin.

"And so did your brother," Hena chided, having just broken the arms of a teenaged lax who was wailing for his mother and swimming straight for the cavern.

"I know. I know. Thank you." Gryshen repeated. This was not the time to think. She had to act. And her brother didn't need any of her guilt.

She admired the matter-of-fact way Jode and Hena battled.

The attackers were thinning. A spike-armored orca

thrashed against them, as if impervious to the blasts of heat from the ground, which were also waning. *They must go in waves.* Gryshen wondered how long the quiet spells lasted.

Jeer taunted a fair-haired lax who bore an unnerving resemblance to Coss, and head-butted a leen, distracting them both while the whale continued to bash them about as if he were a machine.

Gryshen surveyed the remaining battle. Theus and Tollo appeared to have an armor-covered warrior under some kind of submission. Tollo had wrapped her delicate fingers in front of his eyes, her thumbs pressed against his temples, whispering something in his ear.

Theus raised a statuesque arm, gripping a knife of abalone. He slid it straight across the soldier's throat, with no protest from the would-be warrior.

Gryshen made a mental note to keep an eye on the Nereids.

Bravis circled the crowd, Jode pulling up beside him.

Hena wrestled with a cross-eyed lax who looked a little young to be there. After several scrapes with her spear, he scurried away, into one of the shadowy cavern doorways.

Who was left?

Gracke gripped his fin in his massive paws. Blood swirled out in a thin line.

The way was clear. All that remained were their own warriors, it appeared. Gryshen swam cautiously back toward the Calaarn leader, glancing downward every few paces to make sure no scorching fountain or hidden attacker lay in wait.

Head bowed, Gracke grimaced in pain.

Gryshen kept back a little. "Can I help?"

"No, thanks, dear," he spoke tensely and softly. "On second thought, one of those healers could make themselves useful."

A small, eager one—perhaps too eager—was already making his way. Gryshen held her hand out flat, in an effort to motion for him to relax. The healer took the anxious smile off his face and replaced it with an anxious stare.

"Ah, great, the new one." Gracke looked upward, accusingly.

"My superior is dealing with his own injury." They all looked in the direction he nodded to see Hena attempting to bat off the lead healer from rubbing ointment on her cut arm.

"I can handle myself." The healer turned back, nervously. "If—if you'll show me the point of injury, I can ascertain—"

"Oh, Mother, shut it." Gracke plied his fat fingers, black with blood, off the "point of injury." The thin line of blood now came out in clumps and wisps, from one long gash on the side of Gracke's fin.

Bravis studied Gracke's wound. "Our makers might be able to build—"

"Ah, it's a war wound. Necessary, really. Be shameful to come home without one." Gracke mustered his frown into a makeshift smile.

"How bad is it?" Gryshen signaled softly to Bravis since she was unable to get a clear view. Jode swam up after checking on Hena and sent bubbles swirling with a low whistle.

Gracke's fin had been torn completely in half, the ripped-off piece long gone. His beautiful deep-blue fin was mangled permanently.

"It will affect your swimming, but you'll be able to do some exercises to help," Hena signaled in that blunt yet reassuring way of hers. Gryshen noted that her friend had finally conceded to having a pinkish goo slathered and stained across her wounded arm.

"You'll look even scarier," Jode told him.

Gracke laughed, slapping him on the back, which promptly sent him sailing forward into Hena.

The jumpy healer was consulting a flat, carved stone. "Torn fin, torn fin . . . torn tail? Yes, the remedy must be the same." His tone didn't sound as sure. He ran a crooked finger over a set of symbols. "Presso leaves. Right." He reached into one of the pouches strapped to his chest. Looking slightly more confident, he began to tug at long purple strands. He glanced anxiously at Gracke, who gave a quick nod of permission, and attempted that awkward smile again.

Gryshen was certain this was to hide the fact that he was bracing himself. His balled-up fists turned deep burgundy as he lay the presso leaves across the wound.

They had a sticky quality, and appeared to attach themselves on contact.

"Gracke is incredible," Bravis murmured to Gryshen in their Rone signal. "It may be a thin piece of flesh, but it's my understanding that losing part of your fin feels like losing a hand."

Gracke turned whiter as the process continued.

"You are my idol." Jode couldn't help himself.

It seemed to raise Gracke's spirits anyway, to strike such awe. Jode's friends floated beside him, mouths open.

Gryshen checked her surroundings.

Tollo was imitating a crab just across from her—one of the few signs of animal life Gryshen had spotted.

Theus was staring. At what, Gryshen didn't know. She followed the path of his gaze and saw only open water.

Hena noticed, too.

"He's pretty crazy, right? Let's leave it at that. Good job, leader." She patted her friend's shoulder.

"With what?"

"Well, keeping us alive, for a start."

"Don't patronize me, Hena. I didn't do anything."

"Hey!" Hena scolded, "Don't accuse me of being false."

"Sorry, it's just that I"—Gryshen threw up her hands —"I needed all this help."

"We all did. But you took out that psychotic leen." She noticed Gryshen wince, and quickly added, "And you went first, Gree. You went first and didn't shy away when we were attacked from all sides by those torch sprays and Rakor soldiers."

"But where *is* everybody?" She hadn't recognized anyone in this battle. And she felt increasingly uneasy here, exposed, with a wounded crew.

Jode pointed toward the dark holes that dotted the entrance.

"What do you want to bet they're waiting just *there*?"

Gryshen stared into the shadows and a cold shiver ran down her spine, filling her tail with ice. Squinting as hard as she could, she still could not see anyone, but Jode's words struck true. She knew they were there.

She could feel it.

Was Coss watching her right now? Another shiver, coupled with a stabbing feeling in her belly.

"Why—why aren't they coming?" she asked her brother and Bravis in their native notes.

"I think they wanted to know what we could do," Bravis replied.

"Now they know. How many fighters do they have left?' Gryshen asked.

"Their pod is a third the size of ours, remember," Bravis said.

"But they're *all* trained to fight. And they all do, except for their very young. Did you see the leen who first attacked me?" Gryshen asked desperately. She had killed a Wise One. She could only hope to Mother the Rakor would keep consistent with what she knew, for

Gryshen was certain she would have to die herself before killing a babe.

"No, no babes. We know that." Bravis answered the prayer she hadn't spoken aloud. "But only because they would see them as a liability in battle."

"That's right," Jode agreed. Their other warriors had gathered closer. Even though they couldn't understand the Rone signal, it was clear what was being discussed as they all eyed the myriad of black entrances to the cavern.

"But Gryshen, me, Hena, Bravis, Gracke, Theus, and Tollo—Did you see what Tollo did? Terrifying!—anyway, we each took out a warrior, plus injured several more, not to mention a couple that swam away. They'll be useless in battle to the Rakor. Probably executed by Morfal for their disobedience," Jode said.

If it wasn't clear before, the difference between their pods was stark.

"So, what does that leave us with?" Gryshen pressed. She was feeling more and more exposed. It was too easy to imagine all the pairs of their enemy's eyes upon her.

Jode thought a minute.

"They only have about sixty in their pod," Bravis signaled.

"Fifty-five now, really," Jode added.

"Yes. True. And perhaps about twenty of those are babes."

"Thirty to fight. And they'll use all of them," Gryshen said.

"Hey, we've got about fourteen. That's not *too* bad," Jode signaled.

"But they're all trained from birth. They were bred for this. Seasons and seasons of warblood in their veins." She murmured the last sentence, a line from a babe song they had all learned about the different pods.

"Yes," Bravis and Jode replied. There was nothing else to say to that.

"And we're back to . . . " Gryshen stared back at the Rakor Cavern.

"Look, they would have come out by now if they planned to fight this battle today. They were just testing us out."

"Tiring us out, too," Bravis added sagely.

"You getting sleepy on me, grandfather?" Jode raised his eyebrows, teasing.

"No, no. I just meant—"

"Strategy." Gryshen nodded.

"Oh, good." Jode winked. "Because we all need you to stay fresh and virile." He shot Gryshen an almost undetectable look—subtle, very subtle for her brother—and the icy eel that had been swimming up and down her spine melted in a simmer, a burning blush that filled her entire being. She dared not look at either of them, especially Bravis.

How did Jode . . . ?

But what was there to even . . .

And now certainly wasn't the time. She clenched her fists, feeling prickles all over. She was sure they were the malignant stares coming from the fortress they were facing.

"So we go now? Just leave?" She stared down at the cloudy white sand floor. "What if they just shoot arrows in our backs?"

"We'll go along the floor, right?" a warrior said.

"Yes, good. We'll work like crabs," Jode said.

Low to the ground, swimming backward, spears at the ready. It was the best option they had.

In the quietest of signals, using code and small gestures as much as possible, the rest of their army was included. The beasts had been farther back, waiting to be called upon. Two of the orcas had spear punctures, not too serious. The healers had tended to them after finishing with the ceasids. Gryshen surveyed the rest.

Misra.

She was covered in dark-purple salve, thin clear weed leaves binding her belly. She floated jaggedly, off from the others.

"Misra!" Gryshen swam over to see.

"She's all right. She'll be fine. Just—" the older healer began to reassure, but Gryshen had already shot through the water and was rubbing Misra's head. Her black braid floated around them, and her back turned straight at the Rakor Cavern.

A low hiss grew into a rumbling cackle. Gryshen turned to see its maker. No one visible, but a signal tone of mirth and a physical laugh sent bubbles flying out the cavern entrance closest to her, and sent that now familiar chill right back into her being. Gryshen turned to signal their code for *Retreat*. They were not prepared to fight more today.

As she did, she watched her brother steady his jaw. Bravis drew in closer toward her. Gracke adjusted his bandages. *Great*.

Nobody was willing to retreat.

She had to switch to universal signal—even if Rakor heard.

"Stay back! That is an *order*." She mustered her toughest tone as the laugh continued from a hollowed-out place. Her ragged army moved back a barely detectable amount. They watched, and waited.

"A Turnic? Their leader is a *Turnic*?" The laughing had paused only to get these words out, the signal raspy, but clear enough to be heard across oceans.

Gryshen instinctively reached her left hand over her shoulder, touching her brand.

The X must have tipped them off. She felt as though everything was sinking.

"She's a half-made! And they still follow her! Look, they don't know!" Horrible laughs, shrieks, and cries came from the fortress's face.

Yes, they were all waiting.

CHAPTER 18

*B*ack to code. *"Retreat. Retreat."*

Gryshen looked to make sure no one was coming out of the cavern, and she swept down to the sandy surface, gliding backward, her hair pooling, exposing her, her secret. She would not look at the others.

She could see them moving alongside her from the corners of her eyes and that was all she needed.

Gryshen kept her eyes ahead, as the signal from Rakor continued.

"A *fraud!* Not fit for banishment—and she their *leader! Idiots!*"

She recognized that wretched, stale tone. Their shaman. Of course. He saw right through her. Perhaps he always had.

Back they moved, no sign of battle.

The Rakor probably assumed it was over for now. After all, who would follow a hybrid?

Who would fight beside her?

The fortress face lay still as the sound of laughter and shouting signals grew fainter and fainter. Gryshen and the rest put space between them. No more battles would be fought today. She turned sharply before reaching camp, and swam, swam away, from all of them.

From everything.

"Come with me," Bravis signaled gently. "To the surface. You can breathe there."

Gryshen followed. "I guess you all are trying to figure out what to do with me."

Bravis said nothing. He floated for a moment, then reached out his hand to clasp hers, tugging her gently toward the open air.

Her fingers shook. "Why do you . . . ?" She searched the smoke of his eyes. "Is it because of my father? You feel obligated to protect me."

"Yes," Bravis signaled, just as they broke the water to meet sky. Gryshen's heart sank low as she gulped in fresh oxygen. Bravis breathed slowly, continuing to speak through his lips, his tone still low, almost melodic. "When we were both small, it was because of your father." He met her gaze, and as much as she wanted to look away, wanted to hide what he might discover there, she couldn't.

"*Was?*" she finally dared to ask.

"Was." Bravis glanced down into the water, then back at Gryshen. "And as for our group, there is nothing to decide on, Gryshen. You are who you've always been. You are our leader."

Sea birds flew in the distance, circling over a patch of water. They had spotted food.

"Gryshen," he spoke quietly. "Why does everyone need to have a reason for loving you?"

Something broke the space between them.

It was her, unable to stop kissing him.

Gryshen was far, far away from the woman who had birthed her. They were near a shore of blinding white sand that seemed to stretch to forever. The sun burned here. She couldn't see how the landkeepers could take it at first, but now, on an overcast day near one of the hundred tiny islands dotting the coast, the water rocking them as long as they'd let it, she felt . . .

Different.

She was still baffled, still frightened, but there was something here that let her breathe, and it wasn't just the swirling air.

"Bravis," she said, and stared.

"Gryshen," he said again, in an unfamiliar tone. "Are you all right?"

"Maybe." She threw her arms around his neck, pressing her lips against his, feeling the sand intermingle, feeling an electric return. She pulled back to stare him in the face.

And here was one more time she felt sure.

Not about the war. Mother, no. Not about getting back the Great Pearl. Absolutely not about being her pod's chief.

She felt something with Bravis that could have been a tattoo, it was as much a part of her as tea with her landkeeper mother, as burying her father, as laughing with Jode, something that was very . . . different.

He didn't tear her open or put her back together.

"I love you." He blurted out the words like they had been trying to crawl out of his throat for an eternity.

Gryshen lay her head against his chest, listening to the swoosh of the water, the stillness of the sky, the hum of his heartbeat.

"Do you understand what I am? I am a Turnic." She could hardly believe that she was using the word about herself, and that the more she said it, the more relieving it was.

"I have to tell you something."

Her heart rolled. *Was he a Turnic, too?*

His gaze took on its usual somberness before he spoke again. "I know. I knew."

"How long?" She couldn't quite figure out what to feel.

"Always."

"Always?"

"I saw your father with your mother. I was very young, but I started my apprenticeship early for my age."

Of course he did. Bravis was probably six going on a hundred.

"I was just learning to help prep royal chambers, carry messages between your father and his father to meet. I joined my uncle on these jobs. But my uncle was occupied with something, and he asked me to help your father get ready. Your dad said he was leaving for a quick solo hunt. He was in a hurry, and said he didn't want assistance. He left in a bolt, and I realized he had forgotten his spear.

"I figured that even if he were going for something small he might need it. I suppose I intended to prove myself, too." He smiled at the memory. Gryshen mirrored his smile at the thought of seven-year-old Bravis trying to take charge.

"I swam with it, trying to call out to him. There was no response. I decided to follow a path I'd noticed him take on the south side, outside the cavern. I swam as fast as I could, and I almost thought I had missed the opportunity when I saw him." He paused for a second, recalling.

"Something told me not to call out to him right away. I stayed back, out of sight behind the ice, watching him rise. I pulled up and followed far behind, until I knew he was going up to the shore, to the only human-inhabited place nearby. I waited behind a large rock and just . . . watched. Watched as he spoke to your mother. Watched them embrace. She was pregnant. About to give birth. And he was about to be bound."

"So . . . it was an affair?" Gryshen felt sick.

"No—no, Gryshie." He spoke her nickname as naturally as if he'd always said it. "No."

"He committed to bind with your—with Jode's—mother after this. After you were in your mother's womb."

"He just left her?" Gryshen asked. Every choice filled her with dread. There was no way that any answer Bravis gave was going to give her a nice, clean picture of her parents, their love, and her birthright.

"He loved them both, Gryshen."

"That's not possible. Not sincerely. Not equally," Gryshen argued.

Bravis considered his words. "What I mean to say is —no, I'm going to stay by that. He loved them both. But at different times, really. Loving your mother came so easily to your father. As natural as swimming. And yet, it was so unnatural, that he simply could not *live* in love with her—do you understand?"

"But could he have chosen a different life?"

"A life of exile?"

"A life of love." Gryshen kept bumping into thoughts, like the rocks near this shore. Of course, if he had even found a way, there wouldn't be Jode. But her father didn't have Jode yet. So why wasn't the love of her mother important enough to him?

"I guess my father and I are less alike than I had hoped." She was willing to face her family's wrath to elope with Coss. She was willing to risk it all for the promise of love. And her father . . . ?

"The crown was more important," Gryshen added.

"It wasn't that way, Gryshen. You're not being fair to him." Bravis's clear dark eyes set upon her, reading her. Sometimes, his steadiness was maddening.

Swirling in this was a desire of equal parts: to keep kissing Bravis, to cradle herself in his arms, and to scream in his face. She couldn't quite make up her mind, so she kept speaking aloud.

"Fair?"

He had already recognized that she was in no mood for measured. He pursed his lips, waiting for something. He took her hand gently in his own beneath the water.

"Gryshen, sometimes we don't have a choice. We had to go to war with the Rakor, no matter how hard your father tried to avoid it. We must get the pearl back for our survival. And your father had to say goodbye to your mother. It wasn't just about his family, his pod that desperately needed his leadership." He focused on the light pouring along the cove of rock they were tucked beneath.

"What else?" All she wanted was answers, and yet she wasn't sure she wanted to know anymore at all.

"Jode's mother, Athela. Adopting you saved her, too."
Bravis looked down into the water like it was showing
him the story.

"What does that mean?"

"She had someone, too. A lax, a bad one. They bound
before she completed her paces."

Something twitched in Gryshen as she recalled how
she nearly did the same.

Bravis looked back at her, never releasing her hand.
"Her family was furious. The lax ended up dying in a
fight over another leen. *That's* betrayal. He wasn't half
the lax Frall was." Bravis took a deep gulp of air,
looking back at Gryshen. She was listening open
mouthed.

He continued, "But she was pregnant, too."

"Jode!" Gryshen gasped.

"No, not Jode." Bravis squeezed her hand gently. "She
was sick with grief. She lost the baby early on. And then
she was sicker." He paused. "She exiled herself."

Gryshen had never heard such an idea.

"Her family feared she would die, far from home and
their pearl, but she survived. She was tough."

Gryshen tried to piece together the personality of her
memory.

"Your father encountered her on a journey to meet
with the Wanaa. I believe it was when he was trying to
let go of your mother."

"Let go?"

"Sometimes it must be done." Bravis stared at her.

"Sometimes, it can't be done." His tone broke, but his gaze didn't.

Gryshen entwined her long fingers in his without thought. "So he felt he had to. Let go."

"Gryshen, he *did* have to. She was a landkeeper. There was no place for them in either world." His gaze fell on the glass pendant he had given her. Gryshen reached to touch it, feeling the sun warm the beads of water that sparkled around the pendant.

"There was a place for her. There was a place for Athela." It felt strange to refer to the leen by her name, instead of mother. But it didn't leave the hole she would have expected it to. It seemed to fill a space instead.

"There was a place for both of them, together. Frall and Athela found hope."

"But there are stories, Bravis. Everyone knows about the leen who fell in love with the human, who found a way to get legs and live on land."

"That isn't real. It's just a story, a romantic idea." He shook his head. "I've never encountered a shaman with that kind of magic. But even if it were possible, your father wouldn't have wanted to. Not after he saw you."

"Because I was born a ceasid . . . is that right? Is it possible I could have been born a human?" She couldn't believe the idea, and she couldn't believe she hadn't considered this.

"Yes. Yes, Gryshie, that is possible. They are incredibly rare, but they do exist. We do not know much about them. At least, I don't."

So that was it. Dad wanted to see what came out, to see if she'd be a leen to lead his tribe, or a girl he couldn't raise. Was the lady . . . was her mother hoping for . . . which?

It was too much, this real possibility of a completely different existence.

"Gryshen," Bravis speaking her name with such a tenderness brought her back to this place, this very real life.

And a very real war.

"We have to get back." Leaving this moment meant setting everything aside, possibly more answers, possibly —no, definitely—the kind of embrace that would make it more and more difficult for her to leave.

"Yes." He sounded wistful. He gave her hand a gentle squeeze. "Before we leave." He leaned his forehead against hers, laying his lips to hers, as if he were trying to melt his heart into her. This love was so different, this romance so foreign from what she had known. It didn't burn her up and burn her out. It gave and gave.

And she wanted to give back.

The light faded as they made their way back toward encampment. This small cavern wasn't a half-bad space to sleep and regroup.

Bravis's hand stayed on hers, never faltering, never attempting to hide when they arrived at the side by the small hub. A few ilorays were standing guard, and just inside, warriors were fashioning nets, tightening spears, while a couple healers sorted through medicine kits, setting potions they felt they could keep back at this post for longer-term healing in protective seal bladders. They had pouches of the same materials slung with thick kelp and membrane across their chests and backs. They filled these satchels with medicines of high urgency.

Some nodded, a couple bowed their heads, but all averted their eyes as Gryshen passed them.

A boom of a signal poured out from the darkness as the light from a lantern brightened the faces of the ilorays ahead of her: Gracke, Theus, and somersaulting endlessly, Tollo.

"What do you mean, you thought we knew?" Gracke's unmistakable tone boomed as he gripped the jellyfish cage with two fat fingers. He spat an explosion of bubbles as he faced Tollo.

"There was no secret we could see. You knew of her mark," Theus answered calmly.

"Yes, but I just thought she was criminally minded! Completely different situation there."

"Our cavern is filled with stories of the ancients. The chieftainess is just one more story. A unique circumstance."

"Unique?" Gracke's brows, so thick, shot up with such a force they actually lifted a whirl of water.

"Theus, she's"—even his attempt at a whispered signal was ridiculous—"she's a motherdamned *Turnic*."

"Let's ask the Turnic what she thinks," Tollo sang and swirled, and Gracke thrust his lantern outward while Theus coolly turned in her direction.

Bravis's grip on her hand tightened, and Gryshen wriggled her fingers a bit for some freedom.

"He's right." She nodded at Gracke, who gaped back at her.

In the distance and gloom, Jode and Hena swam toward them.

"I'm an X. We all knew that. But it turns out that I'm not the good kind of mystery. I'm the . . . I am an anomaly."

Bravis began to signal, and she broke past his. "I am a freak. I am the freak chieftainess with the landkeeper mother and the bent father. And I lied to you." Now she looked straight into her brother's eyes, the look of hurt and betrayal in them piercing into her stronger than any signal. The silence sat a moment.

"So did I. So did Chief Frall," Bravis spoke calmly, looking at the bewildered faces that had now multiplied to their entire army. "The most beloved chief in many, many seasons, the one we all universally trusted, kept the truth from you."

Tollo was trying to coax Theus into playing some kind of a puzzle with strands of sea kelp, weaving Xs in and out between her fingers.

Gracke turned to the twins again. "I still don't understand. You knew?" He looked at Theus, and then reluctantly glanced Tollo's way as she began to sing.

"Arrow for a hunter true,
Palm for a maker crew,

> *Minstrel gets marked with a bright star of sea,*
> *Healer, an eel, swimming free,*
> *Carer's mark is a circle round,*
> *Chieftain bears the wave like a crown . . . "*

They all knew the old song. It was taught at a young age. But Tollo continued,

> *"And the mark of the X for the Great Unknown, another*
> *Babe from Mother's home,*
> *Stranger, outcast, criminal he*
> *Or something we made, that we just cannot see."*
> *She continued in her childlike nursery tune.*
> *"A twist, a curse, a stab in the night,*
> *Or a vessel, a keeper, a shiner of light."*

And back she went to her finger weaving, trapping her brother's pinky in a tiny net and laughing with delight.

A little fish made its way into Gracke's cavernous open jaw, then, startled, popped back out to rejoin his school.

"I think we know which one our chieftainess is." Bravis folded his long arms across his broad chest, matching eyes with the group.

"Why didn't you tell me?" Jode demanded in a croaking signal.

"I didn't know what to say." Gryshen bowed her head.

"I just found out in my paces, and I still didn't know . . . didn't want to know."

"What could she say?" Hena took Jode's arm gently in her strong hands. "She almost died. Then your father died. Then she almost died again. Sometimes there are things we don't know how to tell ourselves even."

Jode looked at her, his bright blue eyes filling with tears. Then he bowed his own head, reaching a rough hand out to meet his sister's. She grabbed hold of it with a fierceness, and pulled him in, clutching her baby brother in an inky, sobbing hug.

The ocean was sure to turn black from the tears shed this season.

There was fighting to do, and Gracke dealt with his unease enough to battle alongside her. The cool water was warming as the sun began to creep its way closer to the earth. Battles had been fought and won and lost, but this was different. This wasn't about territory. At least, not for the pearl. This was about life itself. Gryshen felt an unease, a restlessness around her heart. She had been so determined to kill Coss—and still was—but what was she to do with what remained? Feelings sat inside of her belly, not all of them ringing clean and clear. Only rubbing war paint on her face and hoisting a helmet upon her head, shell chest-plate across her wrap, steeled her senses. Misra was wrapped, too, in her reins, and whale jaw thrust atop her head. She kept twisting from side to side as if it were scratching.

"I know it's uncomfortable," Gryshen cooed a signal,

adjusting her helmet to lay back a bit farther. "But it's not just about looks. It will keep you safe. We'll keep each other safe," she promised, offering a vine of fat berries. As they floated up, she gobbled them in one bite, nudging her affectionately with her snout.

The rest of their band was sorted according to Jode's attentive eye. Three or four at a time, some astride their beasts, some beside, they swam slowly toward the open sea.

Gup gulped an ocean between them.

The sea had a blinding quality to it. The sand took over here, threatening to sweep anyone crossing into its beige diamond pools. The water continued to warm—unseasonably so—and Gryshen wondered at it. Could it just be the rage surrounding the Rakor cavern? Could their own poison seethe, and the torrent coming their way, actually light a fire in the salty sea?

This battle had to be fought once, and it had to be won. There was no room for discussion of the recent revelations of their leader. They had come for this war, and they all intended to finish it. It was near wordless, their preparations for dawn.

A thought that had nudged the back of Gryshen's mind now turned itself over in her head.

What was whispered to me at my naming? It was a pointless question, but there it was. There was no one left who could answer it, so she started asking herself new questions, questions about the fight ahead.

Everyone set their weapons and armor near their

sleeping spots, made sure the beasts were well-fed and properly tended, and all agreed, silently, to pretend to sleep.

When the light of day sparkled through the water, Gryshen felt like she could finally stir. So did the rest of her crew.

"They are getting ready, like us, aren't they?" she asked her brother, who, amazingly, looked as if he had rested.

"Oh yeah. Kidding? They may never have gone to sleep. Just waited for us. But that's all right." He wiped paint across his sister's cheeks, then his own. "We'll be ready." He thrust a sea-lion skull over his head, and pulled at his grass satchel. "Gotcha something, Gryshie." There was that grin. Like there was no difference between them today. Like they were as much brother and sister, of the same scales, as they had always been. Gryshen wanted to scoop Jode into a fierce hug. But instead, she sank her shoulders in relief, and looked to see what surprise waited.

"The makers wondered if I wanted one, but I'm purely a spear lax, myself. I did think you might like it, though." He picked up a deceptively small rock, tightly bound in some kind of wire, which braided into a rope. "Feel this." *Plunk!* The weight of the rock helped it move more quickly against the water, sinking Gryshen's hand when she caught it.

"Whoa."

"It's like this." He demonstrated, winding the rope

around his tan fist, once, twice, and *smack!* A crack formed in the coral beside them.

"That could be some Rakor's head, Gryshie. Just be careful, and don't swing it at the wrong team." He winked, and finished going over everyone's supplies, gathering them for a plan. Gryshen felt as though there was something else she should be doing, but her brother was clearly the best one to take the lead, and she wasn't sure half of their army really wanted to follow her anyway.

They agreed to post a lookout—Goshen volunteered —to time the eruptions at the entrance to Rakor. When he saw them spout off, he would alert them back at camp, and they would swim to battle, at least knowing they wouldn't be burned just before the fight.

Then?

"We kill them all," Gracke growled.

CHAPTER 19

"Good plan." Jode smiled.

"No babes. No young," Gryshen repeated.

"No," Hena agreed.

Gracke looked offended. "Course not. What, you think I'm like them?" He was already more suspicious, and therefore more defensive, with the Turnic chieftainess.

"I didn't—please," Gryshen signaled. "I just needed to say it."

Gracke relaxed a bit. "Ah."

They saddled their beasts, ready to leave at notice. When their lookout returned, the slightly wounded, mostly sleepless army set off, awake in the way only those about to kill or die recognize.

She just wanted one thing. *Wait,* she reminded herself. Two things. Gryshen gave herself a shake to break free of the singleness of mind, the desire to kill

Coss, which kept capturing her. If she stayed too focused, too selfish, she could risk losing the thing they had all come for, the only thing she was really expected to do, the only thing Rone truly required.

The Rakor were hunched over great sharks, waiting. A rasping signal pulsed across to Gryshen's crew, as this tooth-covered army seemed to shoot out in sprays from the Rakor Cavern. She spotted Lefke among them. *Traitor*. It was like they were bred for battle, the way they made a perfect line of unstoppable strength. Spears carved sharper than Gryshen had seen pointed outward, aimed to kill. They wore shark's jaws like brutal crowns atop their heads, and their fins, and even the sides of some tails, were lined in teeth that were apparently sewn into the top layer of their flesh.

So much for secret weapons. Gryshen could have disappeared when the thought of her own defenses crossed her mind.

How clever they had thought they were. She could feel all her sureness fading.

But Bravis came up on her right. "I'm here." Hena sipped across the front, like a shield.

And Jode screamed like a hunter about to ace his meal.

It wasn't long before she saw him, just beside his father, in synchronicity with the rest of them.

His pale ice-blue eyes showed between the spikes.

How could she have ever thought he was anything else?

And the next cry was hers. A wild animal could have

stolen her body, pushed her forward and propelled her to tear into this creation of perfect terror.

To her left, she saw a Rakor slice into the face of a dolphin with no rider—then Tollo appeared astride, stunning the hunter with her camouflage, reaching her delicate hands to twist his neck.

To her right, Misra was shielding a Nereid who came in and out of disguise. The tall lax shrieked a signal to disorient a pair of elder Rakor approaching. One of them punched the white whale in her back with a spiked fist grip, while the other waved its arms to find the hidden, teasing iloray.

Misra. She couldn't stop to check. Gryshen had one purpose. She couldn't stop when two Rakor lanced Sol and Ry, the little whale siblings, with massive spears. She couldn't stop when she saw a young leen slide a blade across Tollo's waist. Gracke promptly cut off the female fighter's head, anyway.

Gryshen scanned for the pearl, trying to keep her focus on finding it. She saw three younger warriors, two Nereids, one Rone, weave their way toward the back via the outside. They could only guess at the pearl's location. Gryshen spied a break in the line when Coss moved toward her, and she took it, pushing through like that rock on a rope that was now in the satchel strapped tightly to her back.

She felt motion behind her, and knew that Coss was in close pursuit.

It took more strength than she would have said she

possessed to keep pressing forward, eyes open for any sign of the pearl.

Instantly, one could see that the layout of their cavern was a fortress—alike in its interior as its exterior. The walls were lined with small openings, and the darkness consumed the space, with almost no natural light coming through. Lanterns provided minimal vision. A quick peek into the chamber openings revealed sparse rooms.

Straight ahead, what she had thought was an outstretching of cave came abruptly to an end, splitting off into three directions. To the west was what appeared to be a small gathering space. Northward as well, judging by shadows of table slabs.

Only a few lights told the story here. Moving on instinct, Gryshen shifted to the right, flicking her tail, and feeling the pressure, the presence rising beside her. She didn't dare look back.

Just go forward. Just go forward. You have a job to do.

"It's the one thing you must do." Gryshen murmured to herself. "It's the one thing."

"I am sorry I hurt you." It took all her strength to fight the need to turn around and face him.

He's just trying to distract you, she told herself. Even though she didn't entirely believe that.

"I didn't want to do any of it. Except maybe be with you."

"Lies!" she hissed. She couldn't help herself. Back she

looked at the lax who had nearly broken her. He was beautiful and burning cold, like always.

But she was made of more. She had to be.

"What if we forgot it all? I could get you away. We could stay close enough to the pearls of the remaining pods."

In the far distance behind him, she made out ghostly glimmers in the dark. An approaching school of fish? She squinted.

Iloray tails, flickering.

Gryshen couldn't tell who they belonged to. She knew she had to move quickly. She turned away, sending a stream of signal behind her.

"You can't stop me from saving my pod. I'll kill you first."

"I know. Gryshen, please." The freezing burn was on her arm, tingling. His hand squeezed firmly.

"Get off me!"

"I'm not going to hurt you. I never meant to hurt you."

"Yes, you did! You tried to kill me!"

"*Never.* That was my father's plan. I never put enough pressure to kill. Just . . . stop you."

Gryshen's mind raced. How could he still be tugging at her, after everything?

"You tried to kill my pod. You stole our survival."

"Listen to me."

"No!" She jerked her arm back, trying to grasp her spear from the rope across her shoulder blade.

Coss held on.

"Listen. We have survived a whole season without our pearl. No one died."

Gryshen's curiosity took over. She kept swimming down the third tunnel as she spoke. "What do you mean? I thought Rakor were sick. Not just in the head, I mean."

There was that earnest look of his again. The one she knew masked everything, and yet the one she couldn't help but believe a little bit right now.

"No one that was healthy. There were a couple weaker members. The ones more prone to dramatics."

Sure, everyone's got a Helda and Velda. Even the most bloodthirsty pods, Gryshen considered.

"What are you saying?"

"I am saying that I'm suspicious of the pearl's actual powers."

"You would be suspicious. Liars are suspicious of everything, because they can't trust themselves."

But something gnawed at Gryshen's gut. Something she couldn't think about right now.

Focus.

"Gryshen. There's a small opening—not big enough to get the pearl through straight off, but I can help you move a big rock of a door blocking the exit. You could get it to your pod. Do you have a meeting place? I could get it out with you, and we could leave."

"You are not going anywhere with me. You are not going near the pearl again." She had freed herself from his hold, but Gryshen was all too aware that it was only because he released her.

"You need me to help you."

"I never needed you." The signal caught and tore a little as it left the back of her throat.

"We need each other. I'm not like the others. You know that. I know you can feel it. I've never been really like them."

"Enough to do your father's bidding."

"Enough to follow the rules. I'm done, Gryshen. I don't want to kill your ilorays. I'll leave with you."

"Is this another one of your twisted marriage proposals?" Gryshen spit the words out, and, suddenly, there it was, hidden from jellyfish, with only the strangest little light to reveal it.

A glass ball contained in a net held an electric eel, pulsating and striking its own tiny lightning, just enough to flash on the familiar white incandescence of the Rone Pearl.

Coss continued beside her. "I'm not trying to marry you."

"That's a relief. You tried to murder me the last time."

"I'm just telling you what I know. We are both outsiders. We can be outside it all together."

Gryshen gingerly touched the glass surface of the sacred pearl, and realized she had no idea how to get it out.

"They're coming," Coss said.

Gryshen didn't know who, and didn't want to ask.

Coss began to push at the wall.

"What are you doing?"

"Helping you."

Gryshen couldn't see another way, and so she joined him, pushing at what felt like solid wall but began to shift ever so slightly to reveal cracks of light beyond.

She knew the others were close, whoever they were.

Using up strength she thought would be required for killing Coss, she was instead working alongside him, now twisting around with her back to the stone, pushing back with her spine and the base of her tail.

Coss grunted as he heaved against the rock.

All Gryshen felt was scratches against her backbone from the edges of black, so she turned again, wrapping her fingers around a lip of rock and forcing the energy out of her body. Murmurs of signal, unintelligible, were closer than ever.

"One more," Coss groaned, and Gryshen bit into her bottom lip until she tasted blood as she thrust her whole weight against the rock, loosening from its place set in the wall.

"There's still not enough room." Gryshen looked around frantically.

"There will be." Coss shimmied his body through the opening they had created. "Get out of the way."

Gryshen backed up, and in a gust of weight and water, the rock fell back toward her, inside the cave. The opening was slightly bigger than the pearl itself. Gryshen wrapped her arms around it, balancing it on outstretched palms. It didn't feel secure, but there was no way she was letting Coss help. She backed out of the opening slowly, holding the pearl, giving herself the perfect view to see them: Jode and two Rakors, possibly a lax and leen, catching up to him even as he rocketed through the water. Then . . . Bravis, spear ready.

And behind him, Morfal.

For a moment, Gryshen froze, halfway out. *Take the pearl and find the warriors who were supposed to be on the side of the cavern? Protect Jode and Bravis?*

She wasn't sure that her brother could see her, as even now that light was getting through, it was back-lighting her, her body forcing out the glow.

She continued backing up and watching the approachers, suddenly aware that she was blinded from behind.

What was Coss doing out there?

In a rush of adrenaline, she pulled through, and the pearl wobbled. From the back Coss lay his hands around the other side.

"Here. Take it." Gryshen realized that Coss was speaking to the pair of her fighters. Baffled, they looked to Gryshen, who gave a short nod.

"Help me get this to safety. Please."

"Get away from her!" Jode burst out, tearing toward Coss, who was still supporting part of the pearl.

"Jode—wait! Not now. We have to get this out of here," Gryshen signaled to her brother.

It brought him back for the briefest of moments, then someone approached.

Morfal.

"Where's Bravis?" Gryshen's sound was strangled, and she felt Coss's stare.

"Dealing with mine. Or being dealt with by mine." Blood billowed from the chieftain's mouth, and Gryshen gasped. *Had he bitten . . . ?* But no, the sunlight soon revealed an opening on the top bridge of his mouth, where he had clearly lost even more teeth.

He took in the sight of his son, who was backed away from the pearl after Jode moved to attack him. He was clearly not interfering in the escape. And then Morfal looked back at the felled boulder, and a wave of understanding crossed his face.

"You *idiot*. You useless . . . "

Gryshen and Jode, seeing an opportunity while Morfal was distracted with berating his son, nodded to the pair of warriors.

"Take it to camp." Gryshen used another code signal they had prepared for this, in case she wasn't able to do it with them.

It was so quick.

Morfal was spitting insults at his son, who suddenly cried out the warning.

"Jode!"

But Morfal had already plunged the abalone dagger straight into her brother's back.

The tip came out the other side, painting the sea with blood.

"No!" Gryshen rushed at him, fingers like claws, shrieking signals, crying the words. "No, no, no!"

She wrapped a protective arm around her brother, who went instantly limp.

No time for goodbye. And she couldn't pause to consider him. She could only squeeze him as he bobbed, as if her crushing grip could revive him.

Morfal had ripped his dagger back out, his mouth curling in a toothless cackle.

Gryshen braced her tail for a moment, then flung the sides of tiny arrows at his chest, piercing him with a hundred wounds.

Morfal yelled, but he still breathed.

Bravis darted out amid her swing, and with an agonized glance at Jode, turned his spear toward Morfal.

One of Gryshen's fighters joined him while the other held the pearl.

Then, the remaining of the pair of soldiers Bravis had been battling on his way out followed just behind him.

Bravis raised the long sharp edge of his spear arrow, wielding it like an ax.

Morfal, blood flowing from holes across his flesh, reached for a stick covered in seaweed. He shook it loose, revealing the swarm of electric eels, tied up and writhing.

He shook with limited breaths, limited blood, limited life.

Gryshen saw the eels coming toward her, and she reached for her own spear.

The leen lunged for Bravis. The spare Rone warrior grabbed her head and twisted it against her neck in a fluid motion, as if it wasn't the first time the young lax had killed anybody.

Morfal thrust the dagger toward Gryshen, only reaching her left hand—and slicing through bone.

Gryshen screamed as she felt three fingers drop.

Bravis flung his ax across the back of Morfal's neck, bluntly removing his skull from his throat.

But not before Morfal took his last breath of energy and slammed the butt of the eel stick into the Great Pearl, sending it out of protective hands, slamming into a wall of coral behind them, and crumbling into ghostly powder.

A pair of small blue fish sampled it, then swam off.

Coss was backed against the coral, face frozen.

"It might be all right. It could be all right!" Hena's signal rang through as she appeared from the same opening. She was looking at the white mist that was all that remained of the legendary pearl life force. "I don't think you need it."

Then she spotted Gryshen, and the dead lax in her arms, and Hena sank to the bottom of the ocean floor.

CHAPTER 20

"*W*hat are you saying?" The accusation hissed and whispered through the water like sand, smoke.

Gryshen could feel the black ink creeping, but she bolted it back.

She wanted to see Hena's face.

"Gree—"

"Don't call me that."

Hena just stared, like she was waiting for directions. Finally, she spoke again.

"Uncle Qoah used to say we didn't need it—everyone thought he was crazy—but none of you got sick after your pearl was taken, and the Rakor seemed strong, and I . . . "

Gryshen seethed. "You knew something else? About the pearl? How long have you known it?" Her signal was reaching a blade's edge, cutting through the water between them.

"I haven't. I didn't. I only . . . wondered."

"Wondered?" The salt water could have boiled in the heat of Gryshen's signal. "You had a *question?* You had *any question? And you never asked?*" The black took over. All blame could be deposited here.

"You never asked," Gryshen repeated. "You never asked, and now he's gone. It's *your* fault." She jabbed her aching finger into Hena's chest.

Hena looked back, without words. Without anything but grief.

Gryshen bit back some more.

"Your fault." She jabbed again. "Your fault! Your fault!" Gryshen had balled up her gray hands into rock-like fists, and was pounding them like she was beating a drum on Hena's chest. She could see Hena's rosy clay skin turn plum in spots, but she wasn't stopping.

"Your *fault!*" Hands firmly grasped her arms, pinning them back.

"Gryshen, come back," Bravis's steady signal was in her ear as he pulled her away from her target. "Come back."

"I'm *here! That's the problem!*" Gryshen shrieked her signal. "I'm here, and he's not, and it's all her fault!" She screwed up her face, trying to twist her arms back out, to grab, to rip apart—in an instant she felt at one with the hag she had killed in her first battle. Maybe the old one was crazed with pain, broken by loss, just like she was.

"That's not the problem. It's our answer. We need you, Gryshen." Bravis's signal moved gently through her heart, in that way his words always went deeper.

"And it's not her fault." The string of his signal had wound within her, and now it expanded, sending pops in every direction through her insides.

Everything was sore. Everything ached, but this did the most.

Hena just waited, her gaze tired, battle worn. Heartworn.

Gryshen's brain felt like it was breaking. She couldn't swallow this truth, not now. It needed chewing, and with Jode gone, she had lost her teeth.

If she had needed to fight more, she couldn't.

And she didn't need to.

The pearl was born from fairy tales, made up in myth.

And now it was gone, so there wasn't even a pretense.

Jode had died for a lie.

For nothing at all.

"I can't." Gryshen swam out of the overhang, to the vast sea, the only place where she didn't feel as though she were being strangled.

Misra was waiting, like she knew. She dipped, and Gryshen flung her body across her back, laying her head and wrapping her arms around the beast, her iloray tail hanging limply. Misra swam up, up, toward the light that pooled over the surface of the water. She carried the both of them, Gryshen clinging on like a ragged child.

Misra bore down, circled the blue, then raised up and burst into open air. All the while Gryshen kept her tired eyes closed fast.

They swam, and swam, and didn't stop.

At some point Gryshen became aware of company.

She heard the calls of familiar beasts, without the playful chirping of Sol and Ry. In came the signals of her busted army checking in on their state of health and supplies.

Bravis. Tollo and Theus. Gracke.

A note of assent from one of Jode's buddies to a healer questioning him about a wound.

The strange clicking of the Nereid pod. The musical tone of the Calaarn tribe.

They were all there, almost.

No Hena to be heard.

Just as well. Gryshen couldn't stomach her sound, not when her most-loved notes were missing from the chorus. Jode's absence stretched across the sea. It must have been felt by every great beast, every mollusk. Even the plankton must have sensed an emptiness in Oceas.

With her left hand she occasionally tugged on the net holding her brother's body, only opening her eyes to make sure it was still secure. It was all that was left of him, and seeing him still, paling blue . . . *Why am I still here?* Gryshen wondered.

"Please, please brother," she murmured, pressed against the beluga's slippery skin. "Please don't leave me forever. Please visit me. You can do it. You're special. I know you can do this. You're the special one." Ink black-ened her hair, and made it easy to close her eyes once more and just ride.

"Special, special . . ." she kept whispering.

Asking the question was pointless.

She had no idea why she lived while the best around her died. She had no idea why her brother had to die at all.

She had no idea why blood was shed on a lie, why the lie was built in the first place, and why no one ever bothered to tell the truth.

Gryshen kept her eyes shut against the pressing waters.

And then, she thought of Bravis. And she could think of no reason why Bravis loved her.

It sat inside of her, this realization, like knowing how to ride a beast, how to gather weedberries, how to speak in her native signal.

She wasn't sure when she learned these things, she just knew them.

She knew this, too.

But now, this knowing was not a comfort. It was yet another occasion Gryshen was not equipped to rise to. She had nothing left to give, and if he persisted in his insanity, she felt sure he would be one more of her bests to go.

The way home felt different, shorter.

Gryshen kept her eyes closed almost all of the time, only opening them a crack to check on her brother. If they stopped for food, she did not know it. She did not eat. If they stopped to rest, she did not sleep. Only a haze of reality was what she permitted herself. If she'd thought about it, she would have known that she was avoiding sleep to avoid dreams, dreams that wouldn't offer her comfort. There wouldn't be clear, cozy visits with her brother or her father. At best, foggy pictures, whispers that she couldn't comfortably trace, and that sense of second-guessing that had rarely left her, even in sleep.

So she kept her eyes closed and rode.

"Let me tighten this." Bravis's signal flowed gently. Gryshen raised her head, which had been pressed deeply into Misra's back, and lifted her lids to see what he was referring to.

Jode's cocoon was stretching, the cord twisting from the weight of his waterlogged body.

"He needs emberry oil!" Her face twisted as she saw his own beginning to shift into something unfamiliar.

"Yes. It's been used up. The healers didn't pack more."

"Idiots. Useless."

"Yes." He spoke tenderly, tugging at a knot to tighten it.

Gryshen began pulling on the other side, tying a new knot where the rope had too much slack.

Gracke, his one graceful feature gone, came bobbing up. "Here, I'll—"

"We've got it taken care of, thank you." Bravis spoke

in his steady, polite way, as he placed himself carefully in front of the cocoon and Gryshen.

"Right. Let me know, then." Gracke's eyes darted Gryshen's way, and he eased back onto his orca.

"Yes, we will," Bravis said. "Thank you." He went back to tugging on stray pieces of net, building new corners. "We're not far from Rone." He glanced up at Gryshen.

Gryshen, half her body still astride her beluga, nodded. She became focused on double, triple knots.

He waited, the glance turning into his usual stare.

"What I mean is . . . how can we help you? I can address the pod while you—while you take care of Jode," his signal cracked. Gryshen was not the only one to lose two bests. "I can explain what happened. And I can explain what we know to be true." Bravis looked at her, waiting, as Misra swam slower now, sensing their work on the net.

Gryshen tightened one final knot, and Bravis tied up a loose rope.

"Let's stop near the island before we get there." She avoided Bravis's question.

"The island?" Almost immediately, understanding registered on his face. Now he was swimming alongside her and Misra.

"You must be exhausted." Gryshen remembered that the orca he had ridden had died in battle. He had been swimming himself the whole way, which was simple enough for a rested iloray, but for a battle-beaten one?

"I'm all right," he reassured her, swimming alongside.

Misra was already carrying two ceasids; she would tire out too quickly with a third.

But Bravis was not leaving her side, now that she wasn't leaving his.

"Bravis?"

"Yes, Gryshie?" It might have stung a bit, the familiar term, but knowing that someone she loved might still call her that name melted some of the ice that had surrounded her even in warm waters.

She thought for a moment.

"You know a little landkeeper speak." It was more of a statement.

"Yes. A little." Again he watched her carefully.

"Will you teach me some of their words? There are some things I need to be able to say."

Gryshen kept her eyes open the rest of the way, as they moved to a place before the little island, far enough out from Rone that they shouldn't encounter hunters. The group had remained virtually silent—even Gracke. The healers worked to change his ointment and redress his wound, but it was only to keep it clean enough to heal into a thick stub. He could still swim, but his movements were jerkier, pained.

Suddenly, Gryshen noticed a strange smile appear on Tollo's white face, and looked down to see the leaves peeling away from her chest, black billowing behind them.

"Tend to her. Now," she ordered the younger healer

who had been rubbing a spiky orange plant on the place where her fingers had been. He joined the older healer at Tollo's side, and Theus, seeing her, rushed over.

Even now, her movements were musical as she raised her arms toward the surface of the water, watching as they went in and out of camouflage with the gray sea, an effect Gryshen was sure had a connection to her injury.

The grave look on the older healer's face left her sick.

She reached for her own brother's limp hand as Theus held his sister's, as it disappeared and reappeared in the foggy ocean.

"There must be spear left. Those sharp-shelled arrows they used . . . " the young healer remarked thoughtfully.

"Those spears had a hundred tiny points on their end!" Gracke cried out, pushing toward them. "You have to help her! We can't lose them both. They're just babes!" Gracke gazed at Jode, then Tollo. He looked to each of them, the healers and Theus, frantic.

"Yes, let's get to work." Bravis began hauling more supplies from the back of an orca.

Both healers just looked helplessly at Tollo as she smiled.

"Fix her," Gryshen commanded. If she couldn't order the saving of this one life, what could she do?

"There's nothing to fix." Tollo offered Gryshen a sympathetic smile.

"Crazy leen!" Gracke roared at Tollo, "Enough! Look at yourself—blood's pouring out of you!"

Tollo wrapped her small hand around one of Gracke's enormous fingers. Then she turned to her brother.

"Meet you later." Tollo's eyes rolled back, her eyelids fluttered, and her whole body shimmered in and out of view once more.

Now they all knew what it was to watch a spirit leave.

"What?" Gracke sputtered.

Theus took his dead sister in his arms and gently kissed the top of her head. He held her as she floated in his hug, then said, "She's had her burial spot picked out since she was a child. Will you help me prepare her?" He looked right at Gryshen. She looked down at her own brother, tucked safely into his net, tied fast to Misra's side. She nodded, swimming over.

Gryshen waited while Gracke held Tollo's other hand, finally releasing his grip and bowing his head. She gently rested her palm on his hulking, shaking shoulder. He kept muttering, "They might has well have killed little babes. Little babes."

Jode's friends moved by his side, along with his pod's warriors.

Bravis unfurled a net and handed one end to Theus, one to Gryshen. The three of them swept the mesh knots like a veil over her head, then like a cloak covering her whole form. They all bowed their heads, while Theus sang something low in their native signal. The remaining Nereids circled them in a kind of dance. Gryshen leaned forward, looking to Theus for approval. He nodded, and she kissed the smooth white forehead of the strange, beautiful leen. Then she swam with Theus to tie his sister to a pair of dolphins that bobbed alongside Misra. They would part ways here, taking her home with his pod's fighters.

"Go." Gryshen took Theus's hand. "You belong with her."

"Oh, but we are always together. I will meet up with this part of her soon. First, I go with you."

There was no questioning it. Theus's words were final.

They began their preparations to settle in their hobbled little encampment before the time came to move home, to explain to Rone that she had gotten their beloved prince killed. That she had not returned with their salvation in some kind of wretched exchange. That she was the reason the pearl was broken. And then, somehow try and convince the mothers, fathers, young ones, the hearthkeepers, and the makers, hunters, healers, leaders, shaman, that none of it mattered to begin with. That their whole wide world grew up on a lie.

"Bravis." He had come by, making sure that Jode's net was still secure as Misra now took the time to rest.

She had to say the words out loud. "I have no idea what to do. And—" She dropped her signal for a moment, then realized how ridiculous it was to try and keep anything secret at this point, when all was laid bare, when what had been hidden in plain sight exploded in front of her entire army.

She used her normal tone again. "I don't even know what's true. I don't know for sure that the pearls have all been a hoax—" That last word felt like a knife sliding along the edge of her mouth. A hoax.

A trick.

Bravis gave her that look, waiting.

"I don't—I don't believe they're what we think they are. The pearls. How could the Rakor have been so strong? And we've had no report of illness, or even excessive weakness, from our pod. And I feel . . . well, war-battered doesn't count. I'm healthy. You're healthy. After they destroyed"—she couldn't say his name, not now. Not yet—"I'm healthy enough." *Except for my heart*, but she knew that kind of sickness couldn't be healed by any outside force.

"I agree with you," Bravis said, simply.

His words brought relief for her pod, and another wave of nausea over the useless war her brother had died in.

"I also don't think it was a hoax," Bravis finally added.

Gryshen just looked at him, puzzled.

Bravis continued, "A hoax would be something malicious. A trick."

"But it was a trick. At least, a deception."

"A deep deception," Bravis agreed.

"Reaching all of us. Killing—" she didn't need to gesture.

"Let's go up," he signaled softly, watching Theus tuck Tollo in her net with the dolphins closing in to hold her as they slept. "Jode is s—secure." It was as if perhaps he was going to say safe, then realized how insane that was. Gryshen nodded, realizing the center of her grief-stricken, war-broken army wasn't the ideal place to continue this conversation. Together they swam up, Bravis taking her hand reassuringly as they moved toward the surface. They hit air just beside Gryshen's rock, the viewing point where she used to watch the woman she now knew to be her mother, in a time that seemed so long ago.

They pulled up against the rock.

The stars were masked by clouds on this cool night. The moon was a thin sliver, only peeking out occasionally.

Instinctively, Gryshen wrapped her arms around Bravis, laying her head against his chest. The air felt damp and clear. It almost promised to clean them of the days before.

Bravis wrapped one long arm around Gryshen, and with his other, gently smoothed back her hair. Something about it reminded her of her landkeeper mother. She looked ahead at the sea. She pressed the side of her head hard against Bravis's chest to listen to the slow, steady drumming of his heartbeat.

And here we are, debating, like me and Jode. Gryshen allowed herself a small smile, sand and salt frosting her lips.

Only instead of arguing about his ridiculous taste in leens, or, when they were babes, who spotted the great blue crab first, they were quarreling over life, destiny, and Mother Herself.

Bravis was family.

Bravis was home.

And though she had known it since their first night meeting under this sky, she now recognized it as the deepest fact.

Her soaked lips reached upward. His were waiting, ready to greet her. His arms formed a gentle net around her, and she couldn't hold him tightly enough. The dark of the sky met the dark of the sea, and they were the light in between.

"He had to die for a reason." Gryshen spoke again finally. "I need a reason. And so does Tollo. She deserves one, too."

"Perhaps they are the reason."

"You're being cryptic." Her words formed ice on the soaked night air. "I can't take cryptic right now."

"I'm sorry." He kissed the frozen cluster of black hairs on the top of her head. "I don't mean to be. It's more that. Do we have to assign meaning to—" His throat caught.

"He was . . . " Gryshen tried to spell out the loss, but there were no sounds for it. And Bravis held her tighter as tiny ink circles formed on her painted cheeks.

They lay as the waves splashed along them, matching the cold of the rock and air. She felt the icy burn of the air, the gritty salt, the warmth of Bravis's chest, the smooth hardness of the rocks that held them, the silk of the sea as it drew up its arctic blanket only to pull it away.

The cold air felt strangely good on the open places where her three fingers had been. All that remained on her right hand, her thumb and index finger, lay against Bravis's shoulder, the slight bow of webbing connecting them.

"You know, I thought I might meet Mother." The words, connecting that sound and experience, felt so foreign on Gryshen's tongue. "I really thought that."

"Do you mean die?" Bravis held her even closer.

"No." Gryshen smiled slightly at the thought. That seemed comfortable and easy. But she shook her head, the shards of frost flecking off her hair.

She refused to give into this. She knew if she gave up, then there really would be a dead brother who died protecting someone who didn't value life. There could be no deeper insult to Jode, to her army, to Rone, to her father, and to this steady heartbeat that seemed to be guarding her own tired, cracked one in its thrumming waves.

"No, not that." Gryshen paused. "In my paces. In the *room*."

"Ah." He clearly knew the one.

"I thought I would meet her. I actually . . . I thought she was there. Somewhere in all these pictures and stories, I swore I could feel her. And then I realized it was all just manufactured. Maker-made."

"What was?"

"What? That cavern. That whole room, of course. You know the place I'm describing, don't you? Didn't you see it in your Forms—the replica of our first home?"

"Who told you it was a replica?"

Gryshen lifted her frozen face to greet his thoughtful one. They could have been floating, swimming up in that great wild sky and space rumored beyond it, and still she could feel connection.

That steady drum of heartbeat was like a lifeline.

But she had to glare at his question.

"Come on. As if I needed someone to tell me that. Yes, I wondered when I was first trapped in there—after having been strangled, electrocuted, dried out in a net . . . " She used her index to tick off the events leading up to that prophetic pace.

She drew in a breath and drew out a signal, hitting more fingers, one by one. "My father had just died and left me. The lax I loved betrayed me, stole what we *thought* was our source of survival, tried to kill me . . . "

"You're out of fingers, Gryshie."

She looked down at her mangled hand, and burst into laughing sobs. He joined her, hiccupping cackles and tears.

"Does it hurt you that I said I loved him?" Gryshen asked after she had calmed. This made the purple fill her cheeks, but imperceptibly, in the night. Or so she thought.

"Not nearly as much as what he did to you hurts me."

Once again he kissed the top of her head, but he let his lips sit there a bit longer.

She lay there awhile before speaking again, this time more gently. "What I mean is that I wasn't in my right mind when I was in that room. But I caught on quickly enough that it was made by the makers or . . . somebody."

"Who?" Bravis asked.

"Come on. What are you saying?" She looked back up in disbelief.

"I am saying that no one knows when that came to be. It is only introduced in the journey of paces, and never visited again, and—"

"You've only been in it the one time? Is that the case for everybody?"

"Well, it's just that—" but Gryshen had already begun swimming in the best direction she could guess. Bravis dipped in the water, following closely behind.

"What are you doing?"

"I'm not abiding by anymore of Rone's rules, I can tell you that."

CHAPTER 21

"*B*ut—" and he stopped. He swam silently behind her. The cavern of Rone was westward, and Gryshen began to slow down, winding northeast. Finally, she stopped and looked toward Bravis. He nodded in the direction she was going, and joined her side, taking her hand as they moved in the direction of the Womb Cavern.

It was easy to miss, blending with the hilly landscape beneath.

A cluster of boulders had been moved to form a ring around the entrance, which upon closer inspection, was blocked not by a large rock, but by a heavy, metal, rusting disk, clearly a retrieval from land. It was marked with a crisscross pattern and unknown, indecipherable landkeeper symbols.

Gryshen reached out to pull it off, but for all her strain, it wouldn't budge. Again, she turned to look at

Bravis, who was watching with one eyebrow cocked and his arms folded behind his back.

He obliged, and once more, his deceptively sinewy figure delivered an unexpected punch of power, as moving the weighty circle became possible. The water pressure made it more difficult, but in bits and inches they shifted it.

Gryshen picked up the lantern she had grabbed on her way and thrust it in the opening. Adrenaline had pushed her through so much, and now that she had forced this open, she was afraid to go through.

What would she find?

What would be revealed?

And, most frightening of all, what would disappoint?

"Let me join you."

Gryshen desperately wanted to tug Bravis down in there with her, but something deep inside her belly told her not to.

Now was probably time to start paying attention to whatever that was.

"I have to begin to trust myself." She held up a hand to ask him to wait outside. "I'm running out of others." And without a thought, except to make sure he understood that he was first on that very short list, Gryshen leaned forward and planted a kiss on his cheek, her lantern in her good hand, blooming blue upon the two.

Down she went.

Since it was night, the opening offered hardly any light from the sky, but blue shone from a cluster of jellyfish that had bordered the outside of the womb as if in a sacred pact of protection.

But why?

Why did everyone leave this room alone?

Gryshen held her lantern forward. Prickles grew up her arms, along her neck. Electricity crawled like tiny crabs from her hair. The large shells were here, like before. Weren't they stone? She had sworn they were. Gryshen reached out her wounded hand to caress the Great Pearl Throne before her; by far the largest oyster shell she'd ever seen.

It was a trick of the light, the way the gloom shifted, and cerulean swirled like billowing locks of hair before her, like eyes that pierced, and burned, and loved.

The iloray could make no sound.

Her heart, dull from endless ache, now throbbed as if awakened from a strange sleep.

Gryshen couldn't resist reaching out to touch—and meet—only more water. And then stone. Or shell. Something, or nothing at all. The markings on the walls could be given a little more time now. She backed away from this shape-shifting, truth-turning cradle, and searched for honesty on the gray walls.

Plant paints could tell her something to believe, if only. So many of the symbols were faded, ancient.

And what of it? Gryshen thought bitterly to herself. *Old doesn't mean wise. Apocay's a lunatic.*

Still, she pored over paintings. Circles of white to represent pearls. A whole section of wall with golden paint in the shape of a vast tail, the scales the size of Gryshen's hand. Something caught in her throat as she hoisted her lantern upward, following the light's path. The mix of plant powders had been crushed with pearls and crystals, and even as bits had chipped away, it still sparkled and glittered. Gryshen turned for a moment to get her bearing, light before her, filling as much of the room as it could. She was directly across from where she had spent the final moments of her paces. So deep in her . . . hallucinations? Visions?

She had never seen the other side of the room.

Up Gryshen went, tracing the luminous outlines with her fingers, up the golden torso, outstretched arms, and blue. Blowing, billowing, blue locks of hair. Gryshen grabbed for it, like an infant reaches for her own mother's tresses, but only cold stone waited. Scraps of what looked like a golden crown atop her head. Gryshen wondered if it felt heavy like hers. She pressed the lantern against the wall, like a spotlight to seek out those eyes she swore she had spotted in the darkness, those piercing, burning eyes full of love.

But there were no eyes.

There was no face. Just chipped-away, washed-away remnants.

Unknowable. Unknowable.

Gryshen dropped the lantern, letting it sink, sink, and thud against the rocks below.

She lay her whole body against the picture.

"What's left?" Small bubbles poured the question out from her lips.

"Everything." The word sounded in the cavern. Was she hallucinating again?

Gryshen looked for a body to the words. She scooped up the lantern, passing it in a sweep, but there was no one she could see. Just an empty throne.

An empty throne. She swam over to it, setting the lantern to rest on a fingerlike rock that acted as a kind of hook.

Gryshen traced her finger around the top of her head, thinking of the crown that awaited her at home.

If her ilorays hadn't already revolted.

If they even saw it fit to not tear her apart, and send the pieces scattering across the seven seas.

If they had the mercy to not banish her completely.

Gryshen gave a slight jerk of her head to shake these thoughts away. She curled her body in the base of the enormous oyster shell, resting her pointed chin on her torn fist, while the jellyfish in the lantern danced a glow upon her and the shadows of this strange, broken, sacred place.

"I might be the only one here. What I thought I heard from outside myself might have been from within." She paused, as if someone might reply. Just the water in her ears, the ripple from two ghostly white fish that seemed to have lost their way. They moved slowly, in and out of view. Occasionally, the captive in its little cage would bob and hit the sides, causing the light to move and flash across shadowy spaces, and more story-marked walls.

Spears and pearls, legs and fins, babes and grown, earth and sea.

The stark black was cast in night-sky illumination, as the stories told themselves, over and over, in new ways. The warriors fought each other, then for each other.

The lantern rocked.

Babes sprang out of oysters and into each other's arms.

The pearls shimmered, sliding together, apart, together.

Gryshen strained her eyes to focus, once more unsure of what she thought she saw before her.

Blue and white and purple washed its pallor over the stories, the tales that had been told and retold, from tongue to tongue, until where they began and what they meant became misplaced. Lost in the waves and stretches of time, of belief.

And when you're looking for something specific, you'll keep finding it.

Over and over. Gryshen watched the light play its tricks—or cast a spotlight on the truth. Up the little pearls twisted, as if ripped out of their inlaid places in the wall. They passed through the arms of those warriors, those babes, those landkeepers and waterd-wellers, through the heart of the center of it all.

The crumbling, golden, faceless idol. The Mother of Mystery. The God with no name.

The question with no answer.

Gryshen ran her fingers over the small white pearls set into the crown on the throne. They were like perfect, miniature versions of the Great Pearl. She could feel a tingling in her fingertips as she rubbed the water-polished orbs.

She flashed back to her first vision of the Great Pearl when she was small. It was so big, and beautiful, and it carried the promise of strength and hope and magic in its circle. She trembled in its presence.

How could it not be powerful?

How could it not be holy?

The jellyfish twisted, and Gryshen looked up at it.

It was dying. The light it emanated turned round the cavern, and the stories kept retelling themselves.

Her hand pressed firmly against the ring of pearls, clinging to the top of the oyster lid, her braid loose, black hair flowing, the glow moved like a lightning storm across the room.

What was it, the electricity? It didn't burn like the eel's sting, that shivering quake she began to feel, like an amplified version of her childhood trembling.

Now her whole body shook, and the pictures whirled about the space, seeming to leap off the walls.

She let go.

Spears and tears and etchings of lovers in their bindings leapt into her arms. They seemed to lift her instead of weighing her down.

Flashes of final glory exploded from the lantern's inhabitant.

Gryshen gathered the visions in her arms, the dreams, the sacred secrets. A tale of beginning jumped off the wall with the rest of them, into her embrace. It wore the round face of a babe, golden hair, eyes of the clearest sky.

She held the infant close.

"Jode," she whispered. Her tears spilled black, and gleamed copper around him in his light. The baby smiled.

Gryshen clutched him, burying her face into the top of his head, kissing his curls. She closed her eyes tightly, and felt him change into something else.

It was larger than the Great Pearl.

She opened her eyes, and floating just above her, resting barely on the palms of her open hands, was the most enormous pearl she had ever seen. It glittered like the sunlight on a wave.

She couldn't quite feel the object itself—it was like grasping a shadow—but its presence beyond vision was clear in the charge running through her fingertips and up and down her outstretched arms. It pinched and popped, and when she couldn't see the pearl anymore, the sensation didn't stop. Gryshen could feel the bursts around her body, like tiny geysers shooting off in her bloodstream, piercing her bones. Gryshen waved her fingers in the water, seeking out the pearl. She whirled around to face the shell throne once more.

There it sat, resting, like it was just born, like it was in the beginning of a legend. It multiplied into shell cradles encircling the cavern floor, producing their own glow.

"You're the First Ones," Gryshen thought, or signaled. She couldn't be sure. "Why are you here now?"

The glow from the shells seemed to jump out and in, swimming around like the pictures on the walls.

"Just coming home." That single voice answered again. "Like you."

Gryshen stared. "But why? Why now?" The glowing orbs shifted into tails, ghostly babes chasing each other in the darkness, twirling around her. "Coming home for what? Forgiveness? Protection?" she pressed, desperate for a reply as she saw them swimming away.

Only murmuring streams of "yes, yes" followed.

The light from the lamp came in sparks that matched the pulses in her body, and in flashes it lit her and the great white sphere before her on its throne.

"What protection? The pearl is nothing," she now signaled to it, hoping for clearer answers. She couldn't help but shudder as she spoke what would have been blasphemy only days ago. "It's just a story!" she barked at the glimmering orb. Water whooshed in her ears, rocking her. The lantern shone in irregular bursts.

A story that's been told wrong. The sound echoed in her mind.

I don't understand.

The truth has many versions.

Gryshen smiled as she imagined Jode's response. "Oh, well that helps. Hugely. Thanks."

The stream of signal continued. *He's with you. We all are.*

She reached to touch the giant pearl again, feeling nothing solid, only a pulling charge. Gryshen swam to it, and quickly following were the gleaming babe swimmers. Gryshen watched, open mouthed, as they were absorbed into the pearl, one by one.

A last gasp of blue seemed to send the whole cavern alight, and the golden crown on the far wall was mirrored in the glass-like surface of the gleaming globe. The popping grew more frequent.

Gryshen gasped, sucking in more water. A jagged surge of lightning rippled through her tail as she caught the image reflected before her. She reached out her fingers to touch the face looking back.

Her face, with the crown of Mother sitting perfectly atop it.

Her body seemed to be electrified, and then everything went out.

"I'm getting Jode's body. I need to tell someone else about him. Before I tell them all," Gryshen answered Bravis's questions in a current as she shot out the sacred cavern's opening, where he was waiting, and moved back toward their encampment.

"Are you going to tell me what just happened? It looked like a sky storm in there, and I called to you, but you wouldn't answer. I finally went in, and all was dark."

"And I found your hand even in pitch darkness." Gryshen reached back, and grasped his hand again.

Gryshen did not go ungrateful that Bravis trusted her enough to let her be. When she was ready to speak more, she would.

Together they hoisted the net, ignoring the questioning eyes of their hobbled crew. Even if some of their group was unsure about Gryshen, Bravis had their trust, and so they let it be, too.

Soundlessly, they pressed on, save for the whooshing of their bodies and Jode in his net. Gryshen motioned for them to swim past her lookout, straight to the rocks on the edge of the small island. She pressed the top of her head above water, darting her eyes around the gloomy, barren place.

It was the far side, where she had first spoken with her mother. Or rather, shared tea with a stranger, in what seemed like a long-ago and faraway place.

"I don't see her," Gryshen said to Bravis as he dared to rest his own gaze upon the surface.

"Does she have a name you call her?"

CHAPTER 22

It looked like rain. The sound of waves crashing against the rocks sang their familiar melody, and Gryshen called out their tune, and waited. The wind sliced past her ears as she heard the sound of rocks tumbling.

The woman appeared, breathless, at the edge of the cliff, clutching sun-bleached linen like a flag of surrender.

The woman gasped when her eyes fell on Bravis, but seemed to relax at Gryshen's nod. Gryshen watched as she glanced backward for a moment, before seeming to fly down the stone path to where the she lay, waiting for something the woman longed to give her, her black hair spilling over the coal rock.

"Gislunn." The woman spoke the landkeeper version of her name aloud, as if it had the power to lift the face of the girl who bore it. And it did. Gryshen lifted her head, the sun escaped the clouds for a moment, and for this instant in time, a shine washed over the mother who couldn't comfort her child, the daughter who was an endless wound, the dead brother in the net, and the advisor who had nothing left to say.

The sea calmed. The glow lit up the clean linen, and the woman draped it around her daughter, holding her. Gryshen watched her carefully. Watched her see the net. The body. The face. Watched recognition splash over her, the familiar features of her love reflected in the dead iloray.

The woman smoothed the wet strands away from Gryshen's trembling face. Bravis held fast to the other side of the net with one hand, the other gripping the edge of shoreline.

"I needed you to see him." Gryshen's voice was steady, but her eyes began to well in spite of herself. The blast of cold air dried them quickly. The gales of wind took over, as if they could sweep her brother up and carry him away on their current. She repeated herself. "I needed you to see him."

The woman nodded, and held her close, as if she understood. Gryshen lay against her, hearing the thud of her heartbeat drum against a beat of thunder in the distance.

Gryshen held Jode's face in her ashen hands. Then she gently pressed the woman's warm fingers against his cheeks, then against her own.

"Brother." She barked the word out, unsure of intonation. But the woman didn't need her to say it properly. She knew. She leaned over and kissed the bloated dark cheeks of the boy, the other child, and she held him and his living sister in her own pale arms. She took her shawl, her braid whipping loose in the wind, and she cradled Jode in it, kissing him once more.

Bravis remained steady witness. The thunder crept closer, but for some time it just matched this rhythm, this beating in their hearts, this clutching and cradling, kind words and whispers silenced by the sea, but clear to the senses. The rain came, and the woman stayed.

Gryshen took her mother's hands, squeezing them as she looked in her eyes. She saw her own eyes, and she saw her own reflection, once more, in this face.

"I keep looking, and turning up with myself," she whispered so that even Bravis couldn't hear her, not above the storm. The woman smoothed a soaking hand against her dripping black locks.

Gryshen threw the cloth from her shoulders, and held her mother in her arms.

Then she took the other side of the net, and she and Bravis retreated back to the deep.

"Gree, please. Please." Hena was posted between the island and the Rone Cavern, thick black grasses bunched up in a large sack on her back. Two warriors from her pod floated on either side of her, keeping watch around the ledge of rock she was hiding under.

Gryshen froze.

"I have—please, Gryshen." There was a broken pleading in Hena's voice. The only friend Gryshen had growing up reached back and tugged at the rope sealing the bag shut. One swift motion revealed a shining dome.

"Your pearl." Gryshen stared in disbelief.

"I had to. We'll be fine. you know we will. Take it."

"Hena, this is—"

"Take it, sister." If the dark-purple circles beneath Hena's eyes hadn't betrayed her, then the ink seeping out of them did.

"But your pod—what will you tell them?"

"What does it matter? I'll go looking for a new one if I must. There are places, caverns I've heard of."

"Like our sacred one," Gryshen murmured, realizing the growing likelihood that the giant shell was not, in fact, a sculpture, but an actual enormous mollusk that may have carried an actual, enormous pearl. It may have carried the Rone Pearl.

"Yes, I've heard of your place. And when I was a child, my own parents brought me to this . . . valley. I thought it was a dream, it was so long ago, so fuzzy in my mind." Hena wore a wistful expression Gryshen didn't recall seeing on her strong features, and Gryshen felt a twist inside.

Hena had always been on her own. She seemed so

strong. She was always the one to put everything in place. But what else could she be?

"I had my father most of my life. I had my brother. I have Bravis." Bravis was beside her, and squeezed her hand gently at this. "You never really had anybody." Gryshen's heart felt like lead. Hena had lost Jode, too—and the hope of family with him.

"But I had *you*, Gree." Hena's broad hands trembled on the glassy surface of the Great Pearl.

Now it was time for Gryshen to lay her own hands on the shaking leen.

"Come with me, sister."

Hena looked at her in disbelief. Gryshen stretched her pale gray arms around the pinkish orb. It looked like something from Hena's pod, exotic, bright. It was a clear change from the ghostly, ethereal white of the Rone Pearl.

Together, Gryshen and Hena guided the pearl to the mouth of the Rone Cavern. Bravis circled them, warriors continuing to flank them as they approached.

Word spread fast. Signals blew through, calling the old, the young, and the in-between. The remaining hunters, and the band of their army that had caught up from behind. Sodaren was waiting for her pets. Proggunel was watching close by. Helda and Velda floated just behind the glass bottles posted in front, waiting. Babes peeked from behind their mothers. All of Rone waited, Apocay farthest behind the crowd, watching, looking awake for perhaps the first time Gryshen could remember.

The sounds of gasps, cheers, and confusion rolled through the crowd.

A wail rose in multiples as they saw, while Hena and Gryshen carried in the pearl, their chieftainess gripping the rope leading to the net that held Jode. Bravis cradled her dead brother.

And they all stopped to weep.

The crowd swarmed, laying their hands on him.

And it didn't anger Gryshen the way it had with her father. It gave her comfort. They were loving him, as she loved him. They were sharing in grief.

This is what pods must do, Gryshen thought. *They need to do this. I need to do this with them.* She looked at Hena and Bravis, who understood without signal, and they tucked the black grasses around the pearl, resting it in a small alcove.

Gryshen joined her tribe. She touched her brother, she held hunter's faces in her hands, she kissed the little ones who had worshiped him, and she embraced the leens who adored him. She held the mothers who wept for a tribe's lost son, and she let the mothers hold her.

She let the fathers wrap her in their arms, and give her words of strength. Words of respect. Words of hope.

For the first time in her life, Gryshen felt like she belonged to them. And they belonged to her.

"We belong to each other," she signaled in a clear voice. She swam to the pearl, pulling the sack from it.

"Is that—is that ours? I thought—"

"No. Ours was destroyed." Gryshen looked them in the eyes.

"Then is that from . . . " Faces turned to the other ceasid who had carried it in with her.

"Yes. It's from the Wanaa."

More confusion. Murmurs of gratitude, and questions.

"They are so far!"

"How will they survive?"

"Why would they give this to us?'

"They are our great friends!"

"But they'll die!"

Gryshen raised a hand to quiet her pod. They waited, watched, listened.

"I need you." She stared each iloray in the face, pausing to receive a silent vow from them. They agreed, not knowing to what. But they agreed. And waited.

Gryshen reached into her pouch, and removed the last gift her brother gave her. She wound the thick weed around her fist once, twice, and with newfound strength, struck the beautiful sphere.

It cracked. Was the crowd silent, or were they screaming? Gryshen couldn't tell. She could only hear the cracking, her heart beating in her ears, the sea holding them all, while she whipped back once more, cracking the pearl in two.

She turned to the crowd. She met their eyes. She spoke to herself as much as the rest.

"My brother was killed right beside the Rone Pearl. I was distracted, and he died. The pearl didn't protect him." She paused. "And they did not need it. The Rakor never needed it. Those creatures were sick because of their misery. And they weren't even all that sick."

"What are you saying?" Helda was near the front of the group, beside her sister. She wasn't wearing her usual implicating expression. Her eyes looked like everyone else's: Haunted. Grieving. Wishful.

"It's not real." Hena swam forward, on an even path with her friend, her chieftainess sister. "We don't know if it was ever real. This one was a replacement for another."

She turned to Gryshen. "I always heard things from Uncle Qoah. He warned, but I wouldn't listen. I was his niece. I couldn't let anyone think I was crazy like he was. I had a pod to lead."

Gryshen nodded. She understood.

"I asked another Elder, one who had agreed to mark Qoah with me. I made him tell me. He and my uncle were the only ones left who knew. They thought we would be safer believing." Hena pressed her plum lips tightly together.

"But illusions don't keep anyone safe," Gryshen signaled. She gazed out at the Rone pod, and joined them in their loss, in their grasp for understanding. "And the story—the First Story. I don't think it was about the pearls." Confusion met her. "Not exactly." Gryshen stared back, searching for a clear signal.

"Is it true you're a Turnic?" A small voice popped out

from the crowd. It belonged to a young leen, not older than seven or eight.

How did such news travel?

"My father fell in love with a landkeeper. They didn't know they would make me, but they did." Gryshen recited the words she had been preparing, shutting her eyes and waiting for the onslaught, bracing for the screams, the inevitable attack.

But only murmurs followed. Gryshen opened her eyes to Rone. They stared; they whispered. No one raised a spear. No battle cry.

"I told you." The young one turned to her open-mouthed sister.

From the back a signal rasped, "The understanding of both sides of our world born into her blood. Difficult to find that, in someone who managed to avoid being outcast. In one who is a chieftainess, impossible. Her father trusted her. So will I." A small smile cracked Apocay's face as the pod turned to face him. From a hip satchel he removed the remains of a white fish and began chewing, watching Gryshen.

Before she could search for the words, her signal poured out of her. "I have wasted seasons searching for answers, destiny"—she thought of her adopted mother's grave, her father beside her now—"qualifications for caring. And I shut you all out. I missed the point. It was never about my destiny, or our security, or secret answers no one would give me. I am a reminder." Gryshen smiled, thinking of Frall. *Now, I understand, Dad. What is worth protecting.*

"The pearl doesn't protect us. It wasn't supposed to"

"Then what will? What is real?" The signal carried up from somewhere in the crowd.

She let the scenes from the Womb Cavern swim through her mind, trying to grab something tangible to offer them.

"Connection." As soon as she signaled, the word settled over them all like fine, warm sand.

Gryshen recalled the thought that had haunted her on her way to Rakor. "I don't know what was whispered in my ear at my naming. No one is left who can answer that question." She closed her eyes for a moment. "So I will answer it myself."

"I am yours. And you are mine." Gryshen didn't have to look, she knew the hands that clasped hers on either side belonged to Hena and Bravis. One by one, soundlessly, the pod of ilorays reached and took each other's hands, wrapped each other in their arms, and watched her, waiting. This was not the cheering mob that Jode had inspired, but it wasn't the broken one who had lost her father, either. Their faces wore her sorrows and hopes, their eyes had reflected her fear, and now they mirrored something else, something Gryshen was finally willing to give them.

Trust. Love.

"I can't give you any more answers. Not any that you will find real comfort in. But I will make you a promise."

Gryshen stared at the crowd from the vantage point of her father before her.

"I may be half from another place, but I am all your chieftainess. Come, and help me bury my brother."

The Rone carried Jode in a silent parade out to the bone pit. There was no ornate container for his body; this had not been expected.

No death ever really was.

The beasts floated in watch, a quiet understanding. Bravis pointed to a spot near her father and adopted mother, a place where the sunlight hit in a bright beam.

Gryshen nodded.

Velda came forward, signaling softly to Gryshen, "My sister and I used this to keep our treasures in. It's beautiful, isn't it?" She held out a salvaged purple clay urn, with a small net affixed to the top, wrapped in seaweed on the sides. "Like your brother. Let him have it. We'll leave surprises for him there."

Gryshen gently cradled the vase and wrapped an arm around the leen. They wept, together.

They were joined by Hena, Bravis, Gracke, and all of Rone.

Their sea turned black that day.

Jode had been placed under a mound of carefully collected beast bones.

Gryshen and Bravis left things for him often, along with others.

He never showed up in front of her, not like his own

visions, but he whispered a joke into her dreams some-times, warming a space in her heart.

Gryshen visited the makers and requested something shiny, something reflective. They had a cracked hand mirror, a long piece of glass that might not hold up, and a large silver dinner plate. She thanked them and took the dinner plate.

There would be peace, even in the broken-open freedom they all faced.

The Rakor were quieter now, keeping to themselves, their young chieftain weighted with nowhere else to go.

The rest would join in the next migration. There was talk of preparing the hub.

A celebration.

Gryshen swam up to the place, the sacred cavern, and shifted the rock on top. The light was bright, and she didn't bring a lantern in. She felt the place by heart, anyway.

When she had suggested opening the Womb Cavern up for visiting pods, Bravis and Apocay agreed. Only those who had been through their paces though.

Some secrets had to wait to be discovered.

Gryshen took the plate, long pieces of metal soldered to the back, and with a rock she hammered it against the wall, taking care not to crack the rock around it. The plate was battered, but it served its purpose.

A ghost-mist of light peeking through the ceiling hole floated along the space. It lit the long, peeling, painted fin. It flashed on the golden crown. It shone on the smiling face, the reflection in the plate.

And everyone who visited would know Mother. They would feel her presence, and see the bit of her they could recognize.

"We were always together," Gryshen murmured.

"And we always will be." A song returned, from somewhere in the room, somewhere in a grave, somewhere in the sea, somewhere on a little island . . .

Somewhere within.

ACKNOWLEDGMENTS

I should probably begin every one of these by thanking my husband.

Thank you for being the man you are. Thank you for your unwavering belief in me. Thank you to my daughter, for being an excellent person, an encourager, a teacher. For loving stories like I do. To my mom, for all her love and for reading more than anyone I've ever known, except maybe her mom. To my dad, for all his love and loud support.

Thank you, Kit.

Thank you to Nicole Ayers of Ayers Edits, for being the greatest of all editors. For reminding me to use actual words instead of made up ones. For her friendship.

Thank you to Kimberly Marsot at KimG Designs for her stunning cover design.

Thank you to Katherine Trail for crisp, lovely formatting.

To all my wonderful friends, for all their love and support. For being the best kind of friends. I love you.

Shoutout to Hayley and Adam Schwartz, for opting to read my last novel on their honeymoon. Twenty bonus friendpoints apiece.

To the readers. Thank you. Thank you again.

PLAYLIST

Just create a Loreena McKennitt station on your Pandora app.

ABOUT THE AUTHOR

Mary Jane Capps writes young adult novels about witches, mermaids, and ghosts-or some combination of the three.

She likes to keep things spooky, magical, and reasonably upbeat.

Mary Jane lives in Fort Mill, South Carolina with her husband and daughter, down the road from her parents, in a house that is probably haunted.

CONNECT

Sign up for book info and fun giveaways:
www.maryjanecapps.com

Follow on Instagram @maryjanecapps
facebook.com/storytellingspark